BURNED AND BROKEN

MARK HARDIE

sphere

SPHERE

First published in by Sphere in 2016
This paperback edition published by Sphere in 2017

1 3 5 7 9 10 8 6 4 2

A CIP catalogue record for this book
is available from the British Library.

ISBN 978-0-7515-6208-8

Typeset in Caslon by M Rules
Printed and bound in Great Britain by
Clays Ltd, St Ives plc

Papers used by Sphere are from well-managed forests
and other responsible sources.

MIX
Paper from
responsible sources
FSC
www.fsc.org   FSC® C104740

Sphere
An imprint of
Little, Brown Book Group
Carmelite House
50 Victoria Embankment
London EC4Y 0DZ

An Hachette UK Company
www.hachette.co.uk

www.littlebrown.co.uk

Mark Hardie began writing full time after completely losing his eyesight in 2002. He has completed a creative writing course and advanced creative writing course at the Open University, both with distinction. Follow Mark on  @MarkHardiecrime

For Debbie

Prologue

Coming back into consciousness ... his senses gradually returning ... but they were piecemeal, disjointed ... disconnected. Both from him and from each other. His sight fogged. A red mist viewed through half-closed lids too heavy to lift. A steering wheel. A dashboard. The bottom of a windscreen. Momentarily he was confused. Back in that other car, the passenger door swinging to and fro. The lights of the radio still on, though he couldn't hear it above the ringing in his ears. The smoke from the discharged shotgun drifting through the interior of the car. The numbing cold spreading through his body as he bled out ...

But this time there was no ringing in his ears. Instead, a distant, rhythmic shushing. No numbing cold. Rather a cloying dampness, a clammy shroud that clung to his skin. And in place of the smell of a discharged shotgun, an acerbic, astringent smell that was somehow familiar. He became aware that he was staring out through a windscreen at a low, white wall in a parking area. The distant shushing the sound of surf breaking on shingle. The clammy shroud his wet T-shirt. The acerbic smell that of petrol.

His T-shirt, his jeans, the whole inside of the car saturated in it. Between his legs, on the car seat, something blue trembled and flickered. This, too, was familiar, though he couldn't quite grasp its significance. It faltered for a moment, then caught, and recognition dawned. Too late, he understood. He was swallowed by the flames, and the pain came – an unimaginable, overwhelming, unbearable pain. That was when he started to scream ...

PART ONE

1

FRIDAY

Detective Sergeant Frank Pearson pressed the Mondeo's electronic fob and opened the driver's-side door. The door handle, the whole car, sticky with the sap from the tree that overhung the drive. A lime, he had been reliably informed. He slung his jacket on to the passenger seat and stood by the open door for a minute to allow the trapped heat inside to dissipate. He lifted the collar of his shirt and knotted his tie, tucking down his collar and pushing his tie up to his throat. In the winter, he thought, you could get away with just ironing part of your shirt, the front, the collar, or you would be tugging at it all day long, trying to get it to sit comfortably. Chances were, if you had to talk to someone in any professional capacity you would keep your jacket on. But in this hot weather you had to iron the whole bloody thing. And a couple of minutes in the car, your back sticking to the upholstery despite the air-conditioning, would leave the shirt wrinkled and looking like you'd slept in it by the time you got in to work anyway. Looking down, he admitted his suit, the trousers at least, could do with a press. They were creased around the crotch, bagging at the

3

knees. This was the sort of weather he disliked the most. Better persistent drizzle, or heavy rain, or even freezing temperatures and deep snow, than hot and humid.

He had been woken by the ringing of his mobile. Groggy, unrested and already irritable, in a tangle of sheets, and having had to go to the bathroom three times during the night. He had a distinct queasiness, a greasy, unsettled sliding in his stomach. Last night he had been late home from work as usual. He had been too late to visit his mother in the hospital and found himself feeling both relieved and guilty. Probably, if he were honest with himself, more the former than the latter. He had rescued a lone bottle of semi-skimmed from the chiller cabinet of the local Premier, pulling up in the car just as the manager, Kai, was about to pull down the screen on the door. He was frowning, hands on hips, head shaking at the metal shutters on the rest of the shop's windows. It was one of several local convenience stores that had recently been targeted because of an upsurge in anti-Muslim feeling. Even though Kai, being a Sri Lankan, was most likely a Buddhist. But the shutters were pebbledashed with the relics of a different religion. Vodka and stomach acid. Blood and snot. Regurgitated sweet-and-sour pork and egg-fried rice. The Via Dolorosa, the way of sorrows of any given night out in Southend-on-Sea.

'Hoodies,' said Kai. 'I had to chase them off.'

Pearson followed Kai's gaze up the street. As if they might just make them out in the distance. On the farthest shutter there was the faintest impression of an enormous spray-painted cock which hadn't been entirely successfully scrubbed away.

'That was last week,' said Kai, shaking his head again. 'Animals.'

The milk had seemed all right when he had sniffed the bottle this morning. He'd shaken it to see if any globs of congealed fat floated to the surface before pouring it into his tea. Now, though, only a few minutes later, he wondered if it had been on the turn. He heard the reverberation of an engine, looked up expecting to see an easyJet plane in orange-and-white livery throttling down on its final approach into the airport. But there was no sign of it, no distant reflection of sunlight from a fuselage, not even the wispy remnants of a vapour trail in the featureless sky. The Hat Lady passed by, trailing her wheeled shopping basket. He put a finger to his forehead in a silent salute and she nodded an acknowledgement. Today she wore some kind of straw boater with a display of brightly coloured birds and flowers on its brim. He wondered what this particular arrangement might augur for the day ahead. But any day that started with a pre-dawn call to a shout wasn't going to turn out well.

Pearson had to lean forward to peer through the windscreen. Beyond the wipers' reach a layer of dust clung to the stickiness of tree sap, coronas of light refracted around the more obstinate patches inside the cleared space. And at its very centre sat a newly deposited splat of birdshit. He could see that a line of blue-and-white tape had already been strung across the road. Behind this, SOCOs unloaded metal boxes from a van and a white forensic tent was being assembled. The crime-scene manager, in a white forensic suit, six foot eight and stick-thin, was in conversation with a man who stood at least a foot shorter. Detective Chief Inspector Martin Roberts, his thinning red hair lifted by the faintest of breezes, had a between-standard-sizes body that left him constantly tucking in his shirt or adjusting some or other item of clothing. His West Country burr and ruddy complexion more suited a farmer or the owner of a garden centre than the senior investigating officer of the Essex Major Incident Team. A uniformed PC in a hi-vis jacket tapped on the side window and Pearson wound it down and passed him his warrant card.

'Sarge,' he said, passing the card back, 'it's pretty busy in there.' He gestured behind him. 'We've commandeered the pub car park across the road. You'd be better off parking in there.'

He opened the car door and got out into air soupy with heat and exhaust fumes as another car pulled in next to him. He shrugged on his jacket and pressed his electronic fob to lock the car as the other car's driver got out. Podgy. Balding. Slamming his door, the man nodded in Pearson's direction: 'Frank.'

Pearson had always thought of DS Alan Lawrence as a decent copper, steady and meticulous. But lately he had begun to wonder about him. These days Lawrence seemed to prefer to stay in the nick, on the phone or the computer. If he wasn't at his desk he would more than likely be in the bog with a copy of the *Racing Post*, studying form. Or on his mobile, making endless personal calls. Seeing out the last couple of years until his retirement. Lawrence had his all laid out. Something to do with horses, Pearson remembered. Or was it donkeys? So what was he doing here? Before he could ask, Lawrence's mobile began to ring and he checked the screen.

'Sorry,' he said, 'I need to take this.'

Turning, he took a few steps away, talking quietly into the phone, glancing now and then over his shoulder. Rather than wait, Pearson made his way over the main road, flashing his warrant card once again at the uniformed PC. He made a beeline for Roberts, who, acknowledging his presence with a nod, finished his conversation with the CSM and walked over. Reaching into his inside jacket pocket, Roberts retrieved a packet of Extra

Strong Mints. Unwrapping them, he waved the packet at Pearson.

'Nah, you're all right,' said Pearson, shaking his head. 'What've we got?'

Roberts put a mint in his mouth and crunched noisily.

'Burnt-out car.' He half turned and indicated with his chin in the direction of the white forensic tent. 'There's a body inside.'

'We got an ID?'

'Not as yet. The body's too badly burned,' said Roberts. 'But the car's an Audi A8. The back index number's still legible. It's registered to Sean Carragher.'

Pearson took this in as he scanned the crime scene. DI Sean Carragher. That explained it. The heavy police presence. It could only be for one of their own. The death of a cop would mean the whole circus would be mobilised. A strategic command-and-control hierarchy established, headed by Gold Command, overseen by the Deputy Chief Constable himself. Politics would necessitate that the death be solved, swiftly, incontrovertibly and with minimum impact on the reputation of the force. This focus on the force's image had, in the past, resulted in an almost irresistible pressure for the cop in question to appear in the public mind as beyond reproach. The retroactive sanitisation of a career. Personal failings and professional misdemeanours airbrushed out. The elevation of an ordinary, flawed human being to model public servant.

'Called in a couple of hours ago,' continued Roberts.

Pearson automatically checked his watch, an old-fashioned Timex on a battered leather strap. For Pearson there were two types of copper: the Timex cop and the Rolex cop. The other sort, the Carraghers of the world, were all of a type. Lairy suits. Gelled hair. Plenty of chat. More like estate agents than coppers. The sort who identified themselves with the image of the cop

7

portrayed in popular fiction. The maverick who 'followed his gut', who didn't mind kicking down a few doors, cutting a few corners, leaning a little harder on a suspect to get at the truth. The sort of copper the public thought they admired. Until that same gut instinct led him astray. Until it was the door of an innocent man he kicked down. Until it was your door. Your head he held under the water. Until it was you who, coming up spluttering and gasping for air, made a confession, said anything to get it to stop. Until it was you who was in the interview room when that same copper leaned across the table, suspended the interview, turned off the tape recorder, made the threat. The sort of cop you might admire. Unless you worked with him. Unless he crossed the line and dragged you across that line with him.

2

Four Days Earlier

MONDAY

The door of the café slowly swung closed behind her and Donna spotted the boy sitting alone at a table, disinterestedly flicking through the pages of a newspaper. Small and slight, his complexion was smooth, baby-like, except for the skin around one nostril and an eyebrow which was mottled and pimply where he had previously had piercings. An attempt had been made to spike his hair but it was too fine, even with product, to stand up properly. In any case, he had been leaning against the window of the café and it was flattened on one side, wet from the condensation.

As Donna approached he glanced up momentarily, the round, wire-rimmed glasses reflecting the overhead lights in two white discs like full moons. On the right lens was a stain of some kind. Tea or milk. He frowned, took off his glasses and untucked his shirt to clean them. The shirt was grey polycotton – the sort of shirt that the boys at their old school used to wear as part of

9

their uniform. Without his glasses his eyes looked weak, the right noticeably duller. Moving more slowly through its own, denser, medium. A white rabbit twitched his nose and peered myopically at her through red eyes. Despite the hot, steamy atmosphere he was wearing a parka. Not the proper fishtail mod-type parka but the cheap, shitty, nylon knock-off with the red lining. Dirty on the sleeves and around the pockets. She pulled out a chair and sat down opposite him, taking off her own jacket and slipping it onto the back. This, too, was too heavy for the weather. Some designer-name thing. Black, naturally. She didn't like it that much really, too old-fashioned. And not in a retro way. But you had to have something to carry your fags round in, it was either the jacket or a handbag and it wasn't so easy to nick a handbag. She had picked up the jacket at a party she hadn't been invited to. It was easy: all those idiots who posted their parties on social media and then were amazed when dozens of people gatecrashed it. You just had to wait for the party to get going, front it out on the doorstep, blag your way in: 'Darren invited me, he's inside.' There was always a Darren inside somewhere. Then mooch through and see what was on offer; everyone was usually so off their face you could walk out with whatever you wanted.

'It's Mitch, isn't it?' she asked.

His last name was Mitchell. At school he had tried to get everyone to call him that. No one had. He didn't look much like a Mitch. Mitch was a lifeguard on a California beach. Mitch was a denim-clad oil worker from Texas. Mitch was a cowboy.

'Malcolm,' he corrected. Yeah, he was definitely a Malcolm. Malcolm Mitchell hooked his glasses back over his ears and blinked at her. A mouth breather – gormless – but he had brightened a little, was obviously flattered.

'You been at the bus stop?' she asked. 'You know who I am, right? Donna. Donna Freeman.'

He stared at her for a moment. 'Yeah. You look different – your hair.'

She tucked it back behind an ear. Black, shoulder-length. At school she'd had it spiky. Black, with streaks. Nuclear red. Atomic pink. Napalm orange. Blue mayhem. She'd grown it out since. Had had it all sorts. Peacock blue. Canary yellow. Flamingo pink. And now, raven black. Fuck knows what colour it was naturally. Mousy, she thought. Malcolm looked down and started running his fingers along the plastic tablecloth.

It had been just an ordinary bus stop. At first. Then there had been an appeal on the telly when Alicia was declared missing. The police asking for any information on her last known movements. They had received a report that Alicia had been seen there on the day she went missing: the last official sighting they had. So it had become an impromptu shrine. A place for serious-faced teenage girls to hold solemn candlelit vigils and read soppy, bad poetry. Hoping to get their teary, mascara-smeared faces on television.

When her body had been found things had changed. Someone had set up one of those Facebook pages where people who never knew her, never cared for her, people who wouldn't have given her the time of day when she was alive, could leave their tribute. 'We all miss you, Alicia'; 'You were beautiful and kind, my best friend'; and the most popular, the most unimaginative of all: 'RIP, Alicia'. Until, over time, everybody had gradually lost interest.

Then it had been revealed on the local news that the sighting at the bus stop had never happened: a bogus report by some attention seeker who might be charged with wasting the police's time. So today she had watched, had watched Malcolm watching,

11

as some council workmen cleared away the shrine. Peeled off the poems pasted there. Scrubbed away the graffiti tributes. Dumped the wilted, dead and dying bouquets of flowers. Thrown away the mouldering teddy bears. Why did people always leave teddy fucking bears?

'They shouldn't have done that,' said Malcolm, 'took it all down.' He was playing with the tablecloth again, running his fingers along the edge, collecting toast crumbs on the tips before rubbing his fingers together and watching them fall to the floor. Then, looking up, he said, 'We used to come in here all the time, do you remember? We always used to sit at this table.' As if he was part of their crowd, as if he had been invited. She looked at the table. Around the café, trying to place it in her memory. Could be. But it was just a table. She had a vague image of him at the periphery of their group. In the same parka. Not saying much. Not joining in. Not really wanting to be noticed in case someone challenged his right to be there. Told him to fuck off.

'Oh yeah, I remember, you always had a book in your pocket.' She hadn't meant it to come out quite that way. Sneering. Taking the piss.

He shrugged. 'I like stories. Something that's not ...' He looked around the café, out of the window.

Something that's not this, she thought. 'Something that's not crap,' she said out loud. He nodded at the tabletop. 'I used to like books,' she said, 'when I was little. But I can't read them now. The words get all, like, jumbled up? Like moving about and stuff. I prefer the telly now. Nature programmes, soaps, films. They're stories as well, right? Cartoons, mostly. Disney. Stuff like that.'

Not really listening, he looked down at the table. Started doing that thing with the tablecloth again. Fidgeting. Looking like he was getting ready to go.

'D'you want another?' she asked.

When he looked up she indicated the dregs of the cup of tea, the Mars wrapper. He nodded. Donna called out to the woman behind the counter and got herself a tea, even though she didn't much like it.

'Is that the local?' she asked, pointing at the newspaper. He held it out to her and she took it from him and started flicking through the pages, trying to find any mention of Alicia. The café seemed to fall silent. Outside somewhere there was a sound. Indistinct and undefined. An indication of movement, a presence. Then as she listened, stopped turning the pages, concentrated more fully on it, she thought she could hear breathing. Then it was gone.

The woman from behind the counter – fat, middle-aged, too much perfume and way too much make-up – put the two teas and the Mars bar in front of them and waited for her money. Donna fished in the pocket of her jacket, pulled out a crumpled fiver. Her last, until her benefits were paid on Friday. The woman looked at it for a moment – an alien artefact – then made a disgusted face. Moments later she was back, dumping Donna's change on the table. Shrapnel. Donna wondered if the woman had deliberately sorted through the till for the coppers. She scooped up the coins and put them in the pocket of her jacket as Malcolm unwrapped his Mars bar, dipped it in his tea and bit it.

She started leafing through the paper again. There was nothing. Not a single mention of Alicia. She scanned every single article, even the tiny ones with only a few sentences. Nothing. Malcolm looked over as she refolded the newspaper and pushed it across the table to him. 'It's like everyone's just forgotten her,' she said.

3

Cat Russell waited for the Scottish detective to speak. He seemed to take an eternity to ask each question, consider her response, then ask the next. Sometimes asking the same thing several times. It was really starting to get on her bastard nerves.

It already seemed a very long time since they had entered the interview room, Ferguson rattling the window in its frame until finally, with an audible protest, it opened. The previously muted susurration of the rain becoming a noisy tattoo on the metal fire escape, overlaid with the *plink-plink* of drips falling from the window frame on to the sill. Ferguson dragged a chair across the linoleum floor, and sitting down, indicating that she should sit in the chair opposite, even though it was the only other chair in the room.

The rain had come as a sudden break in the weather, several weeks of unbearably hot days followed by equally uncomfortable nights. She suspected, though, that it would not be enough to clear the air. The atmosphere in the room was already beginning to feel too close. The man was talking. Or perhaps he had just

15

cleared his throat. Ferguson had an annoying habit of talking into his paperwork. Addressing the table top, as if he were reading from a script at a first rehearsal. As if he didn't quite know his lines. He hadn't actually looked at her once since they had entered the room. Cat had spent most of that time looking at the top of his head. Thick black hair shot with silver. As was the moustache, like the ones favoured by footballers in the seventies. He had ruddy cheeks but was the sort of bloke who grew a five o'clock shadow by lunchtime. According to Pearson, not exactly the fount of all knowledge when it came to these things, there were two types of officer from the Professional Standards Department. The ex-Job, the misfit with a grudge against the force. Or the pencil pusher who, in Pearson's words, 'avoided making mistakes by doing fuck-all'. But then again, for Pearson there were two types, and only ever two types, of everything. And everybody. She wasn't quite sure at the moment into which of Pearson's categories Ferguson might fall. He riffled through some sheets of A4 notes, then cleared his throat again.

'So, Detective Constable Russell, how would you describe the relationship between yourself and Detective Inspector Sean Carragher?'

'We were partners.'

'"Partners"?' He paused. 'What does that mean?'

There was a vague insinuation in the question. She had caught it in some of the other questions he had asked, his attitude towards her, as if he were in possession of an as yet unacknowledged fact. As if there were more to her relationship with Carragher than she was letting on. Could there be some rumour going around the nick that he'd picked up on? Or, if he was one of Pearson's misfits, maybe he'd never had a partner, was genuinely unsure of what the term meant. Then again, maybe he had

had a partner at one time, before she'd finally had enough of his irritating fucking habits and left him, so that now he had no kind of personal life at all, had nothing better to do than spend his time sitting at his desk shuffling paper. And wasting the time of proper coppers. Russell heaved a sigh.

'We were "partnered" together. As a mentoring process? In the hope, I suppose, that I would gain something from DI Carragher's experience in the Job.'

'OK,' said Ferguson, 'so how would you define the term "partners"?'

'We were partners. We looked out for each other.'

'You looked out for each other.' That was another annoying habit Ferguson had. The repetition of a statement. There was no inflection to indicate as to whether he doubted its veracity, but the implication was there all the same. Cat was beginning to realise that everything this man did needled her in some way.

'And would that include lying for each other?' he asked. She did not answer. 'The problem I have, DC Russell, is that if you were "partners", if you "looked out for each other", as you say, then I find it hard to believe that you wouldn't know exactly what was going on with DI Carragher.'

After a minute he finally looked up. His eyes blue. But bloodshot.

'Sorry,' she said, 'was that a question?'

This time it was Ferguson who didn't answer. He looked back at his notes, lifted the top sheet, studied the one beneath.

'I understand that DI Carragher did not turn up for duty this morning,' he said.

Cat said nothing. The standard procedure in cases where an officer was under investigation was that they were 'removed from the possible chain of evidence', to ensure that their presence did not contaminate any potential criminal trials. In the meantime the officer in question would be asked to limit himself to filing or clearing out the property room. She could guess how that would go down with Sean Carragher – 'Call me Sean. Surnames are for old farts.' Old farts like Pearson being the implication.

'Had DI Carragher given you any indication that he might be intending to report sick?'

Again that insinuation. She took a breath, tried to sound cool, but even so her answer was delivered through gritted teeth.

'No. Why should he? I have no contact with Detective Inspector Carragher outside the Job. I worked with him for around six months and at the moment, as you well know, I'm back working with DS Frank Pearson.'

Detective Inspector Neil Ferguson looked down at the notes in front of him, not really taking anything in. He cleared his throat. He wished now he'd picked up a bottle of water on his way in. And taken some painkillers. He had a banging headache. He was wearing the same shirt that he'd worn the previous evening. And the same underpants, come to that. It was only meant to be a quick drink with a mate. But this morning he had woken up on a strange living-room floor, already hungover, fully dressed but frozen, and late for work. He could smell last night's booze on him. Lager. Scotch. Some kind of rum-based cocktail. And his unwashed body. He hadn't had time to shave. The trouble was, he wasn't used to drinking, wasn't a drinker. But when an old mate left the Job, you had to have a pint or two with him, didn't you? Especially if you were in his debt. If that mate had done you a big favour. If that mate had arranged, at your request, a temporary secondment. A move from the 'cultural wastelands of the north', as he had put it, to 'southern civilisation'. Though if this was 'civilisation' . . .

If they'd left it at just a couple of pints he'd have been all right. If they hadn't gone on to shorts. If, on falling out of the pub, they hadn't decided to go on somewhere else, he might have had some chance of doing his job properly this morning. Of carrying out this interview and asking the right questions. He was the one supposedly responsible for upholding standards of conduct. Instead he'd become a cliché, a stereotype: the Scottish Alkie. Worse than that, the Scottish Alkie Detective. DC Russell by contrast had her long brown hair tied back in a loose ponytail. Somewhere in her late twenties, she had the sort of complexion that would be English Rose in the winter, tanning to a golden brown in the summer, and make-up that was immaculate and minimal. Just a little mascara around her large hazel eyes. The merest hint of lippy. She was dressed in a black suit and white blouse and looked totally comfortable in the oppressive atmosphere of the room. DI Ferguson had no idea where he was in the interview, what questions he had asked. And he had the feeling he'd repeated himself on more than one occasion.

He made a show of studying his notes again, lifting a sheet of paper at random, pretending to read from it. Christ, he felt bad – he wished he'd followed Carragher's example and called in sick himself. He needed to wrap this up, go home, take some painkillers, drink a pint of orange juice and go back to bed. He started to shuffle his papers into a pile, recapped his pen.

'Is that it?' asked Cat.

Ferguson picked up the pile of papers, tapped them on the desk, turned them ninety degrees and tapped them again. He picked up his briefcase from the floor and put his paperwork in it. Snapped the locks shut and slipped his pen into his inside jacket pocket. Finally he spoke. 'No, Detective Constable Russell, that is not it. That is far from "it". Unfortunately I'm due elsewhere and I'll be tied up tomorrow. Shall we say we'll reconvene on Wednesday morning?'

Cat nodded. 'Sir.'

'DI Carragher has a number of very serious charges to answer.' For only the second time, he looked directly at her. 'It would have been better for him if he hadn't signed in sick today. It would be better for all concerned if he were here himself to answer any questions we might have. Don't you agree?' Cat managed to say nothing. 'Until he does, his actions might be seen to cast a shadow across the reputation of all his colleagues.' He paused. 'And, as his partner,' he lifted a palm to forestall any argument, 'or one-time partner, you can see how it might not reflect well on yourself in particular.'

Cat deliberately did not watch him leave the room. But as she heard the door close behind him, looking out at the rain, she shivered.

4

Donna stood at her half-open window, staring past her face, reflected in one of the rain-spackled panes, and out into the street. She struck a match and lit her cigarette, watching the match burn down to a blackened stump between her fingers before flicking it through the window. She ran an index finger absent-mindedly through the water that had pooled on the sill. The window had been painted shut when she had moved in and she had had to chip away at it and then lever it open with a big, flat-headed screwdriver. But it still didn't move freely. Maybe the wood had become warped or something. It was a struggle to get it open and once it was open it was a struggle to get it closed again, so mostly she didn't bother. Outside, the rain had stopped and the street was already nearly dry, the temperature back up in the thirties.

There it was again. That smell. Of course, it could be the black bags of rubbish piled up outside. Late afternoon and they still hadn't been collected. Some of the bags were split. Eggshells. Teabags. Bloodied, plastic meat wrappers. Dirty, disposable nappies. Spilling onto the pavement and into the road. Last night the foxes had come. Mange-ridden and panting, padding on chafed and split paws. Calling out to each other. The rasping bark of a dog with a sore throat answered by a sound like babies crying. Then it had sounded as if one had had a baby in its jaws, worrying at it, the baby being tossed about like a rag doll, screaming in pain and terror. She had had to crawl down under the covers then and put the pillow over her ears and wait for it to go away. In the past Alicia would have lain with her in the cramped single bed, holding her, stroking her hair, singing softly to her. And everything would have been all right. Alicia made everything all right somehow.

Alicia had been the only person who had noticed she existed. The only person to have paid her any attention. The only person who had ever cared for her. Although their backgrounds were similar, with absentee dads and junkie mums with a string of violent and abusive boyfriends who came and went – fucked up, basically – somehow it hadn't mattered to Alicia. Even being in that crap care home. The Abigail Burnett. She had no idea who Abigail Burnett was, didn't want to know really. If Abigail Burnett was still alive she would probably be some stuck-up cow like the headmistress at their old school. A sink school where kids went who couldn't get in anywhere else; kids from the local care homes like her and Alicia, or kids who had been disruptive or underperformed at their primaries, like Malcolm. Some stuck-up cow who looked down her nose at the likes of Donna and Alicia.

Maybe not Alicia. Alicia was beautiful and cool. Alicia could sing and play the piano and write songs. Alicia was going to be somebody – somebody rich, somebody famous. Now she was gone it seemed that everything good in the world, all the light, all the colour, had gone with her. Now everything seemed dulled, tainted and sickly.

There was a smell that had been driving her mad for weeks. It wasn't the rubbish bags and she couldn't for the life of her find out where it was coming from. She had turned her small room upside-down looking for it. Something rank, putrid, decaying, the smell of something rotting.

And someone had their telly or radio on again. Lately it seemed to be on constantly. She could never quite make out what programme it was or whose room it was coming from. And if she concentrated on the sound it seemed to get quieter rather than louder. Voices. People talking. But what they said was indistinct, muffled. It was always just loud enough for her to hear, but not quite loud enough for her to make out properly what the voices were saying. She had thought that it might be The Pervert from down the landing. But standing in the hall a few times outside his room, listening, she hadn't been able to hear anything behind his door. And in the last few days she thought the voices might have followed her out on to the street. She took a last drag of her cigarette and ground it out in the ashtray on the windowsill. A small pottery ashtray she had made at school. Dark brown, it was supposed to have been a hedgehog. But something had gone wrong and it had sort of folded in on itself. Even she had to admit the end result looked more like a turd.

She turned back into the room. It was cluttered, cramped. An unmade single bed. Next to it, on the floor, a small lamp with a wonky shade, a cardboard chest of drawers with a cheap clock radio on it. Boxes and plastic shopping bags containing clothes, toiletries, tampons, make-up. On the wall an antique mirror with the silver peeling behind the glass, hung on wallpaper that hadn't been changed since the seventies. The only decent thing in the room was the telly. Appropriated from another party. There had been a fight, someone had pulled a knife, cut someone else, so the Old Bill had been called. During the confusion, the wait for the police and ambulance to turn up, she had gone into one of the bedrooms and managed to walk out with the flat-screen TV with built-in Freeview, and the remote.

In the narrow strip of floor space remaining, on the threadbare carpet, lay Malcolm, asleep under his imitation parka. Without his glasses, his face at rest, he looked younger. He lay on one arm, the other balled into a fist near his face. As if he had wanted to suck his thumb in his sleep but resisted the temptation. His head lay on the book he had been reading to her earlier. An illustrated encyclopedia of Greek myths. He had read the stories and pointed out who each of the characters was in the drawings, explained them all to her. Malcolm's mouth was hanging open, a string of dribble pooling on the open page. He looked kind of sweet, she thought, like a little toddler. Earlier, though, when they had come back from the café, Donna sitting on the edge of the bed and him on the floor, she had caught him trying to get a look up her skirt. Dirty little bugger.

She kicked the bottom of his trainer. 'Oi!' There was no response, so she kicked him again. 'Oi, Malcolm!'

His eyes opened and he blinked a couple of times. 'What?'

'I've been thinking,' she said.

He got himself into a sitting position, took a clean cotton handkerchief out of his pocket and wiped his face. He looped his glasses over his ears, noticed the dribble on the page and dabbed at it before closing the book.

'About what?' he said without looking up.

'Alicia, of course.'

She had been thinking about Alicia. And not just today. But today she had followed Malcolm from the bus-stop shrine, had let him come back with her to the bedsit. From his position on the floor Malcolm watched as, tucking her hair self-consciously behind an ear, she moved from the window and sat down on the edge of the bed.

'What about her?' he asked.

'It's like what I said in the café, Malc. It's like everyone's forgotten her. It's like no one gives a fuck.'

Malcolm shrugged. 'S'pose.'

'It's not right though,' she said.

Malcolm picked up his book, turned it over in his hands, touched the plastic covering the library had put on it, scratched at some stain or other.

'Someone should care, Malc, someone should give a fuck about her, shouldn't they?' Malcolm opened his book. 'We should do something,' she said.

'Like what?'

It was a good question. She had no idea.

'I don't fucking know. Something.'

She shifted on the bed, parted her legs slightly. Watched his eyes move along her thighs. Let him see her knickers.

'C'mon, Malc. What else have you got to do?'

Transfixed, he said nothing. Casually she closed her legs again.

'We ought to do something,' she said.

5

Sean Carragher drummed impatiently on the steering wheel, both front windows wound down to try to take advantage of an intermittent and ineffectual breeze. The air outside was still, heavy with the smell of frying doughnuts. Over the sound of the incessant seafront traffic he could hear the high-pitched shrieks of passengers on the rollercoaster and, every now and then, a vaguely unsettling repeated melody – a sinister calliope motif which seemed more suited to a black-and-white film featuring a Victorian freak show than a late-summer afternoon on the Essex coast. Southend, in common with most of the country's seaside towns, seemed to him in terminal decline. Despite some attempts at regeneration. New paving along the esplanade. The planting of tropical palms that already looked withered and dying. The new observation platform at the entrance to the pier. Southend Pier, at one and one-third of a mile, he had read somewhere, was the longest pleasure pier in the world. When he had first transferred from the Merseyside force he had walked the length of it – half demolished by fire, the other half creaking wooden planks.

Buffeted by a biting, blustery wind. Only to find that there was nothing at the end of it. Apart from a large and all but empty community arts centre containing four badly executed paintings of local landmarks. And a tiny café that served the worst coffee he had ever tasted.

At the sound of approaching footsteps he checked the rear-view mirror. The passenger door opened and closed and he felt the suspension shift as someone got in. When he turned, Cat Russell was rummaging in her handbag.

Out of the corner of her eye she saw him check his watch. A Rolex. Cat thought about the Timex and Rolex cop speech that Pearson was forever trotting out, and smiled to herself.

'Been waiting long?' she asked.

'A while.'

Good, she thought, but instead she asked, 'It's so hot in here. Why haven't you got the air-con on?'

'I like to hear when anyone's coming,' Carragher said. 'I don't have the windows closed. I don't listen to music. Not when I'm parked. Not since I got this.'

When Cat looked over he was pulling his white T-shirt up and she saw once again the silver tracery of the shotgun wound. A peppering of lighter, puckered indentations littering his tanned stomach. She went back to searching her handbag and finally found her digital cigarette. She put it in her mouth and took a drag.

'Do those things work?' he asked.

'You get a nicotine hit. But it's not the same. I miss the tar.' And like all junkies she missed the ritual. The sparking up of a lighter or striking of a match. The setting of the flame to the end of the tobacco. The flicking of the ash into an ashtray. The attenuated exhalation of the final draw. The grinding out of the cigarette.

Carragher, looking out through the windscreen, watching the pavement traffic, said, 'I heard they give you eczema.'

Cat scratched her ribcage just under her bra cup, took the fag out of her mouth and looked at it. 'Mmm, lung cancer or skin disease. Great choice.'

'At least you don't smell like an ashtray.'

'There is that,' she said, putting the fag back in her mouth and taking another drag. She looked out of the window, following his gaze as he tracked a group of teenage girls. Too much make-up. Roots showing. Too-short skirts.

After a minute he asked, 'So, what happened today?'

She shifted her handbag on her lap, took the fag out of her mouth and regarded it again. It was the size and shape of a cigarette, but heavier. The artificial glow you got when you inhaled wasn't quite convincing. The vapour you breathed in – well, it wasn't really smoke. So it wasn't really smoking.

'Not a lot.'

As she had hoped it would, this response needled him.

'They must have said something.'

'Yeah,' she nodded, 'they said it would have been better if you had come in.'

'To do the filing? Tidy up the evidence room? Sit around on my arse and answer the phones, take messages for the rest of the team while they're out? Come on, Cat, can you really see me doing that?'

She turned to look at his profile. She had to admit, despite everything else, that he really was great-looking. His features were chiselled: prominent cheekbones, a strong jaw. As he turned to look at her, taking off his sunglasses, she noticed how long and thick his eyelashes were. His eyes were strangely soft in such a masculine face. A grey so pale as to appear almost colourless. But they made him look cold, too. Dangerous.

'They said it would have been better for everyone, for me, if you'd come in and answered their questions for yourself.'

Carragher said nothing. She could smell his aftershave, despite the open car windows. Something expensive, subtle.

'It reflects badly on me,' she said. 'They've said as much.'

'I can appreciate that.'

'Can you, Sean? I'm not sure you can.'

'Look, it's just how they operate—'

'And,' she interrupted, 'they implied that they knew there was a relationship going on. Outside of the Job.'

'So?'

'So I'm here, aren't I?'

After a minute he said, 'Look, I can't come in yet. There's things I need to sort out. But you've got nothing to worry about, Cat.'

'Haven't I? That's just the thing, Sean. I don't know if I've got anything to worry about or not, do I? I've already told lies for you. And really, I have no idea what you've been up to. Not a clue.'

'Nothing. I haven't been up to anything. You've got nothing to worry about.'

But at that precise moment, in the oppressive confines of the car, with the sickly, cloying smell of frying doughnuts drifting in through the open window, the shrieking of the passengers on the rollercoaster, and looking into those colourless eyes, she experienced a sudden pitch and lurch in the pit of her stomach.

6

Frank Pearson sat in the hospital car park behind the wheel of the Mondeo. Looking out through the windscreen, he noticed again how dirty it was. He pressed the button and squirted water across the glass, turned on the wipers, watched them for a minute or two. Up in the main part of the building, on one of the wards, was his mother. He had driven here with every intention of visiting her. Now he was actually here, though, he wondered if he could go through with it. The constant struggle to think of things to say. Conversation between them had always been stilted – the two of them usually at cross-purposes. They had little enough in common, little enough to talk about, at the best of times. And now her world had been reduced to the activities and routine of the hospital ward. Even before this, his world had always been totally unfathomable and inexplicable to her. Add to that the overly hot ward. That underlying smell of boiled cabbage and human waste. He shot a cuff and checked his watch. His day off. His first day off in weeks. He hadn't done much with it. Got up late. Switched on the box – daytime TV – switched it off again.

Opened a book he had been meaning to read for months. After a few pages, he had put it down again. Emptied the laundry basket into the washing machine. Considered, then rejected, doing some of those 'little jobs around the flat' that he kept putting off. Wandered aimlessly from room to room for a while.

Finally he had picked up his sax. A second-hand Saramande tenor he had got off the internet. It was amazing what you could find on the net. He had downloaded some lessons, too. The kind where you didn't have to learn to read music. He had a decent tone, he'd give himself that. It sounded nice to his ear. He'd played as a kid. Then he'd wanted to be 'Cannonball' Adderley, or Lester 'Prez' Young, or Charlie 'Bird' Parker. Maybe, he had to admit, what he'd really wanted was a cool nickname. But mostly he'd wanted to be Jonny Hodges. 'Rabbit'. So, maybe not. He'd played alto as a kid. When he'd thought of taking it up again though, he'd fancied a tenor. He could play the notes, follow a tune. But that, really, was as far as it went. There was no ... emotion. No *duende*. It was unfeeling. Mechanical. Perfunctory. What had he expected? It was why he'd given it up in the first place. If you couldn't manage it when you were younger, when you had that obsessive infatuation and, above all, when you had the time, what chance did you have when you were middle-aged? It wasn't helped by the fact that he always got home late, didn't get enough practice. You couldn't play the thing late at night. It was too ... it was too fucking loud, was what it was. But, he admitted to himself, no end of practice would change the fact that he wouldn't ever be able to play the thing the way he wanted. It was never going to happen. Having said all that, he was reluctant to sell the sax. Couldn't quite bring himself to part with it. For him it was a thing of beauty. A feat of engineering: the brass, the rods and pads, the mother-of-pearl inlay on the buttons. He liked to just handle it. Feel the body of it warm beneath his touch. To rub a soft cloth over it and bring it to a high polish. It reminded him, up close, of some kind of steam-punk machine. The sort of thing you might find in the *Nautilus*: the crew gathered round a giant saxophone set like a column in the instrument panel. Nemo adjusting the dials, the rods moving of their own volition, the pads opening and closing and emitting soft peeps, whistles and breaths of steam as the giant submarine headed for the bottom of the ocean. The bell retransmitting the strange, alien emissions of the bio-luminescent jellyfish and giant squid outside.

He checked his watch again. Visiting time had started. Ten minutes ago, in fact. He couldn't sit here all night. For one thing, he was starting to feel uncomfortable, like he had to go for a piss. Although he knew he didn't. Knew that when he did go, an ineffectual stream squeezed out of a seemingly full bladder, it would burn and sting and ten minutes later he would feel like he needed to go again. From where he sat he could see the Oncology Department. A Portakabin in the hospital car park.

Pearson had, along with at least half the population, he suspected, self-diagnosed – looking for a solution on the internet, putting his symptoms into Google and being presented with two possibilities. The first being a water infection. The other: prostate cancer. He had visited his GP, an oddly reticent man, wary of human contact, reluctant to leave the safety of his chair for the precarious business of diagnosis. If pushed he might dart a glance – his expression a mixture of revulsion and apprehension – at the offending body part but his gaze would dart back just as quickly to his computer screen. In the past Pearson had often wondered whether one day he might be reduced to shouting his symptoms through a keyhole, then waiting in the corridor until a prescription was slipped under the locked door. Now, after the

33

same doctor had conducted the first of several prostate examinations he had endured at the hands of several different people, he felt nostalgic for that lack of intimacy. On his first visit he had been prescribed a course of antibiotics, which had had no effect. He returned to his GP a fortnight later, when he had been sent for a blood test – 'I'm ready for my tea and biscuits now' – to check for elevated SAR levels. Pearson had read on the internet that heightened levels of SAR, a prostate-specific antigen, could be an indicator of prostate cancer, but wasn't quite sure what SAR stood for or what exactly an antigen was. His blood test had come back and showed raised levels. Then came his first visit to the Oncology Department: tests for urine flow, an ultrasound scan of his lower abdomen – 'Is it a boy or a girl?' – and he had been prescribed another course of (stronger) antibiotics.

'Finish the course and then we'll send you for another blood test, but if these don't clear it up,' said the specialist, 'we might have to do an internal examination of the bladder.' The specialist held out his hand. After a moment's hesitation, Pearson considering where that hand had just been and the threat of what it might be doing on his next visit, he had shaken it. Surely, he thought on his way out, no matter how small the camera was supposed to be, that particular hole was never designed to have anything inserted *into* it?

He was going to have to have a piss – or at least try to – or go home. Either way he'd have to go into the hospital: he needed to pay for the car park ticket that he'd collected on the way in. The machines for that were inside. Pearson sighed, turned off the windscreen wipers and opened the car door.

7

They entered the room without knocking. The door handle yanked down before they barged through. There was the sound of the door hitting the wall opposite and then rebounding. Papers fluttering on a noticeboard. A man stood up abruptly from behind his desk. Hair cropped close to the skull, the colour of old steel. Watery, blue eyes. Sickert Downey, Director of the Abigail Burnett Children's home. And, as such, always 'Mr Downey' to Donna. He had the tanned face of a man who spent a lot of time out-of-doors. Mr Downey could bore the tits off you about his garden. But a grey shone through. A weather-beaten building starting to reveal a previous layer of paint. He rehearsed a series of expressions. Fear. Anxiety. Confusion. Before, swallowing, recovering his composure a little, he settled on annoyance.

'Expecting someone else?' Donna asked.

'Miss Freeman,' he said, sitting back down. Now merely irritated. 'How did you get in?'

'You should change the code on the outside keypad occasionally.'

Downey picked up a biro, wrote on a Post-it note then stuck it to his computer screen and pointed with the pen. 'Who's your chum?'

Donna smiled. *Chum*.

'That's just Malc,' she said.

Malcolm wasn't listening. Standing instead with his hands in the pockets of his pretend parka. Looking around. And, in Donna's view, taking an overly keen interest in his surroundings. They hadn't changed much. Stained, green carpet tiles. Once-white walls, now yellowing with age. Cork noticeboards containing colour-coded calendars, fading newspaper clippings, council circulars, fire regulations; two grey metal filing cabinets; two mustard-coloured leather-look armchairs on either side of a Formica-topped table which bore the debris of a meagre working lunch. Inside a plastic sandwich wrapper, a balled-up paper napkin and a sliver of buttery ham. A plastic cup with the dregs of tea in the bottom. There were blue plastic moving-crates, cardboard cartons stacked two or three high along one wall. Downey arranged things on the desk, squaring paper and putting pens in the desk-tidy. Opening his top drawer to drop a paperclip into it and shutting it again; letting Donna know how unimportant she was. Finally, lacing his fingers and placing his hands on the desk, he said:

'So, Miss Freeman, what exactly is it that I can do for you?'

'I just wanted to see how things are with you. Just wanted to visit the old place. Make sure it was still here.' He eyed her suspiciously but said nothing. 'So,' a slight edge to her voice now, 'how are things with you?'

Malcolm opened the top drawer of one of the metal filing cabinets. Peered inside, closed it again, opened the next drawer down. Sensing the silence behind him, a tension in the room, he turned.

'I'd really rather you didn't do that,' said Downey. 'Those cabinets contain sensitive personal information.'

Malcolm shrugged. Closed the drawer. Not bothered one way or the other. Downey turned back to Donna.

'As delightful as it is to see you, Miss Freeman, I'm not sure what I can help you with. You're no longer a resident and therefore, technically, you're no longer my responsibility. If you have any problems, with money or accommodation, with your ...' he smiled condescendingly, 'educational needs, your personal adviser is the one best placed to help you. I take it the Social Services Department have put you in touch with a personal adviser?'

She said nothing. Donna had been assigned a personal adviser. He had sorted out her benefits so she got some kind of extra allowance. Found her a place to live. Even if it was a shitty bedsit. He was OK. Mostly. But he talked to you in that voice they had all been taught. The voice they all used. The voice that was supposed to keep you calm, but just sounded patronising and ended up winding you up. So nowadays Donna tried not to have too much to do with him. Malcolm had produced a disposable lighter from somewhere. He flicked the wheel absent-mindedly a few times. Then he put the lighter in and out of his mouth as if he were smoking a cigarette.

'Malc,' said Donna. He looked over at her questioningly. 'Sit down, eh?'

He looked round for somewhere to sit, then went to one of the low leather armchairs.

'Alicia Goode,' said Donna, picking up some official-looking report from Downey's desk and flicking through the pages. Suddenly she was aware of her own breathing, but she thought she could hear something else underneath, a breathing that seemed to echo hers. She held her breath for a few seconds, listening intently. Seconds stretched out into a minute. Silence. But, somewhere, an inference of shuffling hooves. Breath suppressed behind wet nostrils. A realignment of heavily muscled animal bodies. The heady scent of a bestial musk. She released her breath and, in that same somewhere, there was an exhaled sigh of relief. When she looked up Downey had his hand out and she gave him the report.

'Ah, yes.' Downey nodded, putting the report back on his desk out of her reach. 'Your little friend.'

'My little *dead* friend,' she corrected.

'Of course.' He nodded again. He studied her for a moment, took in the clothes she was wearing, her make-up, her hair. He was about to say something. Then thought better of it.

'We were all sorry about her ...' He trailed off.

'Her what? Her disappearance? Her death? Her murder?'

'Murder? Well, I'm sure we're all quite sorry—'

'Sorry? Seems like no one really gives a fuck to me.'

Downey's expression became cold. There were rules. No drinking. No smoking. And definitely no swearing. He was a regular churchgoer, a Christian. That was another thing Mr Downey would bore the tits off you about.

'Miss Freeman,' he said, 'I can assure you that—'

'Don't you fucking dare say you care!' Ear-piercing, shrill, desperate. Reverberating around the walls. Making her ears throb. The buzz and rattle of cheap speakers at maximum volume.

In the silence that followed, Donna became aware of a clicking sound. When she looked around Malcolm had the plastic cup in his hand, holding the disposable lighter under it and flicking the wheel. Finally it caught. Malcolm watched the plastic retreat from the lighter's flame and tea dribble on to the floor. Aware suddenly that they had stopped talking, he looked up and then blew out the flame. Stood up and dropped the burnt plastic cup into the waste bin, then sat down again.

'You leaving?' he asked Downey. 'Only you seem to have a lot of boxes,' he said, pointing with the lighter, 'and the filing cabinets are empty.'

Donna turned back to Downey.

'I've been offered early retirement.' Flat. Impersonal. He turned to Donna. Adopting the tone of the long-suffering, a man who had explained the same thing many times before: 'As you are aware, Miss Freeman, there was a police investigation and they found no evidence that it was anything other than a tragic accident. We are all sorry for your loss, Donna. I can assure you that I regret as much as anyone that it happened. But accidents do happen. Tragic and sad as they might be, they are a fact of life that we must just accept and move on from.'

The picture of fair and reasonable. The matter closed. Dealt with. After a minute Donna realised she was crying.

'You were in charge,' she said.

'As I said before, both you and Miss Goode had left. Technically you were no longer my responsibility.'

'You were supposed to make sure we were safe.'

'You were—'

'You were supposed to look after us.' Donna's face was wet. 'Somebody's supposed to look after us. Aren't they?'

When she had entered the room she had been angry. She was going to make Mr Downey ... she didn't know what she was going to make Mr Downey do. But she was going to make him do something.

But looking at Mr Downey now, he just looked old. Old and sick and very tired. The grey underlying Downey's tan seemed to have become more pronounced. The face underneath. Something already dead. Or dying. Beginning to reveal itself. And Donna had to look away.

8

TUESDAY

TUESDAY

Although it was still early, not even seven, it was already almost unbearably hot again. Dave Cowans could already feel pools of sweat dampening his shirt under the suit jacket. He always wore a suit jacket and suit trousers. But generally not from the same suit. This morning the trousers were grey. Charcoal, maybe, when he had bought them. But they had been in the washing machine so many times that the colour had faded to something indeterminate and washed-out. Almost not a colour at all. He had slept in them, dozing off during some late-night film on the Movie Channel. Had woken up on the settee fully dressed, his shirt and trousers creased to buggery.

The jacket was a sort of brown. He wasn't used to seeing it other than in the crepuscular dimness of the club. In the stark light of the morning, even to him, it looked grubby. Dirt-shiny on the cuffs. Some kind of light-brown stain on one of the lapels. Curry probably. He held up the lapel with one hand, scratched it with the other and sniffed. Definitely curry. Indian. Most likely a prawn madras. That's what he usually had. But

41

he hadn't had an Indian for at least, what, three days? Kebab and chips last night. Actually, now he looked at his jacket, that looked like kebab grease round the bottom edge. He was going to have to put the thing in the dry cleaner's. Cost a bloody fortune these days. Probably cost the same to buy a new jacket, but he hated shopping; he had the kind of body that clothes, no matter where he bought them, just didn't seem to fit. Short legs. Skinny arse. Thick round the middle. His trousers invariably hanging down under his belly, slipping down at the back, always showing his pants. His shirt always hanging out. This morning his socks had migrated down his feet and bunched damply in his shoes.

His head banging. His mouth dry. What sort of fucking time was this to be up and about? Seven o'clock. Christ, when was the last time he'd been up this early on a regular basis? But someone had to let the workmen in. And who else was going to do it but him? Terry's club, but you wouldn't catch Terry getting up to do it. At least the workmen were nearly finished. The club was reopening on Thursday, and he'd help himself to a Scotch or two from the optics when he got in. Why not? He deserved it.

Standing at the front door to the club, searching his pockets unsuccessfully for his keys, he wondered if he might have left them at home again. On the worktop by the toaster. But he hadn't had any breakfast this morning. Had just about been able to force down a weak cup of tea. A raindrop fell, hitting him smack dab in the centre of his bald spot. He started checking his pockets once again. He really could do without having to walk back to the flat. Last night's forecast hadn't predicted rain and on his walk in the sky had been clear and blue. But it would be just his luck to get caught in a downpour. It stank here. Piss. The outside of the club was regularly used as a public toilet. And who had to go out with a bucket of water and disinfectant and a broom and scrub it all down?

What was that? The sound of ... like something creaking? Rummaging in his right-hand jacket pocket, he finally found his keys. They had slipped down through a hole in the lining. He pushed his fingers into the hole and fished out the keys, ripping the lining of the pocket a little more in the process. That creaking again. He sorted through the bunch, trying to find the one that fitted the front door. Another raindrop fell, once again hitting him smack dab in the middle of his bald spot. Then Dave Cowans took a step back and looked up.

9

Pearson adjusted the position of the portable fan on his desktop for the fifth time in as many minutes. The trouble was, if he had it pointing away all it did was move the hot air around in the couple of feet immediately in front of the blades. The incident room was stuffy at the best of times, but in the current weather it was almost intolerable, even with the windows open and fans on every desk. There had been a desultory attempt to decorate – magnolia emulsion for the walls and gloss paint, white, for everything else – but not recently, and it was already starting to look shabby. Pearson watched Wendy Simpson, the team analyst, gather together the photographs from the death scene, walk slowly across the room and attach them to one of the portable whiteboards-on-wheels that Roberts preferred to use. These would be arranged at right-angles to the wall to save space, forcing officers to walk up and down between them to study maps and crime-scene photographs, like some bizarre exhibition that you might find in a particularly macabre public library. Simpson was petite with permed blond hair and a doll-like complexion, still very attractive, Pearson thought, despite the weight she'd put on since becoming pregnant. A year ago, during a celebration after the successful completion of another murder investigation, she had been in pieces and confessed to Pearson that she was about to leave her husband, Ronnie – a gambler, and to make things worse, a loser. Pearson had been tempted, but in the end declined to take it any further. There had been any number of reasons why it would have been wrong. They had both had way too much to drink, for one thing. She was too young for him, for another. And she was married, of course. Obviously, since then, her and Ronnie had made up. Pearson wasn't quite sure about the status of his own marriage. And hadn't been for a while, truth be told. When she glanced over Pearson looked away and adjusted the position of the desk fan again. If he pointed the fan directly at his face it gave him sinus trouble, swiftly followed by a headache which no amount of pills would shift. Plus he had to weight down all the paperwork on the desk, otherwise it lifted and flapped annoyingly or—

Several sheets of paper fluttered to the floor and he started to pick them back up and slap them on to the desk where Cat Russell, having entered the room without him noticing, sat with a face like thunder.

'Morning,' he said. Then, wondering if he would regret it, 'What's up?'

'While you were out yesterday, enjoying your day off, I was interviewed by Professional Standards.'

'Yeah,' he said, 'how did that go?'

She shrugged. 'Hard to tell.'

'Did they give you a hard time?'

'No. Not really.'

Pearson, with the last of the sheets of paper in his hand, looked over at her. 'So what's the matter?'

'The matter is that he seemed to think that me and Carragher were in some kind of relationship.' She searched his face for a reaction, then said, 'So where might he have got that idea?'

'Don't look at me. I haven't said anything.'

'There isn't anything to say anything about.'

'Look,' Pearson said as reasonably as he could, 'even if there was, it's nothing to do with me.'

She eyed him dubiously for a moment and then said, 'But you knew about these rumours?'

'I'd heard them,' he conceded.

'And you didn't think to tell me about them?'

He'd thought about telling her. He'd definitely thought about telling her. Then he'd thought about what kind of reaction he might get, and decided that that might not be such a good idea; that it would very definitely be a bad idea.

'So who had you heard it from?'

Pearson shrugged. 'Just around.'

'Oh, it's common knowledge, is it? The whole fucking nick thinks there's something going on?' Pearson didn't say anything. 'So, if you just heard it "around", who's been putting it around?'

Pearson felt a bead of sweat pop in his scalp, run down the back of his head and gather in his hairline. Russell, in the meantime, was still staring at him, waiting for an answer. Luckily for Pearson, DCI Martin Roberts chose that moment to enter the incident room, a few strands of his thinning red hair sticking to his forehead, his tie at half-mast, making an effort to tuck his shirt into his trousers, to roll up his shirtsleeves. There was something comforting, Pearson thought, about a scruffy copper, something right, something reassuring. Roberts clapped his hands.

'All right, all right, let's get on with it, it's too fucking hot in here to be hanging about.' Roberts waited a moment for the noise in the room to subside. 'OK, at seven twenty-four this morning the emergency services operator received a call reporting a male suspended from the scaffolding around the Avatar nightclub in the town centre. Myself and DS Pearson attended the scene, the uniformed duty inspector having sufficient misgivings surrounding the circumstances of the death that he felt unable to sign it off immediately as a suicide.

'As you are no doubt aware, there are now three classifications into which a sudden death may fall: suspicious, non-suspicious and unexplained. For those of you who may be new to the team, let me explain my position as regards the category of "unexplained". Utter bollocks. The very least, in my opinion, that any family, friends or colleagues of any deceased deserve is an explanation. If we are in any position to provide one.'

He paused to let this sink in and Pearson's mind went back to the previous year. The MIT had been called in to investigate a sudden death where a mutilated body was found on a rubbish tip. Forensic examination ascertained that the injuries were consistent with the body having passed through the tip machinery. The refuse surrounding the body was traced back to a skip in the town centre. Investigation revealed that the young man had been drinking heavily with friends and had been seen to jump into the skip and, it was presumed, had then fallen asleep. Pressure had been applied to declare the case unexplained in order to reduce operational budgets. Roberts, however, had persisted, and eventually CCTV footage had been unearthed of the young man climbing out of the skip before being attacked on the street by a group of youths, forced to the floor and kicked viciously in the head. He had then been upended into the skip and left for dead. The four attackers had subsequently been arrested, charged and convicted of manslaughter.

'So,' continued Roberts, 'we have two options left open to us. It is either suspicious or non-suspicious. In this case there is enough uncertainty that I intend to declare it suspicious until we can prove otherwise.'

When Pearson had arrived at the scene that morning, Roberts, in white forensic overalls, was in conversation with the crime-scene manager. He nodded an acknowledgement at Pearson and held up a couple of fingers to indicate that he wouldn't be much longer. When he walked over, slipping off the hood and unzipping his suit, Pearson asked:

'So what've we got?'

'Man in his sixties found hanged. Discovered by the assistant manager coming in to open up for the workmen refurbishing the nightclub.' Roberts indicated the green netting that obscured the building.

'And he is . . . ?'

'Already en route to the nick to give a video statement.'

'Any indicators that it's anything other than a suicide?'

'We've got some abrasions to the left side of the deceased's forehead,' said Roberts, struggling to remove his arm from the sleeve of the suit. 'Pathologist won't say at the moment whether they're ante- or post-mortem.'

'Anything else?' asked Pearson.

Roberts finally extricated himself from the white forensic suit, his sparse red hair standing on end, his face ruddier than usual.

'Scuff mark on the scaffolding board where he went over. As yet they can't be sure whether it was made by one of his shoes or not.'

Pearson peered up at the netting, squinting into the sun. 'Plus you've got to ask yourself how easy it would be for a man in his sixties to get up there in the first place.'

10

'It's not that much cooler in here, is it?' said Pearson, dropping into the chair in the SIO's office. Roberts wiped a paper towel down his face and looked at it.

'Wasn't it only a few weeks ago it was winter and we were wondering whether we'd ever have a spring? Now it seems like this weather has been going on for fucking months.' Roberts wiped the back of his neck with the paper towel and dropped it into the waste-paper bin, then opened his top desk drawer and took out a packet of Extra Strong Mints. He unwrapped it and waved it in Pearson's direction. Pearson shook his head. Roberts put a mint in his mouth. 'So, you wanted a word?'

'Yeah,' said Pearson. 'It's just that I know the owner of the club where our deceased was found.'

'Go on,' said Roberts, sitting back in his chair.

'Name's Terry Milton. My brother-in-law.'

'OK, I'll ask someone else to talk to him. Lawrence. If I can prise his arse out of his chair.'

'No,' said Pearson, 'I can talk to him. I just thought I should clear it with you.'

Roberts picked up a pencil and started bouncing it on his desk. 'You don't think there'll be any ...' he searched for the right word, 'issues?'

'No, why should there be?'

'You and ...'

'Ruth,' supplied Pearson.

'Ruth.' Roberts nodded. 'You're separated, right?'

Pearson shrugged. 'Yeah. But Terry's got no problem with it.'

'You're sure?'

'Yeah, and I might be able to get more out of him,' said Pearson, 'being as he knows me.'

Roberts rolled the pencil across the desktop, considering.

'It's that or send Lawrence out,' he said, almost to himself. Then he sighed, coming to a decision. 'All right, you can talk to him,' Roberts examined the point of the pencil and then pointed it at Pearson, 'but I want proper records, right? Everything written down. And I mean everything. Make sure you get an "action" raised on the system. By the book. We've got enough fucking trouble on that score as it is.'

There was a knock on the open door and a uniformed WPC stood in the doorway.

'The room is ready for the video interview of your witness, sir.'

'Thank you,' Roberts said. 'Penny, isn't it?'

'Sir.'

Turning to Pearson, he nodded at the door. 'Off you go then.'

Dave Cowans, not for the first time since they had entered the interview room, touched the back of his head. An involuntary tic that he appeared almost unaware of. There was nothing vaguely engaging or attractive about him, Cat thought. Not to put too fine a point on it, he was a minger. His hair was lank and straggly at the sides and he was bald on top except for an island of unruly hair stranded in the middle of his forehead like the full-stop under a question mark. It gave him the air of someone who was constantly baffled by life. The forehead itself was misshapen and half covered with a port-wine birthmark which made it look like he had been in a collision with a very heavy object. Like a bus. His eyebrows, in contrast to his hair, were heavy, and under these were eyes that were pouchy and raw. His whole face, in fact, was slack and bloated. A drinker's face. His lips were wet and rubbery and he had a tendency to dribble. There was something on his unshaven chin. Toothpaste, Cat realised.

'Listen. How many times? I've told you, I didn't see anything,' he said, looking between her and Pearson. 'I was looking in my jacket for the keys to the club and I felt something land on my head. I thought it was raining, that's all. I thought it was, y'know, a freak raincloud or something, I don't know. Then I felt another raindrop. Or what I thought was a raindrop, and I like, looked up. It took me a minute to suss what it was. I mean, you don't expect to look up and see some old geezer swinging above your head, do you? So it took me a minute to work out what was going on. That he'd, like, hung himself. Then I saw the crotch of his trousers was all wet.' He touched the back of his head. 'Listen, when someone dies like that, does something happen to their piss?'

It was quiet and then Pearson said, 'There's a lady in the room. I'd appreciate it if you'd mind your language.'

Cowans looked across at Cat. 'Urine then. Does it? Only, since it happened, it's like my head's been burning or something.'

Cat ignored his question. 'Had you ever seen this man before?' she asked.

He shook his head, 'Nah. Never seen him before. Look, I told the uniform copper this already. They showed me his ID. Some weird name – Cyril? Sidney? Something like that. But like German or something.'

'Sickert Downey,' Cat corrected.

'Sick heart?' He looked to Pearson, as if the two of them were in cahoots. 'What kind of a name is that?'

'Sickert. Like the painter? Walter Sickert?'

Cat thought about clarifying his identity more. Informing Cowans that he was a member of the Camden Group and had been implicated by at least three books as being, or being the accomplice of, Jack the Ripper. But the face staring at her already said, *What the fuck do I care?* Cowans turned away from her and looked at Pearson, his eyes almost pleading.

'I've washed my head loads of times, right, and it still feels like it's burning or something. You sure nothing happens to your pi—' he caught himself – 'urine when you die? Some kind of, like, chemical reaction or something?'

This time it was Pearson's turn to ignore the question.

'Do you open the club at that time every morning?' Cat asked.

'You're joking, aren't you?'

'Then why did you happen to be there at that time this morning?'

'The guv'nor asked me to open up. Let the workmen in. They've been doing some work around the club for the last couple of weeks. New lighting, dance floor, poncing up the outside.' He touched the back of his head again. 'Listen, can I go now? I think I should go to the hospital. Just in case. If you need to know anything else, why not ask Terry? He'll be able to answer your questions better than me.'

Cat looked across at Pearson, who nodded. Pearson would do just that. His brother-in-law had quite a few questions to answer. Not the least of which was, if Terry was pleading poverty, living rent-free in the house that Pearson was still paying the mortgage on, where was he getting the money to do up the club?

11

'It's nice here,' said Alicia.

It looked nice to Donna. The room behind Alicia. The room in the mirror. Well, to be honest, it looked like Donna's room. It was the same room, the same wallpaper, the same bed, the same carpet. But it was ... clean. Fresh. New. That was it: it looked new. Like it might have done when the walls had originally been decorated, the carpet first laid. Only that wasn't quite right either. It looked sunny. Bright. Some of the colours were so bright Donna could barely stand to look at them. The faded piss-yellow of the skirting boards a bright primrose. The grubby grey bedclothes a radiant white. And the flowers on the wallpaper: large blossoms of reds and purples, they looked as if they were actual real flowers rustling and trembling on their vines. There was a light from somewhere. Donna couldn't quite make out where it was coming from. But it made everything in the room glow, somehow. Like the light that had come through the stained-glass windows in the church that Donna had gone into once. Not because she was religious or anything. She hadn't gone in to pray or anything like that.

Just gone in to see what it was like. She had enjoyed it in there. It was quiet. Peaceful. Sort of safe. Until some pervy bloke had come up. Dressed in black, with that old-lady smell of violets, and mints on his breath. Asking if he could help her. All the time looking at her as if she was going to nick something. Trying not to look at her legs in her miniskirt. So after a minute or two she had had to leave. Donna had woken in the murky afternoon light. The room was at the front of the house and by this time of day the sun was round the back so it was always gloomy. Lying there, not moving, listening. As if a noise had woken her up. She couldn't be sure that she had been asleep. Lately she wasn't always aware of when she slipped in and out of sleep. But she assumed she had been asleep because time had moved on according to the luminous digits of the clock radio. She didn't feel rested at all, felt just as crappy and tired as ever. This had been going on for a few days now. Or was it longer? Lying there, not moving, listening, she had become aware of the noise. Voices. People talking. Different this time, though. Soft, soothing voices. Usually the voices were angry, accusatory, rowing. Or insistent – urging her to do something. But she couldn't make out what it was she was supposed to be doing. Couldn't quite hear what they were saying. Only she knew that she should be doing something. And the voices were unhappy, disappointed in her, that she wasn't doing it. Only the voices today were different. The voice. Because she realised that it was only one, and she recognised whose voice it was. As soon as she twigged that it was Alicia, the voice changed; it wasn't talking any more, it was singing. Singing to her in that soft, beautiful voice of hers. It wasn't quite so gloomy now. There was a dim glow from somewhere. The mirror. Gradually the glow brightened and Donna got out of bed and went to it.

'Hello, you,' Alicia said.

'Hello, you.' Donna's own voice was barely a whisper. Her throat dry, a lump there that she could barely force her words around. When she blinked she realised that she had started to cry again. Not angry or sad tears this time, but happy tears.

'I miss you,' Donna managed.

Alicia smiled. 'I know, babe, that's why I'm here.'

Alicia tucked a strand of her shoulder-length hair behind an ear and Donna found herself mirroring the action. Alicia noticed Donna looking at the room behind her.

'It's nice here,' Alicia said.

'It looks nice,' said Donna.

'You'd like it. It's quiet. Sort of peaceful.'

'Yeah?'

'Yeah. You could live here, if you like. Just you and me, hun. Like it used to be.'

'How?'

Alicia smiled again. 'You know how, hun. You know what you've got to do.'

Alicia reached out a hand. Donna hesitated and then did the same, and for a brief moment their fingertips touched.

'Yeah, I know what I'd have to do,' said Donna, 'but not yet.'

'Why not?'

'There's something I've got to do first.'

'It doesn't matter,' said Alicia. 'I'm dead, hun. Nothing matters now.'

'You're dead cos someone killed you.'

Alicia shook her head. 'It doesn't matter. Really, babe. Nothing matters any more.'

'But someone killed you. Someone ought to do something about it.'

'It doesn't matter,' said Alicia again.

'It matters to me.' Alicia glanced back over her shoulder as if she had heard a sound.

'Who are you talking to?' asked Malcolm. Alicia winked and Donna winked back and then Alicia was gone.

'No one,' said Donna. 'I wasn't.'

'You were,' said Malcolm, sitting up and turning on the little lamp on the floor, hooking his glasses over his ears. He stared at her, waiting for her to say something. She wasn't going to tell him. It was private, between her and Alicia. She deserved something private, didn't she? She didn't have to tell him everything; after all, it was her who had let him sleep on her floor. Let him share her room, her space.

'It's all right,' he said, 'to talk to dead people.' Donna said nothing. 'Really, there's nothing wrong with it. People do it all the time.' When Donna still said nothing he said, 'I do it. I still talk to Alicia.'

What do you talk about? Donna wanted to ask. You didn't know her, she thought. Not really. What would you two have to talk about? She wanted to ask him. But she didn't really want to know the answer. In case they did talk. In case Alicia answered him too. Instead, Donna nodded. She didn't want to talk about it any more. Didn't want to say what she and Alicia talked about. Not with Malc. Not with anyone, probably.

'Do you think it might've been our fault?'

For a moment Donna was confused. Then Malc nodded at the copy of the local paper on the floor next to him. The headline read: MAN FOUND HANGED IN TOWN CENTRE. The paper had just said, 'Police would only confirm that the body was that of a man in his early sixties,' but it had been all over Twitter who it was. And later the local radio and the regional TV news had confirmed it.

'Mr Downey?' Donna asked.

Malcolm nodded, his eyes flitting away from hers.

'Dunno,' she said, 'what makes you say that?'

Malcolm shrugged. 'Dunno. We went to see him. Next thing he tops himself.'

Was that their fault? She had been the one who'd asked Mr Downey about Alicia. It had been her idea to go there in the first place. So not their fault. But hers maybe?

'Nah,' she said, 'it's just a coincidence.'

But was it? Could she have caused it somehow? First Alicia, and now Mr Downey. Could she somehow have caused them both to die?

12

Pearson, sitting in his car outside a semi-detached Edwardian-style house in a quiet tree-lined street, checked his watch again. He had been sitting here, watching this house for nearly an hour now. The road was a rat-run, a short-cut for rush-hour traffic. In the last sixty minutes the number of cars had increased considerably, reaching a peak where they were almost bumper to bumper before tapering off to virtually nothing. He opened the glove compartment and fossicked among the detritus of past surveillance operations. Burger wrappers. Plastic spoons. An empty family-size packet of Starburst. The screwed-up silver foil from dozens of mint-flavoured Viscount biscuits, until he managed to find a half-full bottle of mineral water. He pulled up the top, one of those annoying sports caps that you had to suck like a teat on a baby's bottle. The water was tepid and had a strange, metallic aftertaste. He wondered how long it had been there. Could water go off or get stale? He supposed it could get stagnant. He looked back at the house and saw the front door open and a woman come out and walk up the street. He picked up his major-incident notebook from the front passenger seat, an A4 exercise book with a soft red cover. He had taken to carrying his in a leather slipcase. Just so it was a bit more 'major incident' and a little less 'what I did on my holidays'. He got out, clicking his key fob to lock the car doors, went over and rang the bell. After a minute the door was opened by a middle-aged man.

'Hello, Terry,' said Pearson.

'Frank?' the other man replied doubtfully. Terry Milton, at six foot one or two, was around Pearson's height, but a good few stones heavier, most of which he seemed to carry in a beer gut that strained the front of his baby-pink Lacoste polo shirt. 'Ruth's not here.'

'Yeah, I know,' said Pearson. 'Actually, it's you I want to talk to.'

In reality there probably wasn't a good reason for Pearson to be here; the case would likely be closed the following morning. Still, no reason not to use the opportunity to nose around, ask a few questions, see what was going on. Terry's face was craggy and red, puffy around the eyes. It looked like he spent an increasing amount of time trying to arrange his thinning blond hair in a more elaborate style in an attempt to hide his baldness. He had on a pair of grey Farah slacks – Christ, could you still buy those things? – which were way too tight. By the look of it he wasn't wearing any underpants. Going commando. For Pearson there was something unsavoury in not wearing any underwear, something unhygienic. Like wearing a thong, only worse. On his feet – very small feet for a man, Pearson had always thought – he wore a pair of white Gucci loafers. Milton lifted a meaty hand and rubbed his cheek. A large gold bracelet slipped down his forearm. He had the sartorial elegance of a used-car salesman, Pearson thought. Or a professional darts player.

Milton considered for a moment, casting a glance up the street in the direction in which Ruth had disappeared.

'You realise if she comes back and finds you here she's going to go mental?'

'Best we're quick then.'

'All right,' he said, sighing and gesturing inside with an air of resignation, 'I s'pose you'd better come in.'

'How is she?' Pearson asked, following the other man along the hallway.

'Not good,' said Milton over his shoulder. 'Smoking too much.' There was an unspoken 'for one thing'. 'Drink?' he asked, crossing the living room and pulling down the front of an antique-looking cocktail cabinet. That's new, thought Pearson.

'Nah, you're all right. It's a bit early for me.'

He sat on one of the sofas and looked around. The rest of the furniture was pretty much as he remembered it, except that in one corner was a massive flat-screen TV, surrounded by various other electronic accessories. A home cinema system by the look of it, that hadn't been put together properly yet.

'So, apart from the smoking?' asked Pearson, as Milton turned to face him, a small Scotch in his hand.

Milton took a drink and shrugged. 'She's all right most days, as long as she takes her medication. She's sort of . . . ' he paused, 'flat, I suppose.' He took another drink, finishing it. 'So, what is it you wanted to talk to me about?'

'The man who was found hanging from the club this morning. I take it your assistant manager phoned you about it?'

Milton stopped pouring himself a second drink – larger this time – and half turned, looking amused. 'Yeah, I heard about that. That what he called himself, is it? "Assistant manager"?'

'He's not?' asked Pearson.

'Nah,' he turned back to the cabinet, finished pouring his drink, 'he collects the glasses, changes the barrels. Serves behind the bar occasionally, cleans the bogs.'

'But you know about what happened this morning?'

'Pretty much.' He took a drink of his Scotch.

'Any reason why a man should choose to hang himself from your club?'

'Not that I can see. Some old boy, wasn't it? Not exactly the sort of punter we usually get in the club.'

'Really?' asked Pearson. 'What type of punter do you usually get?'

Milton took a drink, shrugged. 'Younger, I suppose. Kids. You know, clubbers.'

Pearson knew for a fact that the club didn't attract many punters of any type, that the place was mostly empty nowadays. How many businesses had Milton tried and ultimately failed at?

'I hear you've been doing pole dancing,' said Pearson.

'Trying it out, yeah. Couple of afternoons a week to start off with. Wednesdays and Thursdays. I originally thought about having lap dancers, but the poles will do a better job—'

'And for half the price,' interrupted Pearson, enjoying Milton's irritation at being denied the punchline.

'And before you ask,' said Milton, 'it wasn't a membership thing, just punters coming in off the street.' Not that there were many of them, thought Pearson. 'So I wouldn't have his name on a list. If he did happen to turn up on one of those days. I was planning to reopen on Thursday. Got some girls booked already. Do you think your lot will be finished by then?' They probably would, thought Pearson. No reason to tell Milton though. He said:

'It's possible. So did Dave Cowans tell you our deceased's name?'

Glass to his mouth, Milton considered the word, took a drink and then said, 'Maybe. But he was making such a fuss about his fucking head . . .'

Pearson flipped his notebook open, slowly leafed through the pages until he found the right one. Wasting some more of what Milton obviously considered his valuable time, conscious of the other man's indifference, his desire to be done with the whole thing. 'Sickert Downey?'

'Sickert? Now that is a name I'd remember.'

'Director of the Abigail Burnett?' prompted Pearson.

'That the place on the local news? Where a couple of the kids had to be taken back to the home after being found drunk on the street or something? Rumours about drugs and underage sex.'

'That's the one.'

'I thought they'd closed that place down.' He considered this for a moment and then suddenly became defensive. 'Look, we check everyone's ID at the door, right? Make a point of it. Last thing I need is to lose my licence.' Pearson waited. 'And,' Milton went on, 'I get all my dancers through a legitimate agency. It's all above board. I can show you the paperwork to prove it.'

Pearson paused for long enough to make it uncomfortable. Then he nodded. 'Any reason why Dave Cowans opened up the club this morning and not you?'

'Not really. I told you, I bung him a few quid to do bits and pieces around the club, so why not? Besides, it gives him a chance to have a go at the optics.' And without a trace of irony, thought Pearson, as Milton finished his Scotch and stared into the bottom of the glass, trying to decide whether to have another.

'Dave said you were having some work done? Renovations?'

Milton's head jerked up. 'Is that what all this is about?'

'I don't want anything to upset Ruth, Terry.'

'Like what?'

'You're not telling me that the insurance is covering everything you're having done?'

'Look, I've borrowed a few quid to tart the place up. Nothing I can't pay back. You don't know what it's like: you have to keep up or everyone goes somewhere else ...'

Pearson held his gaze for a moment or so and then gave a nod. 'I just don't want to give her any excuses to ... y'know ... that's why I waited till she had gone, to talk to you. I don't want her upset by any of this.'

Milton nodded. 'All right, Frank. And she won't be. She doesn't even watch the news or read the papers any more. So she won't hear anything. Not from me.'

Pearson was about to press him on the loan when they heard the front door open and then close again.

13

'Got all the way to the shops and realised I'd left my bloody purse here,' his wife called out from the hallway. His ex-wife, he corrected himself. Possibly. Probably. Then she was standing in the doorway to the living room. She looked from Pearson to her brother and then back at Pearson; reached into her coat pocket, pulled out a packet of cigarettes, lit one with a cheap disposable lighter.

'What are you doing here?' she asked Pearson. Her movements were jerky, nervous. He noticed how pale she was, the bags under her eyes. She looked as if she'd lost weight.

'You've had your hair cut,' he said. 'I like it. It suits you.'

Involuntarily her hand went to her dark hair and touched the short pixie cut. She went across the room and stood by the mantelpiece, picking up an ashtray in one hand and flicking her ash into it. She looked at Pearson's reflection in the mirror above the fireplace. She put the ashtray back down and rolled her cigarette around its edge. Then she looked back up at him in the mirror.

'Why not just call it a day, Frank?' When he said nothing she went on, 'Why are you still paying the mortgage on this place?'

Pearson's eyes cut across to Milton, who shifted uneasily on his feet, then went and sat on one of the armchairs. 'Terry's doing all right, why not let him pay it? You can't possibly afford the mortgage on this place and the rent on your flat. Can't you just let it go?'

He didn't have an answer. He couldn't let go. He certainly couldn't afford the upkeep of both places. He could barely afford the mortgage itself. It was one of the reasons, he told himself, that he did so much overtime. But it felt as if it was his last tenuous link with his wife. That if he was to let that go it would be the final admission that it was all over.

She took an angry draw on her cigarette. 'You never could tell when it was time to pack it in, could you? Saint fucking Francis of the lost causes, that's you.'

That was true, too. He never knew when to give in. Even when it was patently obvious that he should. But that was a good thing, wasn't it? Something to be admired rather than belittled. Then she looked at his face and blinked, seemed to reconsider and soften a little.

'Sorry. That was unfair. You're a good man, Frank. You were always a good man. You always managed to do the right thing, the decent, proper thing.' She sighed. 'That was always the problem. Have you any idea how difficult that is to live up to? To be with someone who is so bloody perfect all the time? I, on the other hand, was a disappointment—'

'I was never—'

'I disappointed myself,' she said, cutting him off. 'So what is it you want, Frank?'

He glanced across at the other man again. Milton gave a slight shake of his head.

'I was just wondering how you were,' he lied. She turned round and looked directly at him.

'Alive,' she said flatly, the word an accusation. She turned to Milton. 'My brother,' this word almost spat, so that Milton flinched, 'had no business letting you in. I know you two talk on the phone, and I want it to stop.' Milton shifted uncomfortably in his seat but said nothing. 'If—' She stopped and then said slowly, deliberately, as if reciting a phrase in a foreign language or something hard to learn and practised many times, 'if I hadn't lost the baby, Frank, then,' she exhaled, 'then we might have had something. *I* might have had something.' She took a final pull on her cigarette, went to the mantelpiece and ground it out in the ashtray. 'You're a copper, Frank. You've always been a copper. Whatever happens you can carry on being a copper. It's what you do. It's what you are.' He glanced away momentarily, unable to meet her gaze. 'What do I do?' she asked. The tension, the anger, in her seemed to subside and her shoulders sagged. 'Without the baby . . . ' she paused, 'there's nothing. You know that.' She turned to face him, putting her hand in her pocket, and he could see she was turning the packet of cigarettes over and over, as if touching some kind of talisman. Then, shaking her head slightly, she said, 'I don't love you, Frank. Don't you get it? I don't love you. There is nothing. I don't,' the next word was drawn out, 'feel anything for you any more.' She looked at the floor and then back at him. 'I don't feel anything. Do you understand? I don't want to see you. Don't come round again.' Then she left, and he thought he might have heard her footsteps on the stairs and a door closing somewhere. After a minute the other man stirred.

'I think you better leave,' he said. He followed Pearson up the hall and as Pearson opened the front door he said, 'Give her some time, Frank, things might change.'

But as the door closed behind him and he found himself back on the street, Pearson very much doubted that they would. And whether he really wanted them to.

14

'What are you doing here anyway? Why do you have to keep fucking following me around all the time?'

When she had turned on him, trailing a few yards behind her, surprising herself with the suddenness, the violence of her anger, he had taken a step back in shock.

'I told you I didn't want you with me, didn't I? You're like a fucking little puppy or something, always following behind me like that.'

'I thought you wanted me to help you.'

'Yeah, well, you're not fucking helping, are you? You're just getting in the way.'

Now Malcolm was blinking behind his glasses. His bottom lip beginning to tremble – Jesus! It was, it was actually beginning to tremble – a little kid smacked by their mum for no real reason, other than she was angry. Angry at the world, angry at having no money, angry at having to live like this, angry at herself for not being able to do anything about it. Malcolm lifted his hands inside the pockets of the parka. A gesture of surrender. Or helplessness.

Just as suddenly as it had arrived, the anger was gone.

'OK,' Donna said, 'but you stay out here, all right?' Malcolm stared sullenly back without saying anything. 'I mean it, Malc. You stay out here, OK?' Looking down, scuffing at something on the pavement with a trainer, he nodded and mumbled something inaudible. Donna pushed herself through a gap in the chain-link fence. On the other side the night suddenly became even darker. The glare of overhead halogen bulbs, the flickering blue glow of televisions in the nearby houses, the approaching headlights and retreating tail lights from the occasional passing car, all replaced by the feeble light of a solitary sodium lamp. Under its dull illumination the children's playground had the look of a painted theatre backdrop. There was no depth to it. Everything was flat, without perspective. It was realistic enough. A rusting metal climbing frame. A half-empty sandpit. A set of three swings, the leftmost dirty, discoloured seat hanging on its single unbroken chain. And all around, clumps of dog shit desiccated and blanched by the hot afternoon, the dogs having taken over during the day. Donna thought she could make out the ghostly outline of the top of the now dismantled slide. The previous year, a five-year-old had got the towelling cape of his home-made Superman costume caught, slipped over the edge and hanged himself, so mothers no longer brought their children here. But as dusk fell even the dogs would decamp, to be replaced in their turn by macabre groups of teenagers who came to share cheap bottles of cider, smoke roll-ups and have sex.

The swings were occupied by a group of girls. Two sitting, the third standing, spinning the last dirty plastic seat on its chain. They were passing a two-litre plastic bottle between them: a mixture of Lilt and cheap vodka. Donna could hear them now, could make out their voices. The girl on the middle swing was saying:

74

'I'm not joking, I ended up with all his fucking jiz in my hair.' She ran a few strands through her fingers in illustration and they all laughed. Donna stopped a few yards off. They had seen her approach and, having assessed the threat, dismissed her.

'Sez?' Donna called.

The girl on the middle swing looked up and stared for a moment before taking a final swig from the bottle and passing it over. As she stood, the girl who had been standing immediately took her place on the swing.

'Donna, isn't it?'

Sez. Serena Gorman. Bleached blonde. But her roots were showing and she had split ends. She wore a vest top and a too-short mini with a single thread of cotton trailing from a drooping hem. And way too much make-up, even in this light. She looked past Donna. 'Who's your little friend?'

Little friend. Something clutched at Donna's heart. She turned and looked, expecting to see Alicia. Instead Malcolm stood about twenty yards away, arms hanging uselessly by his side. Looking gormless. As usual. She'd known this would happen. It was why she hadn't wanted him with her tonight. It was why she had told him to stay outside the fence.

'That's Malc,' she said, turning back.

'Looks a bit of a prat.'

Donna shrugged. 'He is a bit.' Only briefly feeling a pang of disloyalty.

Sez smirked. 'He your boyfriend?'

'Nah, nothing like that. He's just Malc.'

Sez leered at the other two girls and Donna endured a moment of communal humiliation, a collective shaming as they grinned back. Then Sez turned back to her.

'We've got some boys coming later,' she said, 'Only I think

there might be one or two too many.' She nodded in Malcolm's direction. 'Why don't you dump Numbnuts there and even up the numbers a bit?'

'No thanks,' said Donna, looking down, her face burning. When she looked up Sez was grinning.

'Never did like boys much, did you?'

Donna shook her head. 'Not really. Couldn't see what all the fuss was about.'

'Some of us thought you might be a bit of a lez, the way you used to follow around that . . . what was her name?'

'Alicia. I didn't follow her around. We were mates.'

'Alicia, that's it. She was always a bit more fun than you. Didn't she . . .'

'She died. Yeah.'

Donna looked away across the painted backdrop of the children's playground. Behind the layer of oil-daubed canvas Donna could hear them. Scratching. A skittering like tiny claws on lino. A gnawing. Their noses pushing against, their pink tongues licking at, the distorted, saturated material. One day they would break through, they would all come tumbling out, as the fabric split. With that smell, the smell of mould, the smell of damp. The smell of old buildings. Dust and plaster clinging to their fur—

'You look a bit like her.' When she looked back, Sez had moved too close. Violating her personal space, studying her. She ran some of Donna's hair through her fingers. 'Your hair. You've done your hair like her.' She smiled again. Not a nice smile. Donna had seen that particular smile before. At the children's home. At school. On the street. 'And your make-up. You've done your make—'

'I need money,' Donna blurted.

'Yeah?' Sez stopped playing with her hair.

76

'Yeah,' said Donna. 'I mean, I get benefits and that, but time you pay for your phone and fags ... '

'Yeah, I know,' said Sez, 'it's fuck-all, innit? It goes nowhere. I know what you mean.'

'Only,' Donna said when it was obvious Sez wasn't going to say anything more, 'you always seem to have money.' Granted, judging by her clothes, you wouldn't know it.

'Yeah, right. It all depends what you're willing to do for it, though. And I didn't think you liked all that. "Couldn't see what all the fuss was about"?'

Donna shrugged. 'I can't really. But I need the money. I don't have to enjoy it, do I?'

Donna looked away again. Malcolm seemed to be scanning the floor for something – stones – then picking them up and trying to skim them across the concrete surface of the playground. When she looked back Sez, too, was watching Malcolm.

'Do you remember Clive, who used to work at the home?'

'Mr Townsend?'

'"Mr Townsend"? Yeah, right, Clive.'

'Yeah, I remember him.'

'Do you remember,' Sez asked, giving Donna a whack on the arm with her elbow, 'when he first started there he used to give us a lift on his motorbike? And when you got off he used to sniff the seat? She sniffed loudly. '"Mmmm, the sweet smell of pussy." D'you remember?'

Donna remembered. Only she didn't think it was quite as funny as Sez obviously seemed to.

'And,' Sez went on, 'when he helped you on and off he used to feel up your tits, remember? If you let him put his hand up your skirt he'd give you a fiver.'

'Yeah,' Donna said, 'I know.' But she didn't. Hadn't gone back

77

on the bike after the first time. After she had got off and he had sniffed the seat like that. It had creeped her out. Made her feel a bit sick.

'After that he'd give you money all the time, depending on what you did. D'you remember? It's a wonder he had any money left at the end of the month.' Sez was laughing.

Donna looked down, shuffled her feet.

'So how much do you want?' Sez asked. 'Only, Clive's got these friends . . .'

'Dunno. As much as I can get, I suppose.'

'Yeah?' Doubtful. She looked in Malcolm's direction, thinking, 'My guess is you're a virgin, right?'

'Yeah,' Donna lied. As the other girl scrutinised her Donna had to affect embarrassment.

'Only Clive's friends will pay more, y'know, for something like that.' Donna nodded. Sez looked across at Malcolm again. 'Won't your boyfriend have something to say about it?'

'I told you,' Donna said, 'he's not my boyfriend.'

'OK.' Slightly dubious still. Her mind not quite made up.

'So you'll put me in touch with him? Mr Townsend? Clive?'

'Maybe.'

'Tell him I'll meet him somewhere. Anywhere he likes. Tell him I need money. Tell him I'm desperate.'

'If I do it, I'll want a cut of what you get. Your first payment. Like an introduction fee or something.'

'All right,' Donna said, 'how much?'

'Half.'

Donna sighed. 'All right, half.'

'OK, I'll give him a ring, see what he says. I'll call you back and let you know, all right?'

15

WEDNESDAY

'How did it go with your brother-in-law last night?' asked DCI Martin Roberts, head down, scribbling notes on a sheet of paper as Pearson entered the room.

'He wasn't much help,' said Pearson, taking a seat. 'Didn't recognise the name. Doesn't hold a membership list. Can't think of any reason for Downey to pick his club to hang himself from.'

'You've got a completed action form?'

'I will have.'

'Make sure of it,' said Roberts, looking up and waggling the pen at Pearson. 'I want it on the office manager's desk straight after the morning meeting.' He moved the piece of paper to his out-tray and dropped the pen on the desk. 'Who did the post-mortem on Downey?'

'Trish Bannister.'

Roberts rubbed a hand across his face and sat back in his chair. He was of the view that even if a victim was found with an axe lodged in their forehead, Bannister might tentatively venture the possibility, but only the possibility, that the victim might have suffered a fractured skull.

To Pearson's mind she simply did her job and no more. She presented the science. Any speculation beyond that, in her opinion, was the stuff of television drama. The kind of television drama where the police were invariably stupid or corrupt – or both – and it fell to the glamorous female pathologist to perform the post mortem, carry out the forensic investigation, interview the witnesses, identify the suspect and solve the crime. Pearson thought, a little cruelly he had to admit, that Trish Bannister didn't really have the looks for television. Her hands, out of her latex gloves, suffered from the incessant application of astringent chemical cleansers and a scrubbing brush. They were the roughest and most lacerated that he had ever shaken, the hands of a bricklayer rather than a surgeon. Her face, too, had patches of dry skin and was red and blotchy. She had hard, brown eyes behind functional steel-rimmed glasses, and her grey-streaked hair was habitually pulled back into a severe ponytail. But she was probably a lot younger than Pearson himself. Probably.

'So, as usual,' said Roberts, the fingermarks on his face only now starting to fade where he had rubbed it just that little too hard, 'she gave us fuck-all and you got your wrist slapped into the bargain. Am I right?'

'There are no indicators of death by asphyxiation,' Bannister had said the previous afternoon, 'no petechiae – pinpoint haemorrhaging – on his chest, neck or cheeks. Nor on any internal organs or either eyelid. Or in the conjuctivas of the eyes.'

Pearson nodded. 'OK.'

'What can be observed, however, are significant spinal-cord and bone injuries consistent with complete strangulation involving a drop considerably greater than the victim's height.'

'Complete strangulation being where no part of the victim's body is touching the ground?' clarified Pearson.

Bannister nodded. 'Correct. The mechanism of death in this case is effective decapitation: distraction of the head from the neck and torso and traumatic spondylolysis of C2—'

'Which is?'

'Fracture of the upper cervical spine,' provided Bannister, 'leading to transection of the spinal cord and a bilateral fracture through the pedicles of C2, the body of which has been displaced anterior to the vertebral body of C3.'

Before Pearson could ask the question, Bannister had added, 'The so-called "hangman's fracture". Although, of course, these days most of these injuries are observed in road traffic accidents where the passenger is not wearing a seatbelt and the chin is in collision with the steering wheel or dashboard of the car.'

'So,' said Roberts, 'either he knew what he was doing or he was just incredibly lucky?'

'Maybe he just researched it beforehand,' said Pearson. 'Plenty of sites on the internet where you can look up that type of thing.'

'Fair point,' agreed Roberts. 'So nothing inconsistent with suicide as far as that goes?'

'No. And something else . . . '

'A non-small-cell carcinoma can be observed in the left lung,' said Bannister. 'As this measures two point four centimetres in diameter it is predicted Stage I. Without corroboration through a biopsy, this is likely to be a non-small-cell pulmonary adenocarcinoma as the deceased was known to be a non-smoker.'

'Would Downey have been aware of it?' Pearson asked.

'Not necessarily,' said Bannister. 'At Stage I the symptoms might be confined to persistent coughing, recurrent bouts of pneumonia, shortness of breath. It's only when the cancer metastasises – spreads – that the symptoms become more severe: fatigue, chest pain and drastic weight loss.'

'On the other hand,' Pearson said to Roberts, 'it could have been picked up on a routine X-ray.'

'And the abrasions on our deceased's forehead?' asked Roberts.

'Bannister said it had all the indications of having been caused post-mortem. But she wouldn't be drawn on how.'

Roberts nodded. 'Probably covering for some ham-fisted fucking SOCO.'

'I've seen something similar before,' said Pearson. 'Hanging at home. Man in his forties suspended from the staircase. While they were trying to get the body down, some poor probationer seeing his first stiff up close lost his grip and swung the body into the outside of the staircase '

Roberts rolled his pen backwards and forwards across the desktop. 'Forensics have a preliminary match between the mark found on the scaffolding board and scuffing on a right shoe retrieved from the street in front of the building. The shoe matches the brand, style and size of the left shoe on the deceased.'

'That scuffing on the board,' said Pearson, 'could just indicate a last-minute change of heart, couldn't it? He's decided to jump, but his legs have turned to jelly and won't quite take him over the edge. So he drags the side of his foot against the scaffolding board in the process?'

Roberts put his hands on his head and closed his eyes. 'It's a possibility, I suppose. We also found some emails on his computer at his place of work. Seems he'd been offered early retirement.'

'Offered?' asked Pearson. 'You mean he'd been politely asked to leave his post?'

'As good as. The Abigail Burnett is going to be closed. "Rationalisation of the provision of children's services".'

'Meanwhile, there's all that stuff in the press and on the local telly about the kids there running wild. Whether it's mostly rumour or there is actual substance to it, everyone will assume he's been given the push. We've had cases before where the end of someone's career, the loss of what they perceive as their good reputation, has been reason enough for them to top themselves.'

'So you're agreed we can declare it a non-suspicious death?'

'Can't see why not,' said Pearson.

Roberts opened his eyes and sat forward.

'OK, if we're agreed about closing that one, I've got something else I want you to do. As it doesn't seem likely that Carragher is going to turn up any time soon, I want you to have a look through all the cases he's worked on since he transferred here.'

'All of them?'

Roberts nodded. 'Yes, all of them. I've asked Wendy to get you a list of case numbers. Make sure everything's kosher. I don't want any nasty surprises. Russell can help you go through them on the system.'

'Where is Russell this morning?'

16

Cat was back in an interview room. A different one this time. The smallest in the nick, it was windowless and hot. Cat wondered whose idea it had been. Had DI Neil Ferguson requested it in order to gain some psychological advantage over her? Or had it been allocated to him – a small discourtesy, some petty show of a lack of co-operation? The latter, more likely. Although it didn't seem to bother the man from the Professional Standards Department. He was probably used to it. More than likely, for him, it was just par for the course.

'DI Carragher hasn't come in again today?' Ferguson looked up from the papers he had been studying on the desk.

It wasn't really a question. Ferguson already knew. He would have made a point of finding out. Why else would she be in here? If Sean had come in then it would be him that Ferguson would be interviewing, not her. But again there was the insinuation that she would have some involvement in, some influence over, whether Sean decided to turn up or not. Briefly, Cat wondered if she was under surveillance, whether they knew that she had met Sean two days ago, but then she dismissed the idea. It was absurd. They wouldn't be watching her. Wouldn't be watching Sean. Not when he was only suspected of over-claiming on a few expenses.

'It is understandable,' Ferguson said, 'how you, as a serving officer with an as yet unblemished record, might feel a degree of animosity at having to answer to Professional Standards.'

As yet? An as yet unblemished record? What exactly was he hoping to find, Cat wondered. A necessary evil, that's how Pearson had characterised the PSD. There had been too many coppers using the uniform, the warrant card to get the susceptible to say the wrong thing and thereby implicate themselves or someone else. Too many coppers extorting money, pressurising the vulnerable into sex, selling drugs or guns seized in raids, even stealing cash and possessions when supposedly searching a suspect's house. So much so that now, investigations by Professional Standards or the Independent Police Complaints Commission had become almost commonplace. The slightest hint of misconduct nowadays and likely as not the force involved would refer its own officers to Professional Standards. 'The needle of social opinion always swings from one extreme to the other before settling somewhere in the middle,' Pearson had quoted from somewhere. Although he couldn't remember where. Then again, Pearson came out with a lot of crap like that. Besides which, he wasn't the one sitting here answering the questions, was he?

When Ferguson had entered the room he had taken off his jacket and slipped it over the back of his chair, undone his top button, loosened his tie and rolled up the sleeves of his shirt. Cat, her white blouse already plastered to her back, damp patches spreading under her arms, regretted now that she had declined his offer to remove her own jacket. Regretted, too, that she had no representation, no 'police friend', a serving officer to advise her on proceedings. But who would she choose? Pearson, she thought, but just as quickly rejected the idea. A Federation rep? But she wasn't the one under investigation. She was just here to answer a few questions. Or so she had thought. Now, she wasn't so sure. Was wondering what exactly she might have got herself into. Precisely how much potential trouble she might be in. Would it come to that, at some stage, some point in the not too distant future? Would she be in the sort of trouble that required her to have a Federation rep, or even, perhaps, a lawyer? She had always pegged the presence of a solicitor at someone's side during an interview as an implicit admission of guilt. Now she was the one facing the questions, was the one on the other side of things, she could see why people did it, why you might be reluctant to answer any question. To implicate yourself in any way. Was tempted to resort to the seasoned recidivist's mantra of 'No comment.'

'I appreciate,' Ferguson went on, 'that we might be viewed as bean counters' – Please, thought Cat, don't trot out that old chestnut about Al Capone – 'that the common view is that we check officers have not been surfing the internet excessively on force computers, or using police-issue mobile phones to make personal calls. Or that money claimed on expenses can be accounted for with the appropriate receipts.'

That was exactly what this was about, wasn't it? She had been asked to reconcile overtime and expenses. Because after all, she had a degree. Therefore, it was assumed, she must be reasonably intelligent. The fact that it was a psychology degree didn't seem to matter. It was a degree. 'You'd be doing me a big favour,' Sean had said. Be doing his job more like. Checking each officer's envelope of submitted receipts against the allocated cost code. Going through the duty rosters and verifying that the recorded units of overtime were correct.

'Can't Gilbert do it?' she had asked.

They had looked across the room. DC Peter Gilbert sat, a baffled look on his face, one index finger hovering indecisively above his keyboard, the other strumming his bottom lip. A toddler sitting cross-legged on the floor in front of his V-Tech laptop. *What letter is for dog?* it asked. *What letter is for dog?* *Dur is for dog. Dur.* Feeling their eyes on him, Gilbert looked up and flushed, his finger leaving his mouth and running along the inside of his shirt collar. Sean looked back at her.

'All right,' she conceded, sighing, 'I'll do it.' But she had found other things to do specifically so she didn't have to ask the other members of the team to produce receipts, so she didn't have to put up with their grumbling and moaning. Their resentment. All the same, she thought she'd better, at least, enter Sean's claims on to the system—

'But,' Ferguson said, interrupting her train of thought, 'sometimes investigating the minor indiscretions leads us to uncover more serious misconduct. For instance when a routine patrol stops a car with a dodgy tail light.'

You pull over a car for a dodgy tail light, or driving erratically, or ignoring a red light, wandering across the lane markings. When the driver winds down the window you notice a strong smell of alcohol, or a slight whiff of weed. When you run a vehicle check you discover it's uninsured or reported stolen. The driver can't provide ID, or he provides ID that turns out to be fake, and when you finally ascertain his real identity he has outstanding warrants against his name. So you nick him. Search the car. Find class-A drugs in the glove compartment. The makings of a home-made bomb in the boot.

Ferguson let the statement hang in the air for a moment, as if Cat might be able to guess at its significance. Then he looked down, shuffled through some papers, the physical activity marking a change in subject.

'You're familiar, of course, with the term CHIS?'

Of course she was.

'A covert human information source,' he added unnecessarily, as if he thought she really might not know. Perhaps he was being deliberately irritating, winding her up so she said something that otherwise she might not.

'An informant,' she said, unable to stop the note of sarcasm in her voice, despite the fact that he was technically a superior officer. 'I've heard the term.'

'You are aware that DI Carragher was issued with a credit card under a covert identity in order to claim travel and accommodation expenses, make payments to covert human information sources and so on?'

Cat cleared her throat. 'Yes, sir.'

'Are you also aware that DI Carragher had authority to make withdrawals on credit cards issued to other members of the team?'

News to her. And suddenly Cat didn't like the way this was heading, felt what she had previously assumed was solid ground starting to slip away and liquefy beneath her feet . . .

'Would it surprise you to know that DI Carragher has made withdrawals – withdrawals that cannot strictly be accounted for – in the past six months that total more than ten thousand pounds?'

Fucking hell, Cat thought, and hoped she hid her shock behind a blank expression. Ferguson's mobile began to ring. Irritated, he picked it up and checked the call display.

'I need to take this.' He put the phone to his ear, said, 'Sir.' His eyes on Cat, he listened for a minute. 'I'm actually in the middle of an interview at the moment, sir.' Listening again. Checking his watch. His eyes going back to Cat. 'Can I not do it later, sir?' A blink of annoyance. 'Yes, sir.' Disconnecting. Then, to Cat, 'Apparently I'm needed somewhere else.' He gathered his papers together and recapped his pen. 'I think we'll leave it there for now.'

Ferguson picked up the pile of papers, tapped them on the desk, turned them ninety degrees and tapped them again. He picked up his briefcase from the floor and put his paperwork in it, snapping the locks shut. Slipped his pen into his inside jacket pocket, shrugged his jacket on as he stood up.

'I shouldn't be more than an hour,' he said. 'Maybe two at the outside. I do apologise for the interruption. But, on the other hand, it might give you a little time to think things over.'

17

She didn't want to. Told herself not to do it. *Willed* herself not to do it again. But once again for the – the exact number of times she couldn't remember, but it was a lot anyway – she couldn't, couldn't not look. Donna looked back towards the mirror. In its reflection she caught a movement by the door to her bedsit. The closed door. Like someone, or something, had walked through. Something unseen, something that could only be discerned by the disturbance of light it caused. A wave, a ripple that caused the underlying image, the grotty, flowered 1970s wallpaper, to bulge and then retreat as it passed. Alicia. But Donna didn't want to see her this morning. Didn't want to talk to her. She didn't want to ask the question in case the answer wasn't what she wanted to hear, so instead she turned away and faced the wall and tried to close her eyes and go back to sleep. Tried to ignore the mirror, ignore Alicia pacing impatiently up and down behind it. Waiting for her.

Donna took the biro from its place under her pillow and started to write on the wallpaper. Adding to, overlapping, obscuring the words already written there. *It doesn't matter. It doesn't matter.* In some places the words were so dense, so intertwined and tangled that she could barely make out that they were words at all. They looked more like some intricate pattern, a complex interlocking machine or some vast alien organism. *It doesn't matter.* Donna picked at a loose shred of the old wallpaper, feeling something sharp embed itself under her fingernail. She put her finger in her mouth and sucked, then spat the thing out. Then she worked her fingernail under the loose paper and began to pull. A strip of wallpaper came away along a seam, bringing with it the words scrawled there, along with ancient plaster and dry dust that got into her nose and throat. She froze. She heard skittering claws. Gnawing. The high-pitched squeal of something furry and nasty. Then it was gone. She looked back to the mirror again. She got out of bed and went over to it.

'Hello, you,' Alicia said.

'Hello, you,' said Donna, trying not to meet Alicia's eyes. But everywhere she looked away, Alicia's eyes met hers.

'What's up?' asked Alicia. Donna hesitated. Alicia smiled. 'You look sad, hun.'

Suddenly Donna was angry. 'Were we mates?' she asked.

'What?'

'Were we mates? Or did I just tag along and get on your nerves?'

'Of course we were mates, babe. We were best friends. Why do you even have to ask?'

Donna swallowed and looked down. When she looked back up and tucked a strand of her hair behind an ear, Alicia did the same.

'We were best friends. We're still best friends, aren't we?' Alicia asked.

Donna swallowed again. 'Yeah.' But that thing that Sez had

said flashed through her mind: *She was always a bit more fun than you*.

What had Sez meant by that? Donna knew. But she didn't want to ask Alicia. Didn't want her to spell it out. Maybe, though, it had just been something that Sez had said. Something nasty. Something spiteful. Something said just to hurt Donna. She wouldn't put it past her. Like that other thing. When she had looked back to her and Sez was smiling. Not a kind smile. A cruel smile. *You look a bit like her*. Right in Donna's personal space. Running her fingers through her hair. Being a bit too familiar.

'Where's, er ... Thingy?' Alicia nodded past Donna and into the room.

'Malc,' Donna said, annoyed that Alicia couldn't remember his name. Pretended not to remember his name. But Alicia wouldn't have liked him, would she? Not cool enough. *Bit of a dweeb*, she would have said. *Bit of a prat*.

'Malcolm,' Alicia said. 'Where's Malcolm?'

'Malc,' Donna corrected.

Malc was gone. Back home, she assumed. But she didn't really know that for sure. On the way back last night, after meeting Sez, after Sez had said that about how she looked like Alicia. But mostly after Sez had said about her looking like Alicia with that look on her face, that smile. Donna had turned on him again, just as she had at the beginning of the night.

'Did I just use to follow Alicia around? Just tag along after her?' *Like you, Malc*, she meant. Like you keep following me around. Tagging along behind like some kind of fucking puppy or something.

'I don't do my hair and make-up like her, do I?'

Malc hadn't said anything. But he hadn't had to. Just the way he looked at her said so. Said that she was weird, mental, for doing

93

it too. So she had hit him. A slap – maybe a punch, she wasn't quite sure – that had sent his glasses flying through the air and skidding along the road. Then, still angry, but mostly embarrassed and ashamed, she had turned and stomped – yes, stomped, and even at the time she had realised how childish she was being – stomped away up the street, deliberately not looking back.

'You're not her, you know!' Malcolm had shouted after her. 'You'll never fucking be her! No matter how much you pretend to be. You'll never be what she was!'

'Malc's gone,' Donna said.

For the briefest of moments the look on Alicia's face said, *Something else you've fucked up. Someone else you've lost.*

'You're dead,' Donna said.

'Yes, hun, I'm dead.' As if it was a stupid thing to say.

'Somebody's got to do something about it,' Donna insisted again.

Alicia shook her head. 'I told you before, it doesn't matter.'

'It matters to me.'

'Why?'

Donna rubbed the side of her face, her eye.

'I don't know.' She pushed a strand of hair behind her ear. 'So what did she mean, "a bit more fun than you"?'

Alicia looked away for a moment. 'Oh, Donna – grow up! What do you think she fucking meant?'

For a second, a few seconds, a minute maybe, Donna was too shocked to react. Then she brought her two fists crashing down on to the mirror, feeling it smash. Feeling it shatter beneath her hands, feeling it dislodge from the wall and slide to the floor. Looking down – small shards of glass embedded in her knuckles, the back and blade of her hand, the cold shiver of the glass, the warmth of the blood against her skin – she wondered how easy it would be to drag one of those big, jagged edges across her wrists.

'You all right in there?' A voice accompanied by a soft knock on the door. The Pervert from down the hall. Donna froze. Without moving, barely breathing, she said:

'Yeah, just an accident. Broke my mirror.'

'Are you sure?' The Pervert hesitated in the hall for a moment.

'Yeah, I'm fine, honest.'

'OK then, if you're all right. I'm just down the hall if you need anything.'

Yeah, right. Like that was going to happen. All the same, Donna found that she was close to tears. Again. How many times had she found herself close to tears lately? Or actually crying, without realising it, just putting a hand to her face and finding it already wet?

Donna upended one of the boxes, scattering its contents across the floor, then pulled out a drawer, rifled through a series of plastic bags until she found what she was looking for. A pair of scissors. Not a good pair, but out of the Pound Shop. So that when she started to chop at her hair they pulled as much as cut it. When she was done she ran a hand through the ragged crop on her scalp. Somewhere, she remembered, she had a set of clippers. A good set. She had nicked them from someone's bedroom during one of the parties she hadn't been invited to. She sifted through the debris of her belongings on the floor and finally came across them. A decent set, with a rechargeable battery and one comb attachment-thing. She wasn't sure what length it was. Boys she knew asked for a certain number when they went to the barber's but she hadn't a clue what the numbers meant. It didn't really matter as long as it did the job. She turned them on, placed them at the nape of her neck and watched as the tufts of black hair fluttered to the floor. When she was done she ran the clippers along the right side of her skull. Starting just above the ear and running them upwards. As she started on the left side of her head the battery began to run down and occasionally the clippers caught and tugged at her hair. And of course she hadn't taken a mains power cable. Before she could finish the rest of the hair the battery ran down to nothing and the clippers stopped completely. Fucking hell, she couldn't even do a simple fucking thing like this properly. What hope did she have of doing anything about Alicia? Not that anyone else cared. Not even Alicia herself.

Donna looked at the shattered mirror. The clumps of her hair. The mess of clothes, make-up, nail-varnish bottles, the rest of the crap from upturned boxes and turned-out drawers. Then she went to her bed, pulled herself into a foetal position and, not for the first time lately, cried herself to sleep.

18

Ferguson took his time to read each page. Pick it up. Turn it face down on the table. Not saying anything. Not looking at her. Cat took a deep breath, forced herself to relax. Just in case it was a deliberate ploy; a device to get under her skin. A tactic to get her annoyed and make her say something she otherwise wouldn't. Just in case it wasn't because he was an irritating prick.

They were back in the same cramped and windowless interview room. Whenever she had been forced to use this particular room in the past, Cat had always found it extremely claustrophobic. That, of course, was when she was asking the questions – when she was on the other side of the table. The right side of the table. Ferguson, on the other hand, appeared completely at home here. He didn't seem to mind the poky conditions, his briefcase open on the table in front of him simply because there was no room to put it on the floor. An extra couple of chairs had appeared from somewhere since this morning, possibly deliberately placed in here as another petty annoyance. The smell of something – the half-eaten remains of a prawn sandwich? – left to fester in the wastepaper bin. It was also, again, almost unbearably hot, airless and stuffy, though this time Cat had accepted his offer for her to remove her jacket.

'It seems DI Carragher is quite determined to avoid being served with a notice of alleged breach of the Standards of Professional Behaviour.'

'A Regulation 15,' Cat said when he looked up, before he could enquire whether she knew what that was. Of course she fucking knew what it was.

'Aye,' Ferguson acknowledged with a slight nod, 'a Regulation 15 notice.' A little disappointed at not having the opportunity to offer the explanation himself. 'It's always better to serve the notice to the officer in person. A matter of professional courtesy. Failing that, to serve it via a recorded delivery. But it would seem that DI Carragher was either unable or unwilling to take delivery.' Ferguson waited for a reaction. When none was forthcoming he went on. 'I appreciate that, as yet, we haven't got very far, DC Russell, and I can only apologise for that.' He picked up his phone, made a big thing of turning it off and placed it in his open briefcase on the table. 'But I can assure you that there will be no further interruptions.' He paused again and looked down briefly at his papers. When he looked up he attempted what Cat presumed was meant to be a friendly smile. She noticed for the first time that his two front teeth protruded. Presumably why he had grown the moustache. 'At present we have no intention of serving *you* a Regulation 15 notice, DC Russell. You are simply here to assist us with our enquiries.'

Assist us with our enquiries? Was he taking the piss? Was he totally incapable of talking like a normal human being? Cat made a conscious effort to ease the tension in her shoulders. To breathe slowly. To lessen the tightness in her diaphragm. She rested a hand on her knee to stop its agitated bouncing.

'It might be just as well in the circumstances,' Ferguson said, looking down at the sheet of paper he held in his hand, rubbing his chin, 'that the notice couldn't be served. Initially we had wanted to interview DI Carragher in the matter of a number of financial irregularities, which may or may not have led to a misconduct hearing. Now, however, a number of other matters have arisen which may lead us into the realm of a special case hearing.'

He looked up to gauge whether she had registered the implication of this. She had. A special case hearing meant gross misconduct. Possible instant dismissal without pension. 'You'll recall my mention of the dodgy tail light?' Ferguson asked. The dodgy tail light had been spotted, Cat thought, and the car had been pulled over. The question now was: were they about to open the boot and find a ticking bomb inside?

'There is a possibility,' Ferguson continued, 'that our investigations into DI Carragher may ultimately result in criminal proceedings being brought.' He paused, holding Cat with a steady gaze. Under her hand the knee that had stilled started to bounce again. 'Loyalty, DC Russell, is an admirable thing. But sometimes you have to ask yourself whether it's the organisation, or a particular individual, that's worthy of your loyalty.'

The white sheep of the family. That was the expression that Pearson had used – about someone else, admittedly, but at the time Cat had thought it might as easily be applied to her. She had worked hard at school, stayed on to do her A levels. Much to the annoyance of her family. Her father in particular. They would rather she had gone to work. Or claimed benefits – brought *some* money into the house. Then she had decided to go to university.

She had had to move out, of course. And the final betrayal, in her father's eyes, she had 'gone over to the dark side' and joined the filth. Now her family would have nothing to do with her. So, given all that she had sacrificed, why was she putting her career in jeopardy for the sake of some perceived loyalty she thought she might owe Sean? But she owed him something. He had been good to her. Been a friend as much as a superior officer. Taken her into his confidence. Surely that counted for something? But how much? How far should you go to defend a friend? And what might she be defending him against?

Fuck, Sean, what exactly have you got yourself into?

Ferguson shuffled one of the sheets of paper from the bottom of the stack to the top. Looking down at the paper, he asked, almost nonchalantly, 'Has DI Carragher ever acted in an inappropriate manner?'

The change of tack – as it was meant to – momentarily took her by surprise. Ferguson looked up again.

'I'm not exactly sure what you mean,' Cat said, hedging her bets.

'I apologise. I obviously didn't phrase that very well. I can understand how you would find it difficult to answer. Has DI Carragher ever acted in an inappropriate manner – say, in a sexual way?'

Cat cleared her throat. 'No.'

'Made a provocative or suggestive remark?'

'No.'

At each answer, Ferguson made a little mark on the paper with his pen. Whether a tick or a cross, Cat wasn't quite sure.

'By that I mean, made a remark to you of a suggestive nature that made you uncomfortable in some way?'

'No.'

'Invaded your personal space in an aggressive or provocative manner?'

'No.'

'Placed his hands on you in such a way as to make you feel uncomfortable or embarrassed?'

'No.'

'Left a hand on you a little longer, in your opinion, than was strictly necessary?'

'No.'

'Been what might be termed "over-friendly" in any way at all?'

'No.'

'Has he ever acted in any way that made you feel uncomfortable, embarrassed, intimidated or vulnerable?'

'No.'

'Not in any way?'

'No.'

'Acted in any other way, other than I might have implied, that you would like to now bring to my attention?'

'No.'

Ferguson frowned. Looking, Cat thought, a little disappointed. Frustrated even. Gave a nod. Made a note on his pad. Then, without looking up, he asked, 'Have you ever witnessed DI Carragher being overly aggressive when dealing with a suspect?'

Cat hesitated. There had always been the suspicion in her mind that, given the right circumstances, with no witnesses present, Sean might be capable of anything.

Ferguson looked up, suddenly interested. 'You seem unsure, DC Russell.'

'Just making sure of my answer, sir,' clearing her throat again, 'thinking it through.' Then she said, 'No.' A lie. She wasn't even totally sure why she had said it, didn't really know she was going to say it until it came out of her mouth. But now she had lied, she wondered how many more would follow. Would have to follow, now that first lie had been told.

'You've never witnessed DI Carragher being overly aggressive with a suspect?' Ferguson pressed.

'No,' Cat said, the answer coming a little quicker this time. 'I haven't witnessed DI Carragher being overly aggressive with a suspect.'

Ferguson held her gaze a little too long. Then he went back to looking down at his papers. Asking his questions. And so it went on. Did she know what he meant by 'overly aggressive'? Yes. Only, different people had different ideas on how to treat suspects during interview. Yes, she understood the term and what it meant within the terms of the Police and Criminal Evidence Act, and no, she did not consider DI Carragher's interviewing of suspects to be overly aggressive. The questions. The denials, the lies, Ferguson making his little ticks – or crosses – on his piece of paper. Had he ever threatened physical violence? No. To a suspect? No. To a witness? No. To the best of her knowledge, to any of his colleagues? No. Yes, she conceded, DI Carragher may have had the reputation of having a short temper. Yes, she had witnessed this on occasion and no, it had never been directed at her personally. Had his loss of temper, in her presence, ever translated into physical violence? No. Had she heard from anyone else of his loss of temper translating into physical violence? No. And on and on. Until finally he did his thing: the capping of the pen, the squaring of the paper, rotating it through ninety degrees before squaring it again and placing the papers in his briefcase. The thing that said the interview was terminated and she was dismissed. No point in asking if Sean had been accused of assault. That, at least, seemed fairly obvious. No point in asking who might have made the accusation or who the assault might have been on. If Ferguson was willing to tell her that, he would have already done so. Instead he said:

'Thank you, DC Russell, for your help. We will, of course, be questioning other members of the Major Incident Team. So try not to take it personally. And, of course, there might be the need to question you again in future. Now, you are free to go.'

Leaving the room, carrying her jacket, Cat was suddenly aware that her deodorant had lost its battle with the heat of the interview room, with the seriousness of the situation, with her nerves. In the ladies' she took off her blouse, washed under her arms and applied the roll-on that she carried in her handbag. After she put her blouse back on and buttoned it up she took out her mobile. Punched in Sean's number. Just what the fuck was she getting herself into here? What had Sean been up to? A sexual assault? A physical assault? Both? And had the allegations come from inside the nick or outside? The physical-assault allegation certainly seemed to come from someone outside the force. A 'suspect', Ferguson had said. Cat had a fair idea who that might be. But sexual assault? The call went to voicemail. She put the phone back in her bag. She needed some fresh air. Most of all she needed a fag.

19

When Cat let herself back into her flat again after her run, the residual traces of furniture polish and air freshener still hung in the air. Arriving home earlier, she had peeled off her official persona, dropping the blouse in the laundry basket, hanging the suit beside its replicas in the wardrobe. Lining up the shoes alongside the rows of black footwear: low-heeled shoes in summer, boots in winter. Running her hands along the ranks of tops: blouses with collars, blouses without collars, T-shirts. All white. After changing into her running gear and before leaving the flat she had dusted and vacuumed. Not that anyone but her had ever been in the place to appreciate how house-proud she was – or OCD, depending on your point of view. That was what you were supposed to do, wasn't it: get rid of all the signs of smoking, clean the house, wipe out the ashtrays and put them in the back of the cupboard, break the old habits. She wasn't sure it was working. Despite the fact that her lungs were still burning, she could kill for a cigarette. The physical exertion of the run hadn't helped, hadn't given her its usual sense of well-being, that release of endorphins which should have cleared her head and allowed her to think. She was still as confused. Only now she was tired and sweaty too. She stripped off and chucked her running clothes into the washing machine.

Fifteen minutes later, after a scalding shower, and time spent in front of the mirror looking for the tell-tale softening and blurring to the outline of her features, or lines forming around her eyes, any signs of the slow downward drag of gravity on her body despite the running, the exercise, the watching what she ate, she stood in her living room, dressed in trackies and a baggy cotton T-shirt, towelling her hair dry. Standing there, she realised how bare the room was. White-painted walls, laminate flooring, two Art Deco-style brown sofas set at right-angles to each other, a wooden coffee table, a flat-screen TV on one wall. But there were no ornaments, no pictures, no photographs. It was totally devoid of any kind of warmth, of colour, of personality. And whenever they shared a car and Pearson dropped her home he made some disparaging comment about the area. Pearson, in his mid-forties, his hair starting to grey, was definitely beginning to show signs of his age. His body, his face beginning to sag. Somehow, though, for men it didn't seem to matter so much. In fact they got better as they got older, seemed to grow into their faces somehow. Men. Well, there was an area in her life in which she had pressed the self-destruct button more than once. That big, red shiny button in her head with the words DO NOT PRESS written in white block capitals. The big red button she just couldn't resist.

She picked up her mobile from the coffee table, considered for a moment who else she might call. Any normal person, from any normal family, might be able to ring their dad. Or their mum. Or an older sister. Talk things through. Get some clear and sensible advice. Or at least a bit of sympathy. Who could she call? Roberts? No chance. Ferguson? Maybe she *should* call the man from Professional Standards. Tell him everything she knew, leave it to him to decide what had happened. Pearson, maybe? In the end she tried Sean's number again. The third – or was it the fourth? – time she had tried since the meeting with Ferguson. It went to voicemail. Every time she had tried it had gone to voicemail. If they were monitoring his calls, or were to get his phone history later on, of course, it might not look good. But what else could she do? There were explanations to be given. And maybe a few apologies to be made. She disconnected and put the phone back on the coffee table. Outside, beyond the closed slats of the wooden blind, some kind of argument had started. Raised voices, the sound of running footsteps, shouted obscenities between two boys and then a scuffle while a screaming girl tried to break it up. Gradually the noise retreated along the street. Half a lifetime ago that could have been her. Who was she kidding? Half a lifetime ago that *was* her. That, though, was a different life. A different Cat. Wasn't it?

There were two types of people, he thought, who when faced with a situation where others were in danger, would act rather than freeze or run the other way. The sound of a child's crying as smoke billowed from the upstairs window of a burning house. A car careering from a waterlogged road and down an embankment into the muddy, swollen waters of a river in spate. A bomb exploding on a rush-hour underground train in the country's capital city. Two types of people who would run into that fire, jump into the river, go down the steps of that underground station thick with black smoke. The first type might gauge the dangers inherent in the situation, the risk to themselves, and nevertheless opt for altruism over self-preservation. The second type did not analyse. Did not weigh up the pros and cons of the situation. They just reacted, with no consideration of the consequences.

It was the second type who had sat and watched through the window. Sat in the car for what seemed like hours now. Sat and watched the comings and goings at the house. The target arriving on his Kawasaki, wheeling the motorbike over the pavement and through the door of a ground-floor flat in a converted Victorian house. Leaving ten minutes later and returning with a carrier bag containing a six-pack of Stella Artois from the local convenience store. Opening the door half an hour later to a pizza delivery. Since then: nothing. The second type of person – the one in the car, the one watching the comings and goings at the flat, the police officer – this second type of person believed it was those who needed the precursor – the pushing and shoving, the verbals, the ramping up of emotions – who lost out in a violent confrontation. Get in first. Get in hard. That was why, having made up his mind, he was out of the car, across the road, leaning on the doorbell, rapping loudly on the brass door knocker. That was why, almost as soon as the door began to open, he was moving forward, his head describing an arc . . .

Standing in front of the open fridge, Cat wondered what she was going to eat. She was hungry but she couldn't be arsed to cook. On the other hand there was a bottle of Smirnoff in the freezer. A bottle of Chardonnay in the fridge, too, oak-matured Chardonnay. If you believed what you read in the sort of magazine you might get free with your Sunday papers, you weren't supposed to drink oak-matured Chardonnay. Or Merlot. Not an indicator of a discerning palate. But then again neither was Smirnoff. Probably. What did it really matter anyway? It wasn't as if there was anyone here to disapprove. Not like there was ever anyone here to say something one way or the other. Chardonnay, she decided. Reaching in for the bottle, she found some prawns, and some chorizo. There was a meal right there. She must have olive oil, and some garlic cloves somewhere. Not like anyone would be likely to smell her breath, either.

She went back into the living room; prawns and chorizo in a bowl, a few slices of a crusty loaf, a large glass of Chardonnay – her second – on a tray. She picked up the remote and turned on the television, surfing through the channels, finally settling on a rerun of some old stand-up comedy show. A fat comedienne whose routine seemed mostly to revolve around cakes. She could just go a cake right now. A custard slice or a cinnamon swirl. Even a Belgian bun. There were no cakes in the flat, of course. No biscuits either, or crisps. What she really wanted, she thought, picking up her digital cigarette, was a real fag. The red eye of the answerphone blinked insistently at her. Her sister Vicky, more than likely. Calling for a chat. At least *she* still spoke to Cat, the only one of the family who did. It was the only way Cat kept up with what was going on with them. By the end of the conversation, of course, she would have let Cat know how hard-up she was, without actually asking for money, so that Cat would offer and she wouldn't have to feel obliged. Tough, though: single mum, two kids. She'd give her a ring. A bit later ...

That was why, almost as soon as the door was opening, he was moving forward, his head describing an arc that connected with the bridge of the other man's nose. By that time it wouldn't have mattered who had opened the door. The chain of events had been set in motion. The result was inevitable. He was lucky, of course, that he had the personality, the disinhibition, of being able to switch on in that way. To not hesitate. If you hesitated you lost. So, if you wanted to win, you just did it, whatever it took, and fuck the consequences. The consequences were for afterwards. The consequences, the afterwards, would look after themselves. If you thought things through too much it would stop you doing anything.

Pushing through the door, his momentum taking them along the hall, knocking over the motorbike. Gripping the other man's neck, smashing the back of his head against the far wall. Slamming the door behind him with a foot. All this before checking whether there was anyone else in the hallway. Let alone the rest of the house. If he had thought through the consequences he might have considered that breaking the other man's nose might result in his shirt being splattered with blood. That this might have enraged him. Enraged him so much that he would pick up the other man's head, drag him up by his hair, smash his head repeatedly on the bare floorboards. He was pretty sure that the man would be alone, having sat outside the house for the best part of a couple of hours before making his move. All the same he made a quick tour of the flat. Living room: grey three-piece suite, coffee table, magazine rack, home cinema. Bathroom: toilet, shower with folded concertina screen. Bedroom: double bed – made – two bedside cabinets, double wardrobe. He checked inside the wardrobe. Knelt down and peered under the bed. Half-glazed door to back garden. Locked. Garden: laid to lawn, well tended, no garden shed. Nowhere to hide out there. Kitchen: table, two chairs, oven, fridge-freezer, dishwasher, wall cabinets; motorcycle parts, rags, cans of oil and petrol on the worktops. The place was empty. Back in the hall, the other man hadn't moved.

'You know what this is about?'

The other man shook his head and said something indecipherable. He moved closer and the man whimpered and pulled himself into a foetal position, his arms covering his head. The second type – the policeman – crouched down and whispered something in the man's ear.

'Do you know what this is about now?' he asked, standing up.

The other man nodded.

Cat looked into her empty glass. Picked up her mobile, tried Sean again. Voicemail. This was fucking ridiculous. What was he up to? All this worrying and she didn't even know if she had anything to worry about. But . . . let's be honest, more than likely she did. Should she tell Professional Standards what she knew? The real problem was, she didn't know anything. Hadn't a clue what Sean had been up to. She looked at her phone again and found Pearson's number in her contacts. Voicemail. What the fuck was going on? Where was everybody? She chucked the phone at the sofa. Watched it bounce off one of the back cushions, hit the arm and ricochet on to the floor where, thankfully, it didn't shatter. She looked at it for a moment and then into her empty glass. She was sure there was at least one more glassful in that bottle.

20

He felt a tapping on the sole of his right foot. Rhythmic. Weak. Tap-tap-tap. Pause. Tap-tap-tap. Pause. Tap-tap—

When he clambered from the dark well, groggy, mouth dry, crick in his neck, he opened his eyes to find himself sitting in a brown leatherette chair with wooden arms. Facing his mother, who was sitting in a wheelchair opposite, kicking his foot.

'Do you want to sit in your chair, Brenda? Or shall I put you into bed?'

Brenda? When was the last time he had heard her called Brenda? When had she ever been called Brenda? Pearson yawned, ran a hand over his face. Worked his fingers into the corners of his eyes. More to the point, thought Pearson, when had she ever allowed anyone to call her anything other than Mrs Pearson? She insisted on it. Usually.

'I think I'll sit in my chair for a bit, Colin, if you don't mind.' Pointedly staring at Pearson with a malicious half-smile. Not really wanting to sit in the chair. But not wanting him to. He got up.

'I'll go and see if I can find another chair from somewhere,' Pearson said. He glanced at the clock. Visiting time was nearly over. Twenty minutes or so left. Where had she been? He had asked the dark-haired nurse on the way in, pointing over at the empty bed, anxious momentarily.

'Mrs Pearson?' the dark-haired nurse asked, before shaking her head. 'Maybe she's gone for some physio.' At visiting time? They had all day – couldn't they arrange it when people weren't coming in to see their relatives? Seeing his expression, the nurse added, 'Maybe she's just gone to the toilet. Or for an X-ray or something? I'm sure she'll be back soon.'

Surely it shouldn't be that hard to keep track of their patients? Even on a ward that contained elderly people, some of whom were confused and might be prone to wander off when the fancy took them. But before he could make his point the nurse had moved away, so he had sat in the visitor's chair by her bed. And evidently fallen asleep.

When he returned with the orange plastic chair the orderly, or whatever he was, was making his mother comfortable in the armchair. He said something and her hand went to her cheek and then flapped him away. She was ... giddy. That was the word. She was giddy. When had he ever seen her like that? It was like she had gone back into her past. She was flirting, he realised. At her age. That couldn't be right. But it was more acceptable for older women. If an older man behaved in that way to a younger woman it would be thought of as inappropriate. Unsavoury, even. He looked at her. He couldn't imagine it somehow. She had gone back into someone else's past instead. Pearson put the chair next to hers and sat down. His mother was watching the retreating orderly and smiling. She turned to him.

'He's such a wag, that Colin.'

114

Wag? Now that was definitely a word she had borrowed from someone else's lexicon, someone else's past.

'Did you notice his eyes?' his mother asked. 'They're a lovely shade of blue.' He hadn't noticed. What he had noticed was that Colin hadn't shaved for a few days. Had a heavy stubble, the beginnings of a beard. Tattooed forearms under a short-sleeved shirt. And, in his opinion, Colin could stand to use a little more deodorant. At the end of the ward Colin turned briefly. His mother waved and Colin gave a friendly wave back. The gesture was slightly effeminate, studiedly camp. There was something not quite right about it. Something that didn't quite ring true.

'And such a considerate boy,' she said.

'Compared to me, you mean?'

She frowned theatrically. As if trying to work out what on earth he might be talking about. In that transparently false way a young child has when attempting to construct a plausible explanation for a broken toy, a crying sibling, a missing packet of sweets. Pearson couldn't be arsed to pursue it. The ward was too hot. He was too tired. He had spent too many visiting times trying to work out whether his mother was hard of hearing, confused, or deliberately misunderstanding what he said. He glanced over again at the clock. It was going to be a long fifteen minutes.

21

'Patrick.'

'Pardon?'

'Patrick,' Donna said. 'He prefers "Patrick".'

'Oh, OK,' the woman said, looking away from Donna and back to the boy, 'Patrick, can you hear me, Patrick? Patrick? Stay with us. Patrick, talk to me. Don't close your eyes, Patrick. Stay with us, please.'

She didn't know, of course. Donna didn't know if he preferred Patrick or not. Didn't know anything about him. Only his name. Patrick Jennings. And that only because of the provisional driving licence that she had found in the inside pocket of his leather biker jacket. The jacket that she now held to her. The jacket that he had taken off before he had sat down next to her on the kerb and said he felt cold and faint and then lain down and passed out. So she had called an ambulance. She had her phone with her, so she had called it in, given the location of the accident, and told the operator how Patrick Jennings was, how he looked, what he was doing. Which by that time was not a lot really. Just lying there on the kerb, his eyes shut, his breathing ragged and irregular. She hadn't tried to move him, exactly as she had been instructed. Hadn't done much of anything really. She didn't know what to do. So she had just sat there. Picked up his jacket off the floor and held it to her. Checked the inside pocket, though, and found the driving licence. Then held the jacket to her. Smelled the old leather, the smell of his sweat. Of oil. Of the embedded grit, the tarmac, the smell of blood. The jacket had a weight to it and lots of zips and those sew-on badges. One sleeve was ripped and badly scuffed where he had come off the motorbike and skidded along the road. She had seen it happen. Seen the bike tip to one side as he lost control, the bike slithering beneath him, hitting the surface of the road before careering on in a shower of sparks and screaming metal. The boy tobogganing in slow motion, his head in its visored red crash helmet bouncing repeatedly on the tarmac. She had seen it happen. Had she caused it to happen? She had woken – at least it had felt like waking up – becoming aware of being in this particular part of town but having no memory of how she had got there or where she had been before. Just the roaring of an engine behind her as she stood in the middle of the road, turning to see the boy losing control and the bike tipping over. 'I'm sorry,' she might have said. Or thought. Or thought she had said.

She'd thought he would be all right at first. After a minute, the front wheel of the bike still spinning in the glare of the headlight, the echo of the screeching metal and the sickening thud fading into silence, he had got up. He had taken off the battered crash helmet and examined it, running his fingers across the scratches, the dents, as if he couldn't quite believe that he wasn't dead, that the crash helmet had done its job. He had limped over and looked at the ruined bike, lying on its side in the middle of the road, something like tears in his eyes. Then, aware of his ripped jacket, he had slipped it off and studied his arm. The embedded grit, the gash oozing blood and some kind of clear liquid.

'I'm sorry,' Donna said again.

The boy had walked over then. Eighteen, it said on his licence. Not that much older than her. He had limped over to her and asked, 'Are you all right?'

So maybe it had been her fault. Maybe she had been in the middle of the road. In his way. He had sat down on the pavement then, throwing down his jacket, putting his crash helmet next to him, running his fingers once more across its surface, and she had sat down next to him.

'Got any fags?' he asked.

She had searched in the pocket of her hoodie. The hood up against the surprisingly cold night, and to hide the ruins of her hair. When she dug out her packet of cigarettes and matches and turned to offer them to him he was pale, his face covered in a sheen of sweat.

'I feel bad,' he said.

'How d'you mean?' It was a stupid thing to say, wasn't it? *How d'you mean?* But what do you say at a time like that? Unless you're a doctor or nurse or something and know the right thing to ask.

'I'm cold,' he said. 'I feel sick.'

Then he had lain down and closed his eyes. Even she had known then that something wasn't right. That it was dangerous if you felt sleepy after banging your head.

'You his girlfriend?'

When Donna looked up the paramedics had Patrick on a

stretcher, a collar round his neck, a mask over his face. The male one was pumping his chest, doing that CPR thing.

'Are you his girlfriend?' the female paramedic asked again. 'Only we're taking him to the hospital. You can ride in the back with him if you like.'

Donna hesitated. She could go with him. Pretend to be his girlfriend. For a little while anyway. What would happen though when his mum turned up, asked her who she was, what she was doing there? She'd thank Donna for calling the ambulance, and then what? Then nothing. She would be forgotten. Or after a little while they might start casting odd looks in her direction, wondering what she was still doing there. She might be able to ask his mum for some money. Only it's not the first thing you think of when your son is involved in a serious accident, bringing out your purse. And Donna wasn't sure, in any case, it was the right thing to do, asking someone's mum for money when they had been involved in an accident. Donna waved her mobile phone.

'I need to phone his mum. Let her know what happened. I'll come along with her later.'

The paramedic checked her watch, looked at Donna for a moment. Unsure.

'The police should be here soon,' she said, looking up the street as if expecting them to turn the corner at any moment. The woman was short and dumpy. The green uniform didn't look good on her.

'It's all right,' Donna said. 'I'll wait. I'll move the bike.'

The paramedic looked at the bike and then at Donna. Weighing up the likelihood of her being able to move it. Then she shook her head and slammed the doors of the ambulance and it drove off.

Donna shrugged on the leather motorcycle jacket. It was way too big, of course, and surprisingly heavy now she had it on. She turned up the sleeves. Its weight was somehow comforting. As she turned to walk away, catching her reflection in a shop window, she slipped her hands into the jacket's pockets. And found the handle of a knife.

22

THURSDAY

Pearson pinched the bridge of his nose between thumb and forefinger, squeezing his eyes tight shut, then massaged his temples. He had a throbbing headache. His sinuses blocked, an aching around his eye sockets so severe it felt as if he had two black eyes. The background hum of many portable electric fans on numerous desks, at first just mildly annoying, had now set off his tinnitus, a constant high-pitched squealing of metal on metal which was driving him mad. On top of which, it was way too hot. Again. Even though today the incident room was barely half full. He had woken sweaty, unrested and irritable. Already in a foul mood before sitting down at his desk to be faced with – what? Admin. He hated these rare days when there was a lull and you were forced to reach for those 'Case Remains Open' files and reread notes for the hundredth, or thousandth, time. Hoping that something you might have previously overlooked would suddenly jump out at you. Worse, today, reviewing Carragher's cases on Roberts' say-so. Seeing if there was anything that might come back and bite them on the arse. More accurately, bite Roberts on the arse, as he was the ranking officer and should, in theory at least, be able to say what his team were up to. He looked over at Lawrence, turned away from the room, hunched over and talking quietly and urgently into his mobile. Another personal call. Some people, of course, preferred to stay in the nick and work the phones or trawl the system. Pearson wasn't one of them. Sitting in the office gave him too much time to dwell on things. Too much opportunity to catalogue the feelings of physical discomfort: the ache in his back, the burning feeling in the end of his penis, the fullness in his bladder. Too much time to brood about the state of his marriage. To think about Ruth, his wife. The fingers of his right hand strayed to the gold band on his left ring finger and started turning it. His soon-to-be-ex-wife, if he wasn't very much mistaken. It was only her inertia, his reluctance to take that final step, that prevented it. Didn't stop him worrying about her. Speculating about her state of mind.

'I was just wondering how you were,' he had said to her when he'd gone to see Milton. At the time nothing more than a convenient lie. Because she had returned unexpectedly. Because he hadn't wanted to worry her with the real reason for his visit. Ruth, turning from the mirror, looking directly at him, had said, 'Alive.' Her tone flat. The word an accusation.

The key is warm in his hand. He reaches out and places it in the lock. The sound of metal sliding against metal, the teeth engaging in the barrel. Tumblers falling. He pushes the door and slowly, agonisingly, it opens. He steps into a hallway that has become so big that he can barely see the far wall. He takes a few steps inside and drops his briefcase to the floor. A bomb goes off and reverberates in the vastness of the space. In the silence that follows, he becomes aware of how quiet the house is. The sound of timbers settling. The tick of a clock in another room. Dust drifting in the air as the house invites him in. Beneath this, however, there is nothing: a lack of any other sound. Despite the quiet, he feels the presence of someone else in the house. Someone upstairs. Then he is moving again. Hears the scuffing of his shoes on the varnished floorboards, the rustle of his shirt moving against his skin, the creak of the risers as he slowly climbs the stairs. His own breathing as it is drawn raggedly into and then expelled from his mouth, the blood rushing in his ears, the heartbeat hammering in his head. As he turns on to the upstairs landing he notices that all the doors are open, bar one. The door to the main bedroom. Time jerks forward and he is now standing outside the room, reaching out, turning the knob, pushing the door ...

She is lying across the bed. Half on her side, her left hand half outstretched, as if reaching for something. Her face is immobile, peaceful. In his mind everything stops. He stands there, not moving. The moment has expanded, become almost infinite. Disparate, inconsequential images come back to him in exquisite, painful detail. The strand of dark hair caught in the corner of her mouth. A shred of cellophane clinging to the grimy sole of a slipper. The play of light along a white shin. The bunching of a sky-blue pyjama trouser leg around a knee. The way the cord is knotted around the waist of the pink dressing gown with the waffle-effect pattern, the same dressing gown she was wearing that morning when he left for work. Left for work because he couldn't take any more time off. But also because he couldn't stand being at home any longer. She had been sitting in the kitchen, staring at the tabletop, dark circles under her eyes. Both hands cupped around a mug of tea she had let go cold, the toast he had made her untouched. Her hair unwashed, unbrushed. His question as to whether she would be all right unanswered.

In his recollection he imagines that he can see the printing on the label of the bottle she clutches in her right hand, can read the name of the sleeping pills, even as another part of his mind registers that this cannot possibly be true. In the same instant time rushes forward, the nature of the light changes in the room as the bright afternoon sun moves into a late-evening gloom. Sounds come to him as if his ears are partly blocked, or he is underwater. A pop song drifts from an open window. Children playing in the school along the street. Birds singing. And somewhere above the clouds the sound of a light aircraft ...

Each time it ends at the same place, with Pearson standing helpless and immobile in the doorway, staring down at Ruth's lifeless body. In reality, the failure to act had not lasted more than half a minute at the very most. Then he was pulling the mobile out of his inside pocket, dialling the emergency services, feeling for a pulse. Tugging the pill bottle from Ruth's hand, reading the contents of the label into the phone, following the instructions being given to him by the emergency operator. All the while the realisation pounded in his head: this was not a cry for help, not a dramatic gesture in order to seek attention. Pearson had returned home early by chance – almost by chance. Because he had been worried about her, worried about what she might do if left on her own. No. This was a genuine attempt on Ruth's part to take her own life. An attempt that Pearson had thwarted. And now she hated him for it. It had become something for which she couldn't forgive him. Something for which she would probably never forgive him. He realised that he was still turning his wedding ring. That underneath the ring, where the finger joined the pad of his palm, a callus had formed.

He glanced over at Russell, who seemed engrossed in

something on her screen. He was desperate to pee. How long had it been since the last time he had gone? How many times had he already gone in the past three hours? It was almost impossible to get up from your seat and leave the room without anyone noticing. Even though they seemed intent on their screens, you just knew they were taking note of everyone else's movements. All right if you were a smoker. Then your need to leave the office, the building, was legitimised by your addiction. When had he started his new course of antibiotics? He had seen the consultant on his day off. Monday. Been issued the new prescription, picked up the tablets the same day, started taking them the next morning. So, two days. Not enough time then for them to work. Or was it? Should he have noticed a marked improvement by now? Sometimes he wondered if in some cases – in this case – the treatment, the very process of reaching a diagnosis even, wasn't worse than the disease itself. It was no good: he couldn't wait any longer, he would have to go and have a piss. He stood up and put his hands on the base of his back and stretched. Still looking at her screen, Cat said:

'You're not going to the loo again? I don't know why you don't just move your desk in there.'

23

A town centre pub with pretensions to being a fashionably cool night spot. A neon sign that when illuminated would flash repeatedly in sequence: white outline in shape of lozenge; upper left-hand corner HIP, upper-case, shocking pink; lower right-hand corner *gnosis*, lower-case, cursive script, electric blue. The sign lights up for a couple of seconds before going out. The neon tubes at present remain unlit. A man enters through the front door. His eyes sweep the room: plain off-white walls, stripped floorboards, leather club chairs and banquettes. The clientele mostly older men. Opposite, a pine bar. To the left, a low stage. At night this might hold a mixed-race woman dressed in a tight-fitting, red-sequinned evening gown, singing a jazz standard in a slightly shaky voice, occasionally going flat. A once-famous singer attempting a comeback, or an unknown actress on the way up who has been sleeping with the producer. The singer following the man's progress through the haphazardly arranged tables and chairs with an expression of recognition and regret. This early afternoon the low stage to the left holds a topless girl, hard face, heavy make-up, bored expression. Going through a set of desultory gyrations around a metal pole. Her expression barely changes as she follows the man's progress and, getting no reaction, she goes back to ignoring the audience.

Reaching the bar, Carragher glanced back across the club, experiencing a feeling of dislocation. As if he had watched someone, himself, walking into a generic crime serial or low-budget British-made gangster film. *Depersonalisation*, his counsellor had said. Since the shooting, the episodes had become more intense, more frequent. The sensation of separation from his emotions, his actions, his self. The conviction that he was living out a role dictated by someone else. Looking around the club, he couldn't decide who was the most bored, the most disinterested: the dancer – Eastern European, narrow-hipped, flat-chested, body piercings and even from here he could see she had bad skin – going through the motions of a half-hearted routine, or the punters sitting at the tables, sipping their overpriced continental lager. This atmosphere of ennui, of apathy, hadn't changed in two decades. When he was in his teens the club would unquestionably have been wreathed in cigarette smoke. The lingerie – nylon, mail-order or from the Ann Summers in the high street – a bit baggier, less salubrious; the women older, veteran strippers of the pub circuit and likely as not to be northerners, wherever in the country they were performing. The height of sophistication in those days consisted of a pubic hair dropped into your beer for having the temerity to rest your pint mug on the stage. But the prevailing mood would still have been one of tedium.

Turning back, he caught the eye of the shabby troll behind the bar, who was pretending to dry a glass with a tea towel and seemed to be the only one taking an avid interest in what was going on onstage.

'Terry in?' Carragher asked.

'Office,' said the barman – Dave something? – his eyes on the stage.

'Can you see if I can have a word?'

'Can't leave the bar,' said – Dave, yeah, that was it, Dave Cowans, still not looking his way. 'Someone might need serving.'

Carragher looked around. There didn't appear to be any great rush. Turning back, biting down the anger, he said, 'Can I go through?'

Cowans shrugged. 'Suit yourself.'

Stepping through the door marked PRIVATE behind the bar, and spotted by Carragher before he could slip back inside, Terry Milton hesitated for a moment, then indicated that the other man should come through.

'I like the new name of the club,' said Carragher from behind him as they made their way along the narrow corridor to Milton's office. 'I'm not sure everyone will get it, though. Could be a bit too clever.' After another few steps he said, 'This is a bit of a fire risk.'

Milton stopped walking and turned.

Carragher nodded downwards, tapping some plastic bottles and containers with his foot. 'Turps. White spirit.' Head tilted, reading the labels, 'Petrol?' Looking up, his expression blank, those disturbing grey eyes fixed on his.

'They use it for the compressor? For the spray-painting guns?' Milton mimicked holding something like a pistol and pulling the trigger.

'Point is, Terry, someone drops a lit fag in here, the whole place is likely to go up.'

Milton cleared his throat. 'The contractor was supposed to

come back today and pack all this away. Check off the snagging list. Only he hasn't turned up. I phoned this morning a couple of times,' he shrugged, 'went straight to voicemail.'

'The club burns down, Terry, that's your problem. But you're putting people's lives at risk.'

'I'll get Dave to move it. Put it out back in the yard.'

Carragher nodded again. 'Make sure you do. We don't want any more "accidents", do we?'

Glad to be free finally of the other man's stare, Milton turned away. They went a few yards further and Milton opened a door. He snapped a switch and as the fluorescent lights flickered into life he dragged a doorstop – pink, cast-iron and in the shape of a lighthouse – across with his foot to wedge the door open. The office was windowless, reasonably sized, the walls wood-panelled, a plush green carpet, a wing-back leather armchair in the middle of the floor. His idea of a gentleman's club. But in this weather it soon became close and uncomfortable, even with the fan. He switched it on and sat in the captain's chair behind the desk: oak, with a red leather inset on the top. Too big for the office. Way too expensive. But even now he couldn't resist running his hand over its surface.

'Scotch?' He took a bottle of single malt from the bottom drawer and waved it at Carragher.

'No thanks,' said Carragher, shifting the doorstop with his foot and allowing the door to swing shut before taking a seat himself. Slowly, deliberately, Milton took a small glass from the same drawer. Unscrewed the lid of the bottle. Poured himself a drink. Screwed the lid on the bottle. Put the bottle back in the drawer. Took a sip of the whisky. Smacked his lips in appreciation. All this time Carragher had said nothing. Not moving, just sitting in the chair opposite. Staring at him again.

Milton spread his hands. 'So?'

'Alicia Goode. You remember her?'

Milton scratched behind an ear. 'The sixteen-year-old who died?' He lifted the glass to his mouth then put it back on the desk without taking a drink. The other man's silence, his stillness, his eyes, making him feel self-conscious. Like he should – needed to – say more. 'You asked about her before.'

'That's right, Terry, we spoke to all of the pubs and clubs in town. But your name, specifically, had come up in connection with the investigation. Or the name of the club. The old name. At the time, I didn't give it much credence. The source wasn't that reliable. And the information wasn't that specific.'

'What information?'

Carragher said nothing. Didn't move. Just kept staring.

'It's bollocks. I had nothing to do with that girl's death.'

No reaction.

'It was an accident, right? They said so on the news.'

Silence. For a beat. Two.

'Well, maybe,' conceded Carragher, 'but when the head of the same children's home is found hanging from the scaffolding outside your club?' A pause. 'Some people might think he was trying to send out a message.' Neither said anything for half a minute, Milton resisting the urge to pick up his drink and drain it.

'It's a coincidence,' he said, 'that's all. A coincidence. Look, I've got scaffolding up. It's just somewhere easy for him to do it. Somewhere convenient. That's all.' Then, lamely, 'It's just a coincidence.'

Carragher nodded slowly. Agreeing. Or confirming something to himself. All the time not moving. His face expressionless. Just those grey eyes. That stare. That wasn't right, was it? Wasn't normal. Finally he said:

'And now, Terry, your name's come up again . . .'

Milton sighed and ran his fingertips around the rim of his glass. Not yet empty. But already he wanted another. He had known it was coming, of course. Had known as soon as Carragher had stopped in the corridor and tapped the half-full containers with his foot. Had made the little crack about accidents, about the club burning down. So he didn't need to hear what Carragher had to say. Not really. He just had to sit and watch Carragher's lips moving. Watch his lips moving over the top of his glass as he drank. He knew where this was going. So he'd just sit and wait. Wait until he could take the bottle of whisky out of his drawer again. Until he could unscrew the top and pour himself another drink. Screw the top back on the bottle, put the whisky back and shut the drawer. Until he could take a sip of his drink and ask, 'How much?'

24

Real nudity wasn't very attractive. Especially past a certain age and BMI. It might be acceptable if you were young, fit, good-looking. Preferably in a glossy magazine, tastefully arranged, artistically photographed, the unsightly bits airbrushed out. And above all, static. But in real life? Late thirties, possibly early forties for some people, those that kept themselves in really good shape, the exceptions – that should be the absolute top limit. A view reinforced only recently when Pearson had caught sight of his own all but naked body. The wardrobe door swinging slowly open, Pearson reflected in the full-length mirror attached to the inside while getting ready for work. He had recognised, in that instant, that he had reached that age when it would be best if he kept his clothes on. Accepted now that it had been a mistake to put his socks on before his underpants. If other people were going to insist on taking their clothes off in public, then shouldn't they at least have the common decency not to indulge in any form of physical activity?

'Is that even legal?' asked Cat.

They had driven to the amusements by the pier because Pearson had fancied some chips – 'fat chips' – and he liked the ones they did in the little kiosk there. Then they had crossed the road, walked past the benches opposite, Russell standing looking out across the estuary while Pearson sat on the sea wall, eating chips from a polystyrene cone, the wind roaring in his ears and small particles of sand stinging his face, the base of his back aching, his bladder full and finding himself uncomfortably in need of a pee again. Russell leaned down, took a chip, put it in her mouth and then made a face.

'Not enough salt. Too much vinegar.'

'I offered to buy you some,' he said, taking a chip himself.

Russell shook her head – 'It's all right. I'm not that hungry' – before leaning over and stealing another.

They had watched in astonishment as the naked cyclists rode by – buttocks overflowing saddles, rolls of fat wobbling, dimpled and mottled flesh, islands of coarse grey hair – until they were nearly out of sight at the eastern end of the seafront.

Pearson put a chip in his mouth and chewed thoughtfully. 'They were all wearing crash helmets,' he pointed out reasonably, putting another chip in his mouth. 'And,' he added, 'I wouldn't fancy trying to manhandle one of them into the back of the car.'

Illegal, no, but it seemed to him that it might be a little uncomfortable. Not to mention unhygienic. There would be a definite interaction between saddle and naked buttock. Not to mention genitalia. Pearson had tried cycling, gone so far as to buy himself an exercise bike, in fact. Gone on it religiously – well sort of. Regularly, at least. As regularly as the Job would allow. But every time had been the same. After ten minutes or so it had resulted in aching thigh muscles, burning knees. Worst of all a certain deadening effect – 'numb penis syndrome' he had discovered later on the internet. Even if he was willing to manhandle an overweight, naked middle-aged man – or, worse, woman – into the car there was the question of the upholstery of the Mondeo's back seat to consider. Better, if it was illegal in some way, to leave it to someone else. Let Uniform deal with it. For a few minutes he concentrated on his chips, saying nothing but wondering how to broach the subject. The real reason he had suggested they grab some fresh air, something to eat. No way to just drop it casually into the conversation. Best just to come out and ask. If she told him to mind his own business then so be it.

'How's it going with Professional Standards?'

'Slowly,' rootling round in her bag, 'but he seems to be finished with me for now.' Taking out a packet of wet wipes and cleaning her hands.

'Who's doing the interviews?'

'DI Ferguson. Do you know him?'

Pearson shook his head. 'Can't say I've ever heard of him. What's he like?'

'Scottish. Fucking irritating. Talking down into the desk, asks a question and you answer and then he takes for ever to ask the next one. He does these long silences. And then he looks up and gives you these meaningful looks.'

Pearson considered this. 'Maybe it's an interview technique.'

'Yeah, I thought that at first. Now I think he's just naturally fucking irritating.'

'Well, as long as he hasn't got under your skin, eh?' He put a chip in his mouth, chewed, swallowed. 'So what's it all about?'

Russell sighed. 'Oh, expenses for the most part ...' Pearson waited, knowing there was more. 'But he's hinting at some kind of assault. Hasn't come right out and said it. I don't know if it's sexual or physical. He's not even let on if the complainant is internal or external.'

'Sounds a bit vague?'

'Yep.'

Pearson shook the polystyrene cone at her.

She waved it away. 'No thanks.'

'You've never . . . ?' Looking at her. Putting the last of the chips in his mouth.

'No.' Russell shook her head.

'So, expenses. Hints at some kind of assault. And this has taken you three meetings?'

'That's what I mean,' she said. 'Everyone's going to think one of two things – either I'm in some kind of serious trouble myself, or I'm busy dropping everyone else in the shit.'

She might have a point. But in truth it was hard to say, not knowing exactly what it was all about. There was obviously something else. Something she was holding back. But it didn't seem that she was in any great rush to tell him what it was. And he wasn't about to ask. Best then, for the moment, just to drop it. Without saying anything she passed him a wet wipe.

'Thanks.' He gripped the polystyrene cone between his knees, wiped his fingers and then dropped the wipe into it. He thought for a minute then said, 'All I'm going to say is: you need to be careful. It's all well and good being loyal. But be sure that the person you're being loyal to deserves it.'

Pretty much, Cat thought as Pearson walked over and dropped the cone into a rubbish bin, what Ferguson had said. The question she had to ask herself now was: was Sean worthy of her loyalty? Pretty difficult to answer if she didn't exactly know what he'd been up to. But maybe that was an answer in itself.

Pearson came back and stood by her. Slipping his hands into his trouser pockets and looking up the beach, he fingered the folded Post-it note in his pocket and his mind went back to this morning in the incident room.

Pearson stood up, put his hands on the base of his back and stretched.

Still looking at her screen, Cat said, 'You're not going to the loo again? I don't know why you don't just move your desk in there.'

Pearson pantomimed confusion. 'What? I was just going to have a look on Carragher's desk,' he lied, nodding over in its general direction. Russell's eyes cut to him, then, pursing her lips and shaking her head, she returned her attention to her screen. Pearson pushed his way through the jumble of chairs. He didn't hold out much hope. There was nothing on the top. A yellow Post-it stuck to the computer screen. The desktop bare save for some dust. He didn't expect he would find much, if anything. He sat in Carragher's chair and opened the top drawer. Pens, elastic bands, a few staples, a blue highlighter pen and a pair of broken scissors. The next drawer held only a glossy brochure for an Audi A8. Pearson took it out of the drawer and turned idly through its pages. Inside the back cover he found a computer printout of a car-leasing agreement.

At this point Pearson imagined Marlowe, lit only by the green-shaded desk lamp, smoke rising from the cigarette between his fingers, taking the occasional sip from a shot-glass of Scotch, his eyes scanning across the text, letting the brochure fall to the desktop, whistling gently through closed teeth. Pearson did none of these. He had thought then that the monthly repayments were steep, had done a rough mental calculation: a fair chunk of a DI's salary. But affordable. Just. Now, he wondered if it might not have been an indication that Carragher was getting money from another source. All right, the monthly payments were doable. But add to that the flashy clothes, the designer suits. The Rolex. The Rolexes – he was sure he'd seen Carragher with at least two different models of the watch, maybe three. Had PSD already searched the desk? It seemed unlikely that they would have missed the brochure. That they wouldn't, like him, have picked it up and looked through and found the leasing agreement. If they had found it, wouldn't they have taken it as evidence? Pearson had put the brochure back in the drawer. If they found it, they found it, but he wasn't about to point them in its direction. The bottom drawer was empty. Pearson shut it, placed his hands on the top of the desk. Pretty much as he'd thought. But nothing at all? Even *his* desk had stuff in the drawers; paperwork for the most part. Admin that he hadn't quite got around to. Out-of-date copies of statements and reports that he should by now have shredded. An absence of personal effects, that was one thing, but a total lack of work-related papers? Perhaps Carragher was the sort of person who was completely up to date and cleared his desk every night before leaving; almost impossible, he'd have thought. He bet even Russell had outstanding admin she had to tackle. Or maybe he was the type of person who played things close to his chest, didn't want others to know exactly what he was up to. Sitting there, drumming his fingers absent-mindedly on the desk, Pearson's eye was caught by the yellow Post-it note stuck to the bottom of the computer screen. Three lines of scrawled biro. The top line, Pearson realised, was the last four digits of one of the case numbers he had given to Russell to look up on the system. The next line read *MONITOR 24* and then a zero – or was it 'two hundred and forty'? The last line read: *AV?* Surreptitiously he glanced across to where Russell sat engrossed in something on her screen. Then he reached out, unpeeled the Post-it and slipped it into his pocket.

'I suppose we'd better get back,' he said. But when he turned he saw that Russell was staring out into the estuary. Following her gaze, he noticed that there was a break in the cloud and sunlight had escaped to illuminate a small area of the water by the far shore. The rolling hills of Kent sloped down to the bank and where the water had caught the light it appeared as if the land had been underlined in silver.

25

The passenger door opened and she felt the suspension shift as someone got in. The door closed again and Cat turned. Pearson was leaning forward. He felt under the seat, found the lever and pushed his seat back.

'Not a lot of leg room, is there?' he asked.

Cat sighed, 'What do you want? I'm about to go home.'

'Really?' Looking out of the side window into the police-station car park, he rubbed away some non-existent specks of dust. Leaving, she noticed, smeary fingerprints in the process. 'Only, I've been watching you for the last ten minutes and you haven't moved.'

She had been sitting in the car after texting Sean again. Need to meet. Name time and place. Hoping that this time he would get back to her. Getting no reply. Deliberating on what to do next. What could she do? Until she heard from him: nothing.

For most of the day she had managed to put the whole Sean business out of her mind, at least for stretches of an hour or half an hour at a time. Losing herself in the routine of reading case

143

files on the computer. Cross-referencing filed reports. Making sure that every bit of paperwork was in order and that there were no loose ends. But on leaving the nick, sitting in her car, it had all crowded in on her again. In the past few days she had assumed, she realised, the role of the cuckolded husband, the wronged wife. She had become someone who suspected their partner of betrayal and was now replaying old conversations, picking apart sentences word by word for proof of infidelity. Re-examining seemingly innocent suggestions or actions, looking for the ulterior motive.

'Listen,' Pearson said, 'if you ever need someone to talk to . . .'

She looked across at him, then looked away. He was still gazing out of the side window. But she couldn't be sure if he could see her reflection in it.

She cleared her throat. 'I'll bear it in mind.' Sarcastic. But she was touched. And, really, she meant it.

'Sooo . . .' Pearson said, looking at her now, 'doing anything nice this weekend?'

If Sean phoned she would be meeting him. So, waiting on his call probably. Like a love-struck teenager. Waiting on a call that in all probability would never come.

'Pearson . . .' shaking her head, 'fuck off.' Attempting a nonchalant tone. But when she looked down she realised she was gripping her phone so tightly that her fingers were actually aching. Pearson glanced down. Casually she put the phone in her handbag. But she was sure he had noticed.

'You're not planning on doing anything stupid?' he asked.

Define 'stupid', she thought. But then the definition of stupid was probably to keep on trying Sean. Even though it was more than likely that Professional Standards had a tap on his mobile by now. Too late to worry about that one. They only had to go back over his phone records to see that she had tried to contact him. To see how many times she had tried to contact him. And if that was stupid, what was planning to meet him if he called? But she said nothing and they sat for a few minutes just staring out of the front windscreen. Pearson checked his watch and sighed. A loud exhalation through his nostrils. Irritated. Or frustrated.

'OK,' he said, 'just remember what I said earlier. About loyalty?'

He got out of the car and slammed the door. Cat sat for a few minutes and watched Pearson start his Mondeo, indicate to pull out, lift a hand in acknowledgement to her as he passed. The Mondeo waited at the exit to the car park, the indicator flashing, then took a right on to the main road. When Cat was quite sure he had gone she reached into her bag and retrieved her phone.

Donna woke back in the bedsit. Back in her single bed and wearing the heavy leather biker jacket over her hoodie. She checked the time on the clock radio next to the bed. Gone five. Across the room, leaning against the foot of the wall, the broken mirror reflected the light from the street outside. Beneath the mirror, shards of glass glittered among tufts of black hair, as if some immense black-feathered bird – a crow, perhaps – had been trapped in the room and managed to beat itself to death in its panic to escape. She swung her legs over the edge of the bed. She was hot. The leather jacket was too heavy really. But she liked the weight of it. Liked its comfort. Liked, too, the comfort of the knife in its pocket. She reached down and picked up a two-litre bottle of Diet Coke. Unscrewing the top, she took a swig. It was tepid, and flat. She stared at the mirror. Something moved behind the jagged remnants that clung to its frame. She screwed the top back on the bottle and crossed the room. Picking up the mirror, she hung it back on its nail on the wall.

Alicia stared back at her. She had done something awful to her hair. The sides were shaved to a stubble and the top had been chopped to a ragged crop.

'Hello, you,' Alicia said. Donna said nothing. 'I miss you,' Alicia said.

Trying not to look at her, Donna picked some of the tiny fragments of glass from the bottom of the frame and dropped them on the floor.

'Yeah?'

'Yeah, babe, course I do. I wish we could be together again. Just me and you.'

'And Motorcycle Boy,' Donna said, nodding at the other figure in the mirror.

Motorcycle Boy – Patrick – had on another leather jacket, she noticed. This too had lots of zips and those sew-on badges. And he had contrived to rip it somehow in exactly the same place as her own. Had scuffed the leather of the arm to match the scuffing on the arm of her own jacket.

'He doesn't matter. I'm so sad without you.'

'Funny, you look happy enough.'

She wondered how long it would take before Mr Downey appeared in the mirror with them. Donna took something out of her pocket.

'What's that?' Alicia asked, panic in her voice.

'I don't want to see you,' Donna said. 'Not for a little while. I've got things I need to do.'

'If it's about—'

146

'Yeah, I know. "It doesn't matter." Only it matters to me.'

Donna undid the lid of the white paint. The sort of paint you used on little kids' faces at birthday parties. Not that she'd ever been invited to those kinds of parties. Those kinds of parties were for the kids whose mums had money. For the kids whose mums weren't smackheads. For the kids whose mums weren't a complete fucking waste of space. She had bought the paints and a brush at one of those party shops. Told the old bag behind the counter some story about her little brother having a party soon and she wanted to practise painting faces so that when they had the party she could do a good job. The old bag hadn't believed her, or hadn't cared. Just took her money without saying anything. Dropping the change into Donna's palm as if she might catch something if they actually touched.

She dipped the paintbrush and started to apply the paint to her face.

'Who's that?' Donna had asked.

Malcolm looked up from the book he had been reading and over at the telly.

'Dunno, some old bloke from the eighties. This video's like, ancient.'

'Nah, not the bloke singing. The thingy, the character he's meant to be.'

Malcolm thought for a moment or two, then he said, 'Can't remember. Show us your phone a minute.'

Malc had looked it up on Wikipedia. Malc said everything in the world was on Wikipedia. That people always took the piss, said it was crap, but he had found out everything he had ever wanted to know on Wikipedia. And Malc had found out who the character was, had read it all out to her. She hadn't understood

147

hardly any of it, to be honest. But she had understood enough to think that the story reminded her of her and Alicia.

Donna watched as Alicia's face disappeared. To be replaced by the white blankness of the painted mask.

'The thing is,' she said, 'I can't see you for a while. You're doing my fucking head in.'

26

Pearson looked across the street at the dingy row of shops opposite. A newsagent's with its window completely obscured by advertisements for cigarettes, lager, ice cream, the National Lottery. An appliance-repair shop. Rows of dusty upright hoovers and old-fashioned sewing machines warped behind yellow-tinted plastic sheeting. A Chinese supermarket with shelves containing bottles and boxes with exotic and baffling labels, open cardboard cartons of gnarly, disfigured vegetables sprouting grotesque tufts of wiry hair. A launderette, the lone shabby customer swigging from a can of Tennent's Extra and having a heated argument with the soap-powder dispenser. The discreetly curtained frontage of a sex shop. For Sickert Downey, his dizzying fall to earth brought to an abrupt halt by the rope around his neck, this, thought Pearson, would have been his last view of the world . . .

He turned and pushed through the front door of Milton's club. His first thought was: All very bright. All very airy. All very bland. Very much the same as every other new pub you walked into these days. If you were going to own your own club, why make it look like everywhere else? Because, he supposed, that was what people wanted. For Pearson, pubs were meant to be dark. Dark-oak bars, sticky tables and a ratty old dartboard with the stuffing coming out of it. The carpets – carpets, not floorboards – were meant to be red. When they were first laid, in any case. Obviously, over the passage of time they passed into the colour of spilt beer, fag ash and chewing gum. Who brought chewing gum into a pub? But it was always there, or at least it used to be. Trodden in, blackened, but always managing to retain the vestige of stickiness. Just tacky enough to stick to the sole of your shoe. And flock wallpaper. Whatever happened to flock wallpaper? They didn't even have it in Indian restaurants these days. For him the smell of his teenage years, the smell of nostalgia, was the smell of stale cigarettes and sour beer. The aromas of the pub in the morning before it was cleaned for the midday trade. Some of the pubs, most of the pubs of his teenage years, never were cleaned properly. What would be the smell of nostalgia in another twenty years' time? New paint? Lavender air freshener? Furniture polish?

Sitting on a stool at the bar, dressed in another Lacoste, baby-blue this one, Terry Milton looked up from the newspaper he was reading.

'Frank.' Not at all pleased to see him.

'Can we have a word?' Pearson asked.

Milton closed his paper and stood up. 'Mind the bar for a minute, Dave, will you?'

Dave Cowans grunted a reply. Already making himself busy, leaning forward and wiping the bar with a cloth.

Pearson looked at the back of his head and sucked air in through his teeth. 'Your head looks bad, Dave.' Feigning concern: 'It's like it's all burned or something.' Cowan's hand went immediately to his bald patch and, smiling, Pearson turned away.

'Cheers for that, Frank,' said Milton, 'he'll be fucking off down the hospital again now.'

'I like the new name,' Pearson said as they stepped through the door into the back of the club, 'but you realise most people will just think you can't spell?'

Déjà vu. Walking along the narrow hallway, Pearson at his back rather than Carragher, passing the rows of half-empty plastic containers.

'I've already asked Dave to put them out the back,' Milton said before Pearson could comment. 'The contractor was supposed to come today and clear it all away but I can't get hold of him.'

He opened the door, snapped on the light. Thought about pulling the pink lighthouse across and propping open the door. Tracy would be in soon to take over at the bar. And, knowing Dave, he would choose this moment to start moving the crap in the hallway. Taking his time to pick up each bottle in turn and test the lid to see if it was screwed on tight. Carefully placing the bottles in a cardboard box. Dave could make a five-minute job last an hour at the best of times. And today he would have the opportunity to hang around and earwig. He wasn't sure what Pearson was here for, but he was sure he didn't want Dave to hear it. So he changed his mind. Let the door swing closed behind him, turned on the fan and went and sat behind the desk. Pearson looked around the office.

'This is all a bit Bertie Wooster,' perching on the arm of the wing-back chair, 'but I can't see Dave as Jeeves. More like Scrotum, the old wrinkled retainer?'

Milton wanted to open his bottom drawer. Take out the bottle of Scotch. Pour himself a drink. He resisted.

'How is she?' Pearson asked.

'Bit down' – best to put Frank on the back foot from the off – 'since your visit.' A minor exaggeration. She had been upset, true. But not that much. And not for that long. More angry than anything.

'She still thinks it was about her?' Pearson asked.

'Yeah.'

'Well, that's something, I suppose. I just don't want her worrying.'

'There's nothing for her to worry about.'

'So you said.' Pearson picked a thread from his suit trousers, rubbed his finger and thumb together, let it fall to the floor. Looking up, he said, 'Have you ever come across a DI by the name of Sean Carragher?'

He really needed that drink. Palms sweating, Milton spread his hands on the desk. Hoping they wouldn't leave a stain on the leather. Hoping it wouldn't show when he took them away.

'Carragher?' he said as if trying to place the name. 'Scouser? Lairy bastard?'

Pearson nodded. 'That's him.'

'He was one of the coppers who came here when that girl went missing. They spoke to all of the pubs and clubs in town, I think.'

'You haven't spoken to him since?' Pearson asked.

Milton gave in and opened the bottom drawer of the desk. Looking down, avoiding Pearson's eyes, he said, 'No, I haven't spoken to him since then.' Taking out the bottle. Shaking it at Pearson.

'No thanks.'

Milton checked his watch. 'You can't still be on duty?'

'I'm not. I just don't fancy it.'

Milton shrugged. 'Suit yourself.' He got out a glass. Poured himself a drink. Screwed the top on the bottle. Took a sip of his

Scotch. All the time watching Pearson for a reaction. 'What's all this about, Frank? I assume there's some point to it? Otherwise I should get back to the club.'

'Carragher's under investigation by our Professional Standards Department. You understand what that means?'

'Yeah.' Milton nodded, starting to relax a little. 'It means he's been a naughty boy, right?'

'We don't know yet.'

'So what's it got to do with you?'

Pearson shrugged. 'We're just trying to see how bad things are.'

'Before this Professional Standards lot find out, right? OK,' taking a sip of his Scotch, 'this Carragher's under investigation. What's it got to do with me?'

'Before your club was Hipgnosis, it was called Avatar, right?'

'Yeah, you know it was. So what?'

'And before that?'

'Monitor,' irritated, 'again, so what? Clubs change their names all the time. You tart it up. Change the name. The punters think it's something new. But in the end it's still the same. Same music. Same beer.'

Pearson got something out of his pocket. A yellow Post-it note. He held it up between the thumb and forefinger of his left hand. It was too far away for Milton to see what was on it. And he wasn't about to get out of his chair and go over and have a look.

'I found this stuck to Carragher's computer screen.' Pearson pointed with his right index finger. 'This, at the top? That's the last four numbers of a case reference. A series of fires, which we suspect might have been arson. This, on the bottom line, a capital A and V and a question mark. I think this is short for "Avatar".'

'AV? It could—'

'Could be anything,' Pearson interrupted, nodding, 'right. Except for this middle line. "Monitor", and then the number twenty-four. And then this ... At first I thought it might be a zero. Two hundred and forty, maybe? Then I fell in. It's not a zero. It's the letter O.' He paused. 'It's a date. The twenty-fourth of October.' Pearson paused. 'You've had two fires in the past two years at the club. One two months ago. When was the other one?'

Milton sighed. 'The October before last.'

'Right. And if I was to go back and check on the system the exact date? What's the betting I'll find it's the twenty-fourth?'

'So what you're saying, Frank,' unscrewing the lid of the bottle, pouring himself another drink, 'is that you think I've torched the club twice to claim the insurance? Is that it?' He sipped his drink. Watching Pearson over the rim of the glass.

'You tell me.'

'*Suspected* arson case, you said. So you've got no proof, right?' Pearson said nothing. Time to push his luck a little. 'Listen, Frank,' Milton said, 'I can see how it might look. Things haven't always gone so well for me. I'm the first to admit that. The club gets torched twice in two years. Both times I redecorate the place and reopen. And in the meantime I'm not exactly going without, am I? So straight away you're thinking, Where's he getting all this money? Right? He must have some kind of scam going. So you think: Insurance. He's got some kind of insurance scam going. But you've forgotten something. You know yourself I've taken out a loan. I told you a couple of days ago. So why would I need to take out a loan to do up the club if I've got some racket going on with the insurance?'

He looked down at his glass, ran his finger around the rim.

154

'Truth is, Frank, I … Had my public liability, all that. All the stuff I needed to run the club. But the rest?' He held his hands up in surrender. 'What can I say? I forgot to do it. I fucked up. Like you've always said, Frank. I'm a fuck-up. Always have been. Always will be, probably.' He picked up the glass. Drained it. Put it back on the desk. 'What's the matter, Frank? Really, you should be pleased. You've been proved right after all.'

Not the complete truth, Milton thought after Pearson had left and he sat alone in his office staring at the closed door once again. He hadn't had insurance, that much was true. But he had intended to have insurance. Had gone to the website, clicked all the right buttons, or so he had thought. Only, the paperwork hadn't come through. There had been no confirmation email. He had meant to chase it up, but forgot. So that much was true: he had fucked up. And then he had had to borrow the money. But what bank would lend to him? Well, he'd tried them all, and the answer was: none. So he had had to go elsewhere. To the sort of people who charged you outrageous rates of interest. The sort of people who took your club, or the best part of it, if you couldn't keep up the repayments. Fair enough, they might let you stay on, let you run the business. Or be the public face of the business. They might even let you earn a living. Just. Or they might ask you to do them the odd favour now and then. At least these days they let you keep your kneecaps. The repayments were extortionate, crippling, but not quite impossible. You could pay off the loan – eventually. But the last thing you could do was waste money. To give it away, to pay people off. Coppers, for instance. Coppers who were already under investigation by their own Professional Standards Department. He took a sip of his Scotch and his eyes fell on the door stop. Heavy. Iron. Pink. And in the shape of a lighthouse. When he had seen it, brought it back to the club, shown it to Dave, they had both cracked up. They'd kept it behind the bar for a while. When the joke had worn thin it had made its way into his office. But it still looked like nothing more than an enormous pink cock. And standing now on the carpet in the middle of his office it seemed to be sending him a message.

27

Sitting in his car and looking out into the dark, he wondered if this had been such a good idea after all. His choice of venue: an area set aside for parking at the very eastern end of the esplanade. A row of beach huts to his right, to his left Ministry of Defence land enclosed by a waist-high wall topped by metal railings. Somewhere in front of him, obscured by the sea wall and the concrete ramp of the slipway, he could hear waves breaking in the estuary. Behind him the occasional car turned on to or off the seafront. Alone in his car, at night, in this out-of-the-way place? If anyone were to drive by now, Carragher realised, they might think he was dogging. Some busybody only had to phone it in. Or a random police patrol stop. Especially as he expected not to be alone for too much longer. He checked his watch again. He'd give it another five minutes. Maybe ten. At the sound of approaching footsteps he checked his rear-view mirror. The passenger door opened and closed and someone got in.

'Expecting someone else?' the girl asked as he turned to face her.

Donna Freeman wore a biker's jacket that was way too big for her. The arm nearest to him was scuffed and ripped, as if its previous occupant had been dragged bodily along a road at high speed. The rest of her clothes were black: T-shirt, short skirt, boots. Her legs, bare, slim, smooth, weren't at all bad, he had always thought. But her black hair had been shaved to stubble at the sides, the top unkempt and irregular in length. And she was made-up kind of weird. Her face painted white, the eyes outlined by heavy black eyeliner. Only half the eyebrows made up. The black lipstick applied to make the mouth seem smaller. It was familiar somehow. A mime? A clown? The sad-faced clown. What was it called? That thing from the Commedia dell'Arte? Pierrot. That was it. She was Pierrot.

'What's all that about?' he asked, nodding at her made-up face. The girl shrugged sulkily, jamming her hands between her legs and settling back into the seat. 'You look fucking ridiculous,' he said. He felt a brief flash of anger. It was ludicrous. Like it mattered to him what she did to herself. Like he should care. The look on her face made it quite obvious she didn't give a shit what he thought anyway. He fought an urge to give her a slap, shake some sense into her. Gripping the wheel, he looked away, making an effort to calm himself, taking a series of deep breaths, consciously relaxing his hold on the steering wheel. 'I told you before, we're finished,' he said.

'I know,' she said miserably, looking down into the footwell.

'So what are you doing here, Donna? What the fuck are you doing here?'

'I don't know.'

She felt in her pocket and took out her fags and matches. As she scratched at her leg above her knee he could see her shoulders start to shudder. She turned to him then, her eyes already

158

shiny with tears. Looking so lost and pathetic that he made an effort to soften his voice.

'What's this all about, Donna?'

'Alicia,' she said. The word barely a whisper.

Not this again. Carragher sighed. 'Your little friend.'

'Everyone says that,' taking out a cigarette, rolling it absent-mindedly along her leg, '"your little friend". And I always say, "My little *dead* friend."' Carragher scratched at his cheek and looked out through the windscreen.

'And what exactly,' he said, 'do you expect me to do about it?'

'I don't know,' she said, 'but you ought to do something. Somebody ought to do something.' She struck a match and lit her cigarette.

'I didn't say you could smoke. It makes the car smell.' He caught the whiff of something acerbic on a sudden gust of wind, some accelerant, petrol perhaps. She watched the match burn down. Then she shook it out and flicked the matchstick away through the open side window.

'You're a policeman,' she said pathetically. 'You ought to do something.'

'Not for much longer.'

'You investigated Alicia's death,' she went on, ignoring what he had said. 'You were the . . . you were in charge.'

'I was the deputy senior investigating officer,' he corrected her, 'but, yeah, I suppose to all intents and purposes I was in charge. We looked into your friend's death thoroughly, Donna. We followed the right procedures. We looked at all the facts. And we decided that there was nothing to indicate it was anything other than an accident.'

The girl had started to shake her head as soon as he had begun to speak, had continued to shake it as he went through it all for the – he couldn't remember how many times it had been – was still shaking her head now.

'We spoke to everyone. Everyone at the party she had been to. We collected CCTV. We put out a media appeal. In short, we did everything we were supposed to, everything we could. It was just an accident. There was no evidence – *evidence*, Donna – to say it was anything else. And the facts won't be changed just because you can't accept it. Because you think it shouldn't have happened.'

'You could find the evidence. You could keep trying,' she said, studying his face through a cloud of exhaled blue smoke.

'And why would I do that?'

She put a foot up on the seat, her skirt sliding down her thigh.

'Pack it in,' he said.

'What?' Shifting her skirt with her hand, exposing her under-wear to him.

'Pack it in, I said.'

She put her leg back down. Took a drag on her cigarette, stared into the footwell. They were quiet for a minute or so, both looking out through the windscreen at nothing. She took a drag on her cigarette and flicked the ash out of the window.

Eventually she said, 'I helped you out before.'

'So?'

'I gave you information.'

'And you think that entitles you to what, exactly?' She shrugged, took a long drag on her fag and then stared at its glowing tip. 'Don't drop that on the floor,' he said. She looked at the cigarette for a moment then flicked it out of the window. 'I meant, use the ashtray.'

After a minute he said, 'You gave me information, Donna. And I gave you money. But the truth is I only gave you money because

160

I felt sorry for you. That's why I told you we were finished. I can't keep on giving you money, OK? I can't afford it.' He dug in his jeans pocket and pulled out his wallet. He peeled off three twenties and offered them to her. She refused to meet his gaze, clenching her hands into fists, so he dropped the notes into her lap.

'That's your lot, OK? That's it.'

Biting her bottom lip, she looked down at the money in her lap. Then she picked it up and pushed open the car door, slamming it behind her.

After the girl had gone he sat, staring at nothing in particular, listening to the waves break on the other side of the sea wall. He checked his watch again. Time to leave, no sense in hanging around any longer. No one was coming now. Out of the corner of his eye he thought he caught a movement. Up by the beach huts to his right. Could that be a slightly darker shadow against the black? Someone standing there? Someone who'd seen the girl get in the car and been scared off? Or was it the girl standing watching him? The passenger door opened again.

PART TWO

28

FRIDAY

Pearson flashed his warrant card at the uniformed PC, who lifted the incident tape and allowed him to duck under. Roberts, finishing his conversation with the CSM, walked over, reaching into his inside jacket pocket and retrieving a packet of Extra Strong Mints, which he waved at Pearson.

'Nah, you're all right. What've we got?'

Roberts crunched his mint noisily. 'Burnt-out car.' Half turning, indicating the white forensic tent. 'There's a body inside.'

'We got an ID?'

'Not as yet. The body's too badly burned. But the car's an Audi A8. The back index number's still legible. It's registered to Sean Carragher.'

Pearson scanned the crime scene: two panda cars, the forensics van, a loose semicircle of coppers slipping on yellow plastic bibs and being addressed by another cop who Pearson recognised as the head of the search team. The other first-responders: a fire engine, an ambulance and a couple of unmarked vehicles. Several firemen sweltering in yellow waterproofs, paramedics in green uniforms. All shuffling uncertainly; feeling redundant but loath to leave.

'Called in a couple of hours ago,' said Roberts.

Pearson automatically checked his watch. A couple of hours. Meaning the call was received not long after 3 a.m.

'By a lady motorist on her way home from her sister's.' Roberts nodded in the direction of the sea wall, where Cat Russell was perched, talking to another woman. Mid to late twenties. Dark hair in a ponytail. Red T-shirt. Black jeans. Black trainers.

'Her sister's been having some kind of domestic. Sounds like the old man's been playing away. She was driving down Ness Road. As she turned right on to the seafront she saw it go up. By the time she'd pulled over and called it in, it was already well ablaze. Unfortunately for her, while she waited for Fire and Rescue to arrive she decided to take a closer look. See if she could help . . . '

The woman was obviously distraught. Shoulders hunched, dabbing occasionally at her eyes and nose with the balled-up tissue in her right fist. Cat, to Pearson's eyes only slightly less pale, only slightly less shaky, but holding it together, leaned in close, putting her hand on the other woman's arm in order to offer some comfort. A blonde female PC hovered uncertainly a few yards away.

'When the brigade arrived,' said Roberts, 'the fire had all but burned itself out. We've only just been given the go-ahead that it's safe to take a proper look.'

Beside the fire tender, one of the firefighters stood chatting to the CSM and another man in shirtsleeves. Pearson knew him from a previous case: the fire investigation officer. The person officially charged with establishing the cause and origin of the fire. He nodded to the firefighter, who opened the door of the cab, took off his jacket and helmet and put them in the front seat before running a hand through his short, damp hair. Getting ready to leave. The paramedics, too, were packing up, stowing their equipment, shutting the back doors of the ambulance. Roberts followed his gaze.

'There's not much for them to do,' he said. 'Body's not ready to be moved yet. Rather than try and separate them here, Bannister thinks she might have to take the seat out. Take that and the body as a whole back to the morgue.'

When Pearson looked at him, Roberts shook his head and answered his unasked question. 'I only caught a brief glimpse, but it's not pretty.'

Pearson felt an unsettled sliding in his stomach again. Globs of fat floating up to a greasy surface. That bottle of semi-skimmed milk on the turn. He hoped.

Roberts sighed. 'Let's go take a look.'

Outside the entrance to the white forensic tent they each pulled on hooded paper onesies. Blue polythene overshoes like elasticated carrier bags; for every pair you got on, you ripped another three. Latex gloves. They stepped inside into an abrupt deadening of sound, a lowering in light levels, the atmosphere hot and airless with the quantity of equipment, the press of bodies. Pearson felt that familiar shift into the unreal as time and movement were frozen momentarily in the glare of a camera flash. Bannister crouched by the driver's-side window, a miniature voice recorder held to her mouth. The car a blackened skeleton. Tiny chips of shattered windscreen glass. The metal of the chassis exposed, the paintwork almost totally burned away, except for irregular blistered and buckled red patches.

The scene lurched back into motion. Bannister stood, directing the forensic photographer to take some shots of the vehicle's interior. This wasn't the first car-fire fatality Pearson had attended.

Not that long ago and not that far away, maybe a few hundred yards from the seafront, a father involved in a bitter divorce had smothered his five-year-old daughter, who was staying on a weekend visit, before setting himself alight inside the car. The speculation at the time being that it was a self-imposed punishment for what he had done. Somehow Pearson couldn't see Carragher as a candidate for self-immolation. If it was Carragher, of course – there was still a chance it wasn't him. But if it wasn't Carragher then it was still some other poor bastard.

The inside of the tent lit up as the camera flash went off: Bannister caught in mid-sentence pointing out a detail to the photographer. A white-suited SOCO adjusting a halogen light on a stand with a screwdriver. Their monstrous silhouettes fixed against the billowing fabric of the tent.

He had also attended when a burnt-out car had been found in a lay-by. At first it bore all the hallmarks of a gangland hit. Especially as the victim was a known user and small-time dealer. It later turned out that he had simply parked up and passed out under the influence of drugs and alcohol, then been overcome from the smoke in a counterfeit car stereo. The car had subsequently burst into flames and he had burned to death before he could wake up. So there was a minimal probability, and Pearson didn't rate it any higher than minimal, that this was an accident.

Some fault with the electrics, maybe? But the driver's door was shut. And from the glimpse he had got, the body was still seated in an upright position. Wouldn't whoever it was have made more of an effort to escape? Surely the fire wouldn't have spread that quickly? Pearson didn't buy it. No. There was no real doubt in his mind that the body in the car would turn out to be Carragher. A serving police officer. A serving police officer under investigation by the Professional Standards Department. The most likely scenario was that Carragher had been killed and the car set on fire in an effort to destroy any forensic evidence. In the short time they had been inside the tent, the temperature had risen noticeably. And with it the smell. Bannister stepped away and for the first time Pearson got a good look at the body inside the car. The smell of melted rubber. Singed metal. Torched paint. Liquefied plastic. Overlaying it all, a miasma of barbecued human flesh. A camera flash went off and the white-hot glare of magnesium burned the image of the thing that had once been Sean Carragher on to Pearson's retina.

Just thirty seconds too late Roberts said, 'We might as well go back to the nick. We're not going to learn anything more here.' Unwrapping another mint from the packet. Putting it into his mouth.

Back outside, Pearson bent down to remove his polythene over-shoes, furiously blinking away the hovering after-image. A body 'burned beyond recognition'. It was a phrase often used. A cliché. A euphemism. A palliative. But seldom grasped unless witnessed at first hand. The smell, however – his nostril hairs cauterised, his mucus membranes coated with a layer of atomised human fat – was likely to stay with him for the rest of the day. If not longer.

Roberts was saying, 'The question is not what happened. That seems fairly obvious. Either it's suicide, which seems unlikely, or he was killed in the car, probably by someone he knew, and then set on fire to hide the evidence. So the question is, who was he planning to meet, right?'

Pearson stood up and glanced over to see Cat helping the lady motorist into the back of a panda. The previously hovering blonde female PC got into the other side and they slammed the back doors in unison. As Cat straightened, she met Pearson's eyes across the roof of the car.

'And,' said Roberts, 'what, exactly, the fucker was up to?'

29

DCI Roberts cleared his throat. There would be a lot of throat-clearing in the coming days, Pearson thought. A lot of officers not quite able to meet each other's eyes, a lot of people keeping their heads down and concentrating on the task at hand. A lot of people not talking to each other quite as much as they might normally. The incident room was already quieter than usual. The atmosphere, understandably, subdued. But there was an undercurrent of tension. Of expectation. They all knew what Roberts was going to say. Or had an idea. Had heard a rumour, knew part of the story. Had been told on their way in; in the car park, on their way up the stairs, as they shrugged off a jacket, slipped behind a desk. There would be those, of course, who, having heard, were still hoping it might not be true. That there might have been some mistake made or some piece of evidence overlooked. Something, anything, that might prove that it had been someone else in the car. Those who were hoping it was not their colleague, their friend, whose body had been discovered this morning. Surely even those who had been unaware up till now would have heard that Carragher had been under investigation in recent weeks? Even if they didn't know why. So there would be others, those who had not had so much time for Carragher, who would be wondering, like Pearson, what his death might mean for the force. For the nick. And there might be some who might have even more personal concerns. He glanced over at Cat, but she was engrossed in something on her computer screen. Looking around, he noticed some new faces: additional resources drafted in to assist with the investigation. Most not yet allocated desk space, in some cases not even chairs. In the corner of the room by the door stood a man in dress uniform. Brass. His black hair so neat, so precise, it looked as if it had been cut with the aid of a ruler. Blue eyes set in a complexion that was boyish and healthy. But he was beginning to look a little jowly, his jawline already softening into the onset of a double chin. Pearson could just make out the crown and pip on his epaulettes. A chief superintendent. He was someone Pearson took an instant dislike to. (Not exactly an exclusive club, even he had to admit.) But there was something about him. Apart from the usual. It wasn't just that he was brass. There were superior officers he had worked for that he had liked. Even respected, on the odd occasion. This man, however, had the look of a political cop, someone who might appear on television with a peaked cap under one arm, a silver-tipped baton in one hand and a pair of brown leather gloves held casually in the other. Except there was also something about him that suggested a man living up to a stereotype. Or hiding behind one.

Roberts took in a deep breath, ran his hand over his face and exhaled a sigh.

'At oh-three-fourteen this morning a human body was discovered in a burnt-out vehicle in the Ness Road car park. The registered owner of the vehicle is Detective Inspector Sean Carragher. While we still await confirmation by way of formal identification, there is no reason to believe, at the present time, that the deceased might be anyone other than DI Carragher.' A simple statement of fact. Unemotional. Impersonal. That way there could be no misunderstanding, no ambiguity. Roberts did a slow scan of the assembled officers and then said, 'Because of the circumstances in which the deceased was found, it has been decided to initiate a murder inquiry.' He paused again for a moment to allow the information to sink in. 'This investigation must be conducted with the maximum of objectivity, professionalism and rigour. We will be subject to intense scrutiny from our fellow police officers in forces across the country, from the top-ranking officers in our own force and from the media. We will also face severe pressure from politicians, both in government and in opposition, who will view the conduct and outcome of this investigation as an opportunity to score political points. Is everybody clear?'

There was a collective murmur of confirmation.

'OK,' said Roberts. 'For the purposes of this investigation, and in the absence of any more senior officer, Detective Sergeant Frank Pearson will be acting as my deputy.'

Pearson stood up and the new additions to the team looked over. He nodded to no one in particular and sat down again.

'This meeting will cover the following,' continued Roberts. 'The murder scene; the fire investigation report; any pertinent forensic conclusions up to this point; viewing of the video footage shot by the Fire Brigade and stills from the forensic photographer. I will briefly outline our lines of enquiry, namely: victimology, deceased's background, personal life and known associates; as well as a review of all cases in which he was involved. Focusing initially on the most recent. As always, we will attempt to construct a timeline of the days and hours leading up to the time of death.'

Pearson's gaze cut across, once again, to Russell, who this time had her head down and was taking notes.

'Lawrence?' Roberts asked, looking over at the detective sergeant. 'Do you have the report from the fire investigation officer?'

Lawrence stood up behind his desk, 'Guv,' picked up a pile of papers, shuffled them together into something resembling order and held them up. 'We've just received copies of the stills taken by the brigade at the scene.'

Roberts looked across at Wendy Simpson, who was fanning herself with a magazine, her face flushed. Some of her curly hair was wet and stuck to her forehead.

'Wendy,' asked Roberts, 'would you mind?'

Simpson heaved herself out of her chair. She took the photos from Lawrence and they waited while she made her ungainly way across the room. She seemed way too pregnant, in Pearson's opinion, to even be working. But Roberts knew better than to attempt to mess with the incident boards. He had been chewed out more than once by her for fixing crime-scene photographs to them in a slipshod manner or writing on them in his indecipherable scrawl.

'We'll make the full fire-investigation report available on HOLMES in the next few hours,' said Lawrence.

'Just give us the abridged version.'

'Guv.' Lawrence nodded. 'This is pretty much covered by the bullet-point summary which is among the stuff that Wendy's putting on the board. I'll assume that not everyone on the team has been involved with a fire death before?' He looked over at Roberts, who gestured for him to carry on. Lawrence addressed the room: 'In order to determine whether a fire may have been started deliberately, that is whether it is likely to be arson, the fire investigation officer will consider several criteria.' He picked up a clear plastic biro and tapped the piece of paper in front of him on the desk as he ran through each item. 'Among these will be: is the rate of growth and spread of the fire inconsistent with the amount of combustible materials present within the vehicle? Are there multiple points of origin? Is there a noticeable smell of a recognised accelerant, for instance petrol, turpentine or barbecue lighter fuel? In the view of the fire investigation officer, the answer in this case to all these questions is yes. There is no doubt in his mind that this particular fire was started deliberately. Examination of the scene suggests that the seat of the fire was around . . .' Lawrence hesitated and then cleared his throat, 'around the body of the deceased. The fire investigation officer has given a preliminary outline of what he considers to be the most likely chain of events. The deceased was first doused with some kind of accelerant—'

'It'll be petrol,' interrupted Roberts. When Lawrence hesitated, Roberts nodded, 'Go on.'

'The deceased was doused with an accelerant,' Lawrence continued, 'the exact nature of which is yet to be confirmed pending chemical evaluation by Forensics.'

'It'll be petrol,' insisted Roberts.

'The deceased' – obviously irritated, Lawrence pressed on – 'was stationary and in a seated position. This is indicated by the intensity of the fire at distinct locations within the vehicle. Notably, the ceiling upholstery directly above the driver's-side seat and the fabric of the driver's seat itself. This was also indicative of a pooling of a fuel accelerant under the victim at the time it was ignited. The assailant would probably have stood outside the vehicle, adjacent to the window on the driver's side, and poured

175

the liquid accelerant from a container, such as a jerry can. This is corroborated by the burn patterning of the driver's seat, the floor covering directly underneath and the driver's-side door panel. The accelerant was then poured over the bodywork of the car: bonnet, roof, boot – this accounts for the reduction in damage towards the rear of the vehicle – before being ignited.' Lawrence cleared his throat again and shuffled through some papers on his desk. 'Uh, that's it. As far as the fire itself is concerned.'

'Well, that didn't tell us anything we didn't already know,' said Roberts. 'OK. Anything else?'

'The pathologist says she won't be ready for the post-mortem till late this evening.'

'When I'm due to attend another meeting of Gold Command.' Roberts took a packet of mints from his pocket, unwrapped one and put it in his mouth. 'Pearson, would you attend the PM?'

Pearson nodded. 'Guv.'

'Lawrence? Anything else?'

'Guv. The SOCOs retrieved a cigarette end from the vicinity of the car. It's been sent to Forensics for DNA analysis. We've asked for it to be fast-tracked, so we should have the results within twenty-four hours.'

'Good. Anything else?'

Lawrence shuffled through the papers on his desk again, then shook his head, 'No, guv, that's it.'

'OK,' said Roberts, 'if someone can dim the lights we'll have a look at the scene video shot by the brigade.'

The senior uniform by the door cleared his throat and turned his wrist to show Roberts his watch. Roberts nodded: 'Sir.' Then he addressed the room.

'As you are probably aware, before this meeting I attended a briefing with Gold Command. One of the things agreed was that all media contact would be handled from this point on by Detective Chief Superintendent Andy Curtis.'

He indicated the uniformed man. As all eyes turned to him he nodded, then stood momentarily, as if unsure what to do next. Wondering if Curtis might be considering the idea that now might be the right time to give a pep talk, Pearson's heart sank.

'Speaking of which,' said Curtis, making a show of checking his watch again, 'I'm due at a media briefing at this very moment.' He nodded towards Roberts again. 'Carry on.'

Most eyes in the room followed Curtis as he left, so only a few, Pearson included, caught the look on Roberts' face.

30

'No thanks,' Cat said.

DCI Roberts waved the packet of mints at Pearson.

Pearson took the packet and studied it. 'Polos?' He took one and passed them back to Roberts.

'I'm up to half a dozen packs a day, thought I'd better try the low-tar option. They'll probably find these give you cancer next.' He put one in his mouth, wrapped up the mints and dropped them on his desk. 'But at least I'll die with fresh, minty breath.'

Cat did her best to avoid Pearson's gaze, which had slid over in her direction again. In the meeting she had pretended to be engrossed in something on the computer. Kept her head down, taking notes, when, in reality, she had no need to. When they had viewed the crime-scene video and the stills taken by the forensic photographer, she had rigidly fixed her stare at the images projected on the screen. Needing desperately to look away, but not wanting to appear weak in front of her fellow officers. Most of all, hoping not to catch Pearson's eye. Internally, though, the shutters were down, her mind in neutral. She had had to visit the ladies' after the meeting. Locking herself in a cubicle, dry-retching over the toilet bowl. Then washing off the cold sweat at the basin with a damp paper towel and reapplying her make-up.

'How did it go with Gold this morning?' Pearson asked.

The other man's glance went briefly to Cat, then returned to Pearson. 'As you'd expect. A complete fucking waste of time.'

He took a piece of paper from his desk and passed it across. Pearson scanned it and gave a short, dismissive grunt before passing it to Cat. Minutes from the Gold Command meeting. At the top was the list of attendees: the Deputy Chief Constable, acting as chair; a representative of Professional Standards – not Ferguson – whose name Cat didn't recognise. Then again, she didn't really know any of the names. Wouldn't have known who any of them were even if they were to pass her in a corridor and nod an acknowledgement. Their titles, though, appeared after each name in brackets. The chief finance officer. The chief press officer. The force solicitor. The head of Crime Division. The head of the Force Support Unit. And then Roberts. And DCS Andy Curtis.

'It's a wonder you didn't run out of biscuits,' said Pearson.

'Jaffa Cakes today,' said Roberts. 'The DCC's favourites, apparently.'

'What do you know about this Curtis?' Pearson asked. 'I don't think I've come across him before.'

'Not surprising: he's only been in post a couple of months. Tosser, in a word. Couldn't find his arse with both hands if you drew him a map. Another product of HPDS.'

The High Potential Development Scheme was a rapid-promotion programme 'designed to identify, develop and progress the leaders of the future' which aimed to 'identify ... those with significant potential to reach the rank of superintendent and above'.

'You'd have thought they'd have learned their lesson after Dougie Ettrick,' said Pearson.

Doug Ettrick had been a previous detective chief superintendent, before Cat's time. But Pearson had told her all about him. Ettrick had appeared a plausible and persuasive senior officer. Until, that is, he had been the SIO on a serial rape case, where his insistence on focusing on a suspect who fitted a textbook psychological profile rather than more compelling physical evidence had almost – almost – resulted in them overlooking the real culprit. Eventually, a forty-three-year-old primary-school teacher with a wife of eighteen years and three children was convicted of the crimes. But not before another three women had been brutally raped. It later emerged that Ettrick had reached the rank of superintendent in seven years, doing two years as a PC, two years as a detective constable, two as a sergeant, one as an inspector and then taking the leap to superintendent. Moving from force to force, applying for promotions and blagging his way through interviews. In the process, according to Pearson's contacts in other forces, he falsely claimed greater responsibility for the successful conclusions to many investigations in which he had played only a minor role. Typically, after the schoolteacher had been successfully arrested, charged, convicted and given a life sentence, Ettrick had somehow contrived to take the credit. He had since moved onwards and, presumably, upwards. The onwards, in Pearson's view, being the most important.

'You would,' agreed Roberts. 'Instead, we're lumbered with another prick who's spent half his life fucking around at university. No offence,' looking at Cat.

'None taken,' she said, looking up from her reading. Inwardly she seethed.

Turning back to Pearson, Roberts said, 'This one's got

a doctorate,' putting it on a par with a sexually transmitted disease. 'But he's going to handle media relations, so I'm not complaining.'

No? thought Cat, sounds very much like fucking complaining to me. She put her head down again. The last section of the minutes contained a number of bullet points. Manage the media. Keep the family informed. Keep the IPCC informed. Work with partners. Solve the crime. Prosecute the offenders. Return to normality. It had the look of something that had been cut and pasted from a PowerPoint presentation, something delivered to the University of the Third Age or the Women's Institute rather than Interpol or the FBI. Cat suddenly felt a profound, almost overwhelming, wave of depression.

'I want you two to go over to Carragher's place. Have a look around before the search team trample all over it.' Looking over at Cat, he asked, 'You know the address?'

Pearson was already getting to his feet. 'We'll find it out,' he said to Roberts, standing between them. Nodding towards the door he said to Cat, 'C'mon.'

From the outside, the house – a Victorian semi-detached in a row of similar – had seemed decent enough, comfortably well off, maybe, rather than affluent. But when they stepped through the front door – paper onesies, latex gloves, polythene overshoes – it was obvious the place hadn't been decorated for quite some time. The furnishings couldn't really be described as minimal, more non-existent. The living room, at the front of the house, contained a large flat-screen TV and a Sky box. The only other thing in the room was a crumpled beanbag. Beside the beanbag a couple of empty cans of Boddingtons and several crisp packets, smoky bacon flavour. In the kitchen there was a sink full of unwashed plates. The fridge was empty save for a half-full plastic bottle of sour-smelling milk without a lid. On the worktop next to the sink a foil container, the remains of a beef chow mein. In the bathroom: shit pebble-dashing a toilet, a cracked bath with a tidemark of dirt, limescale stains around the plughole. On the windowsill hair gel, an exclusive aftershave, designer moisturiser. And a razor blade speckled with some kind of white powder. Russell turned to him, a troubled look on her face.

Pearson shook his head, disappointed. 'I know . . . moisturiser.'

Next door there was an empty room. The spare bedroom, presumably. In the other bedroom a futon lay on the floor. An ironing board with an iron on it. A clothes rail from which hung a row of designer suits. Under the clothes rail a line of expensive-looking shoes. On the floor, neatly folded, jeans, T-shirts, boxers, a pile of balled-together socks.

Russell stood in the middle of the room, shaking her head as she took it all in. 'It's all a bit sad. A bit . . . tawdry.'

'Yep,' agreed Pearson, 'what might be termed a craphole.'

Privately he wondered how much better *he* lived. What someone would find looking around his flat if he were to die in the line of duty. Not an ironing board ready to use, that's for sure. No designer clothes either. He had more furniture, at least. But not that much.

Russell said, 'How can someone live like this? It's like he's . . .'

'Squatting,' Pearson said. And he bet when they looked in the cupboard under the stairs that they would find that the electric meter had been bypassed. The official search unit and Forensics, both of whom were waiting outside for them to finish, would take the place apart. But Pearson didn't think they'd find much, other than what they could already see. He went to the clothes rail and turned over one of the ties hanging from it. Silk. Hermès. He rifled through the pockets of each pair of trousers, each jacket in turn, reading the inside labels. Boss. Armani. Conran. Boss. Another Boss. Another Armani. Pearson had two suits, in effect, the third being in a heap, covered in chicken curry and awaiting a trip to the dry cleaner's, which he doubted it would survive. He squatted down, picked up a roll of notes from inside one of the shoes and showed it to Cat.

'Fifties. Must be a couple of grand, at least.'

'I don't get it,' said Russell, shaking her head again, standing by the Mondeo. Looking across the street at Carragher's place, both of them reluctant to leave. 'The money. The designer clothes. The flashy car. The Rolex. And then he lives like that.'

Pearson looked away up the street. Further up, on the right, was a Premier. He considered whether it would be worthwhile going in, showing Carragher's photo, asking a few questions. It was a fair bet that that was where he bought his Boddingtons and smoky bacon crisps. But Carragher didn't strike him as the sort of person who would stand around idly chatting with a shop assistant, much less divulge intimate secrets to a complete stranger. He put his hand to his mouth and stifled a yawn.

'Kippers and curtains, my mum would say.' Probably still did say, given the opportunity. To anyone who might listen. Colin, maybe, at the hospital. He might listen. He would at least pretend to listen. Or was it 'fur coat and no drawers'? No, that was more to do with how someone got their money. Mind you, in this case, it could be the more apposite phrase. Pearson checked his watch and then his mobile for messages. When he looked up Russell had a cigarette in her mouth.

'You back on real fags?'

'Yep.' She took the cigarette out of her mouth and regarded it appreciatively. 'Those other things just didn't do it for me.' She put it back in her mouth and took a drag. 'Kippers and curtains? What exactly does that mean?'

Pearson thought for a moment and then said, 'I have absolutely no idea.'

31

'**O**h God! Has something happened? Is Sean all right?'

They turned to see a woman with a pushchair staring across the road at Carragher's house – marked police cars blocking the road outside, uniformed officers stringing up blue-and-white incident tape, SOCOs in white suits unloading metal boxes from a van – hand to her mouth, an anxious look on her face. Russell dropped her cigarette on the pavement and ground it out as Pearson slipped his hand into his inside jacket pocket and took out his warrant card.

'Police. And you'd be . . . ?'

Her eyes slid over the warrant card and across to Russell before settling back on him. 'Lorna. Lorna Jeffries.'

Lorna Jeffries had cheap black plastic sunglasses pushed up on top of wispy, strawberry-blond hair. Freckles across her forehead, nose and cheeks. Amber eyes. Ginger eyebrows and lashes so fine they were almost non-existent. She wore a strappy yellow dress, her bare shoulders showing the first signs of sunburn. In the pushchair a toddler in a grubby white baseball cap worried at the strap of his right sandal.

'I take it you know Mr Carragher?' Pearson indicated the house opposite with the warrant card before tucking it back into his pocket. Careful with the tense. No sense either in letting on that Carragher was – had been – a copper. Not yet.

'Yes. Well, sort of – he's my next-door neighbour. Has something happened to him?'

In his pushchair the toddler had managed to wriggle out of his sandal and drop it on to the pavement. He gave up trying to take off the other and instead started standing up on the footrest and throwing himself backwards. Lorna Jeffries dragged her attention back from across the street and took a firmer grip on the pushchair's handles. Pearson bent down, picked up the sandal and gave it to her.

'Do you mind if we ask you a few questions?'

'OK. Can we go indoors? It's already past his teatime, he'll start really kicking off any minute.'

The toddler slowly raised a sticky, accusatory finger and pointed it at Pearson. 'Man!' he said. 'Man!'

Inside the house the layout was the same. The other half of the semi. A mirror-image, except next door had had the stairs blocked off to make the upstairs flat. The floorboards here, however, had been professionally stripped and varnished, the walls sanded and emulsioned, the skirting boards and doors taken back to the original wood. She showed them into the front room and said, 'Do you want some tea?'

'That would be great,' said Pearson. 'White, no sugar, please.'

'The same,' Cat said. 'Thanks.'

'Sit down,' Lorna said. 'I'd better get this little monster sorted.'

'What's his name?' Cat asked.

'Jack. My ex's choice, not mine. I wanted Owen – y'know, like the actor? Jack, what do you want for tea?'

'Sammidge.'

'Sandwich. Please. What kind of sandwich?'

'Grumpy bread and ham and that jam they call crabry.'

'Grumpy bread?' Cat asked.

'It's what he calls a crusty loaf. I don't know why he asks for it, he never eats the crust.'

Their tea was brought in and they tucked it out of the way behind their feet on the floor. They waited for a few minutes while the little boy, washed and in pyjamas, eating his sandwich, was settled in front of the television on a floor cushion to watch a DVD. From what Pearson could make out it seemed to involve some kind of red wooden cylinder who had, apparently, misplaced his moustache. Disturbingly, it was voiced by an actor Pearson recognised but couldn't quite place. Lorna Jeffries picked up her own tea from where she had left it on the mantelpiece and sat in the armchair opposite.

The yellow sundress, Cat noticed, was creased. Damp around the hem. The cork soles of her canvas shoes wet. A few blades of grass clinging to her right ankle.

'So,' she said, looking first to Cat and then to Pearson, 'you wanted to ask me about Sean?'

Pearson open his notebook, took out a pen: Cat's cue to take the lead.

'I'm sorry, is it Mrs or Miss Jeffries?' she asked, picking up her cup of tea. Accept the offer of a cup of tea, appear friendly. How many different sofas did she sit on during the course of a year? How many cups of tea did she drink? Sometimes she felt more like a vicar than a copper.

'Mrs Jeffries,' Lorna sipped her tea, 'makes me sound like my mother,' cupping the mug with both hands, staring down into the steam. 'Actually, it's Miss. Why don't you just call me Lorna?'

'OK, Lorna it is. Can you tell us how you came to know Sean, Lorna?' This was generally how they worked. She would talk to the women. The younger witnesses. The more vulnerable.

Looking up, Lorna shrugged. 'We're neighbours. We run into each other occasionally. You know, I'm coming in, he's going out . . .'

'So just to say hello to? That sort of thing?'

'I suppose so, yes. He pretty much keeps himself to himself.' Great. The cliché TV interview quote from the neighbour of a serial killer. 'He's pretty quiet, y'know? I mean, I never hear loud music or anything. You can hear the telly sometimes, but I don't always have the telly on at night. After Jack goes to bed I quite often just sit and read.'

Suddenly bored by the DVD, Jack got up and stood by his mother's knee. She reached out and stroked his hair, pulled him close to her.

'Do you ever see anyone else go into Sean's house?' Cat asked.

'With him, you mean?'

'With him. Without him. When he isn't there?'

'No.' Lorna shook her head. 'Never.'

'Have you ever been next door yourself?'

'Bug-a-bye,' said Jack.

'Hold on, sweetie,' she said, stroking the little boy's hair. 'No, like I said, he's quite a private person. I know he's a policeman, and that's about it.'

'Bug-a-bye! Bug-a-bye!' Jack said again, shaking his mother's leg.

'Magnifying glass,' Lorna said to Cat by way of explanation. She got up and went to the bureau in the corner of the room.

'He told you he was a policeman?' Cat asked.

'Well,' she opened a drawer, 'it sort of came out in conversation really.'

Sifting through the contents, not looking up, she got something out and gave it to the little boy. A magnifying glass with a big, round lens and a handle. Jack held it at arm's length, leaning forward, studying the floor. Taking slow, deliberate steps. Looking for clues. A cartoon Inspector Clouseau. For some absurd reason it made Cat think of Pearson. She resisted the urge to look across at him.

'Came out?' asked Cat. 'In what way?'

Lorna sat down again, hands in her lap, lacing her fingers. 'I'd been having some problems with his,' she nodded towards Jack, 'dad. There was a bit of a shouting match on the doorstep. Sean pulled up just at the tail end of it. I was in a bit of a state. He asked me if everything was OK, waited until Ray had gone. So, Sean came in and we talked. Well, I talked, he listened. Sean's a good listener, don't you think?'

Next to her, Cat sensed the scratching of a pen. The underlining of a phrase. Multiple question marks being added.

'Well, I don't need to tell you that.' Lorna looked Cat in the eye. 'You probably know him better than I do.'

'And this is when he told you he was a policeman?'

'Yes, he asked me if Ray had done that sort of thing before, if I wanted to report it or anything, make an official complaint, at least get an incident number so it was all on record.'

'And did you?'

She shook her head again. 'No. Look, Ray's a good man really. A hard worker. He did this place. Like, single-handedly? The whole house. At weekends, in the evenings. That's what he does. Building. Decorative plasterwork, painting and decorating mostly.'

'So you didn't report anything?' Cat asked.

'No. Like I said, Ray's a good man. Older than me, you know, late forties – no: early fifties now. It's just, he lost his little girl. When she was about thirteen or fourteen? It's made him a bit ... he's a bit funny. Y'know, sort of ... over-protective? Possessive, y'know? He doesn't mean it in a nasty way. He's just terrified that something like that might happen again. I suppose, him and me, it just got a bit ... overbearing? He wanted to know where I was all the time, what I was up to. It was hard to live with. In the end it got too much, y'know? Then, after he moved out he started pestering me about seeing ... ' She nodded again in the direction of her son. 'Parking up the street, wanting to take him out, pick him up from nursery, have him stay over at his place ... '

'Your ex-partner,' said Pearson, 'Ray? What's his surname?'

'He's not going to get into any trouble, is he? I don't want to get him into any trouble.'

'We probably won't even need to talk to him, Lorna,' said Pearson, 'but just in case?'

'Ray – well, Raymond. Raymond Walsh.'

'And do you know where he's living at the moment?'

Lorna told him the address.

'Nothing else came of it?' Cat asked.

Lorna shook her head again. 'I asked Sean not to do anything. And I haven't heard any more from Ray. I mean, lately he's been out there every night, but sometimes you don't see him for weeks. It's like that. It depends how much work he's got on. If he's busy working he's less of a nuisance. I know he's got a couple of big jobs on at the moment. He's refurbishing a place in town, the Hip-gernosis club? Have you heard of it?'

*

Pearson looked up from his notebook to find a massive, alien eye regarding him. An octopus floating behind the flecked, dilating glass wall of an aquarium.

'Jack,' Lorna said, 'leave the nice man alone.'

'He got lots of lines,' Jack said seriously, studying Pearson's face through the glass.

'It's already way past your bedtime, little man. So if you want to stay up you better be good, OK?'

Pearson's phone buzzed in his pocket and he took it out to read the text.

'Is there anything else you can tell us about Sean?' Russell asked.

'I don't think so. I suppose I don't know him that well really,' Lorna admitted, 'It's just a shock, you know, when something happens to someone you know. Even a little bit. I take it it's bad? Otherwise there wouldn't be so many police here, right?'

Pearson got to his feet and Russell followed his lead. 'Sorry,' he said, 'I'm afraid we're not allowed to say.'

On the way to the car Cat, rummaging in her handbag for her cigarettes, asked, 'What's up?'

Pearson shook his phone at her. 'They're ready for the PM.'

'So what do I do?'

'Ah,' said Pearson, 'you're forgetting. They'll have had the media conference by now. In which they would have given out several phone numbers and asked the public for their help. So, Detective Constable Russell, for the next couple of hours you will be answering calls and logging them on the system.'

Cat swore under her breath.

'C'mon,' he said, 'I'll drop you off at the nick on the way.'

32

Donna checked the reflection in the broken glass of the mirror. Once again it was as if the silver at the back had melted away. She was looking at a film set, artfully arranged and dressed to look exactly the same as the room she had been living in for the last year. But now the room was empty. Motorcycle Boy was missing. Alicia, too, was absent. As if her non-appearance was an admonition, a punishment for letting her down. The only thing reflected back to Donna was her own face. Free now of the white paint and the black lips, the mask removed.

It was quiet too. She couldn't hear the television or the radio or whatever it was through the walls. The voices had gone. She couldn't hear anything. Just the silence. She couldn't stand it, the quiet. The walls were already closing in. She needed to get out for a little while. Go for a walk. It didn't matter where. She snatched up the leather jacket and her keys, running down the stairs and out on to the street, the events of last night – was it really only last night? – coming back to her.

*

'Expecting someone else?' she had asked when he turned to face her with an expression which said that, if she wasn't the last person on earth he wanted to see, then she wasn't that far from the top of the list. There was something in it, in him, that she recognised only too well. Had seen in countless numbers of her mum's boyfriends. A tension. A barely suppressed anger. An almost irresistible compulsion towards violence. And after she had struck a match, lit her cigarette, let the match burn down, let it burn her fingers for a moment before shaking it out and flicking it out through the side window, he was saying, 'We looked into your friend's death thoroughly, Donna ...'

But he was talking to her as if he were explaining it to a child. As if she were some kind of retard or something. And he was saying the same things, the things she'd heard before. Saying that it was an accident. And she didn't want to hear it. After a while he stopped talking and she had said, 'You could find the evidence. You could keep trying.'

When she had drawn on her cigarette. Breathed it out. Through the cloud of exhaled blue smoke she had seen two faces. Slightly indistinct. A blurring at the edges, the policeman's face and, underneath, something inhuman ...

' ... on which the soft tissue has been partially burned away,' Bannister, mask down around her chin, spoke into the microphone suspended from the ceiling of the mortuary, 'in places exposing the skull beneath. The torso and limbs have suffered fourth-degree burns over ninety per cent of their area. The buttocks, however, have been spared due to the deceased being in a seated position at the time of death. The skin is stiff, yellow-brown and parchment-like.'

From his position in the viewing gallery Pearson, leaning

forward on the handrail, his chin resting on his folded arms, watched the pathologist circle the body on the stainless-steel table. Positively identified by partial fingerprints as Sean Carragher. Less than a day ago he had been a colleague. There was no way Pearson could claim a friendship, he didn't like the bloke. At best he had tolerated him. But he had interacted with him, as another human being. Now that human being had become something else. An exhibit. A mummified relic that might have been recovered in an archaeological dig, the desiccated remains of a long-dead pharaoh buried for millennia in the desert sand. Or the charred carcass of an overcooked chicken.

'And why would I do that?' His face, his human face, regarded her with a studied indifference. Waiting for her to make the next move. She put a foot up on the seat, allowing her skirt to slide down her thigh. 'Pack it in,' he said.

'What?' Meeting his gaze. She lifted her skirt with her hand, shifted her hips forward provocatively, allowing him a good look at her knickers. It was what they wanted, wasn't it? Men. Boys. The only thing they ever seemed to want.

'Pack it in, I said.'

Except for him. Apparently. When he dug in his jeans pocket, took out his wallet, flung some notes across at her, she had looked down at the money in her lap. It was no use. No one cared. No one gave a fuck about Alicia. Except her. And what could she do about it now? She bit her bottom lip. She wasn't going to let him see her cry. She wasn't. She looked at her lap and the money stared back. Even the face of the Queen seemed to be taunting her. Mocking her uselessness. She didn't want his fucking money. That wasn't what this was all about. Then she snatched it up and pushed open the car door, slamming it behind her.

'Due to the dehydration and contracture of the skeletal muscles, the body has assumed a characteristic pugilistic attitude.' The arms had flexed at the elbows and wrists, which positioned the hands in front of the body. The hands claws rather than fists. This was always referred to as 'the boxer's stance'. He could see it. Sort of. Laid on his back, arms in front of his body, hands in loose fists, the knees bent and the feet flat on the surface of the table, it reminded Pearson of a boxer in a gym, working on his abs, halfway through a sit-up and waiting for that heavy medicine ball to be thrown into his guts. On this occasion the contraction of the knees had been hampered by the seated position at the time of death and the body appeared to be sitting on an invisible chair.

'Heat rupturing can be observed. The skin has split near all joint surfaces, including at the elbows, shoulders and knees. These splits have extended to the underlying adipose tissue and skeletal muscles. The soft-tissue splits are full thickness, particularly on the abdomen. Due to the expansion of gases within the intestines and the corollary enlargement of the abdominal wall, there has been a resultant charring of the exposed bowel surface.'

Pearson sat up, clearing his throat, and Bannister switched off the microphone and looked up at him. He yawned and put his hand over his mouth.

'Sorry. Long day.' He checked his watch – very nearly the next day.

Bannister looked exhausted. Her day had been just as long. And at least he hadn't been poking around in dead bodies.

'In terms of a cause of death,' he said, 'with all that damage, would you be able to tell if there might be any stab wounds or bullet holes, or anything?'

Donna had pushed open the car door, stepped out, slammed the door behind her and walked about ten or fifteen paces before becoming aware of her balled-up fist. Opening her hand, she saw the crumpled notes and stopped. She didn't want his fucking money. It was obvious that he didn't care. That nobody cared about Alicia. That Alicia was gone and there was nothing she could do about it. Nothing that anybody else seemed prepared to do about it. She was crying. Fucking crying again. Crying in frustration. Crying because she was angry – angry at his indifference, at her humiliation. Her hand closed around the notes and she pushed them into her pocket, scrabbling for her cigarettes and matches. And felt the knife. She took it out of her pocket. Felt the weight, the heft of it, in her hand. Slid it out of its metal sheath. Examined the blade, its dull glint in the dim light. Somebody should fucking do something. She turned back towards the car.

When the passenger door opened again, Carragher had started. Turning to her as she got in, the suspension shifting as she sat down, looking even more annoyed than before.

'I told you we were done,' he said.

'I know.'

She saw his knuckles blanche as he squeezed the steering wheel and then released it. 'I've told you. There's no more money. That's the last of it.' When Donna didn't reply he said, 'Oh Christ, this isn't still about your little friend, is it?'

'My little *dead* friend,' Donna said.

Carragher sighed, his fingers drumming irritably on the wheel. 'Look, I've told you before—'

'Alicia was killed. Everyone knows who did it.'

'*You* know who did it,' he said, 'or at least you think you know who did it.'

Beneath the jacket Donna gripped the knife. Ran her thumb along the top edge of the blade. 'Alicia was murdered,' she insisted, 'and I told you who did it.'

He almost laughed. Sounded like he wanted to laugh. 'Clive Townsend? From the home?' And again, as if he were explaining it to a child, as if she were some kind of retard or something, he said, 'We spoke to him. We spoke to everyone. There was no evidence. Evidence, Donna. Not just rumour. You can't charge someone with murder just because you think they might be a bit . . . '

He looked across at her and she could tell what he was thinking. *Just because you think they might be a bit of a fucking weirdo. A bit of a fucking weirdo like you, Donna.*

Under the jacket her grip tightened on the knife.

'There was no evidence,' he said again, 'that Alicia's death was anything other than an accident.'

'If he didn't kill her,' she said, 'then he was involved. He made it happen somehow.'

Carragher exhaled, like a sigh, but annoyed too. 'How exactly?'

'I don't know.'

'Look,' he said shaking his head, 'you've got to stop this.'

'Stop what?'

'This. This . . . you've got to accept that it was just an accident. A stupid, senseless accident. As far as anyone else is concerned it's over. Finished. We're not investigating it any further.'

Donna took out the knife and pointed it at him and this time he did laugh. 'What are you going to do with that?'

She was going to make him do something. Something about Alicia's death. Alicia's murder. She was going to make him stop laughing at her.

'I'm going to make you take me seriously,' she said.

'I did take you seriously. Maybe a little too seriously.'

'You need to talk to him.'

'We spoke to him. I've told you – Christ, how many times?'

'You didn't do it right. You didn't ask the right questions.'

He looked to the heavens and then said, 'Enough. The case is closed, Donna. Closed. It was an accident. That's all. Nothing else. And no silly little girl is going to change that. It's over, OK?'

She lunged at him with the knife. He batted it away. She lunged again. This time he caught her wrist. He was laughing now and it made her even more angry. She struggled against his grip. The more she struggled, the more he laughed. And the more he laughed the angrier she got. So finally she stopped struggling.

'You're hurting me,' she whined.

'OK,' he said. 'If you promise you'll behave yourself I'll let you go, OK?'

'OK,' she said.

'You sure?'

'I said so, didn't I?'

When he released her, while he was off guard, she lunged again, quicker this time, before he had time to bring his hands up and defend himself. When she looked down she realised that the knife was caught up in his T-shirt. And a red stain was starting to spread across the white material. He looked down at his stomach, a stupid, surprised expression on his face. And as he lifted his shirt to check the wound she was pushing the door open again.

*

201

'The splitting is quite extensive,' Bannister said, indicating the abdomen of the body on the table. 'It's possible that this has occurred along an ante-mortem puncture wound. Also, I understand that DI Carragher had pre-existing abdominal scarring from a shotgun wound, which may further confuse the findings. So, unless there is damage to the vertebral column or to T11 or T12 ...' she looked up at him and when she saw his expression she clarified, 'the spine and the lowest two ribs – then I'm afraid the answer is no, it is highly unlikely that we will be able to ascertain whether there are stab wounds. At least, not definitively.'

Pearson stifled another yawn. 'Yep. I'm assuming it isn't going to be that straightforward.'

'Probably not,' she agreed, 'but let's not concede defeat just yet. We carried out a full-body radiograph before you arrived. So if there are any extraneous objects, such as a bullet, within the body we'll be able to see them. We'll have a look at the X-rays as soon as I've completed the gross examination.'

'Fair enough,' said Pearson, refolding his arms on the handrail and resting his chin on them.

Bannister switched the microphone back on and turned back to the body. 'Fracturing of bones can be observed where the muscle, tendons and soft tissue have been charred, resulting in exposure of the underlying skeleton to extreme heat.'

She moved along the table to a position by the head. After a moment she leaned forward as if something had piqued her interest. Then she retrieved a torch from a tray of instruments and shone it into the open mouth of the corpse. Pearson sat up, suddenly alert. Bannister took something else from the instrument tray and leaned over the body. For a moment his view was obscured. Then she stepped back, holding something up and studying it intensely. A cotton bud.

'Found something?' Pearson asked.

Bannister turned off the microphone again. 'Soot. In the nostrils and trachea.'

'Which means—'

'Which means,' Bannister interrupted, 'that he was still breathing at the time of the fire. I'll confirm it when I do the internal. We should observe a cherry-pink coloration to internal organs, such as the liver, indicating heightened levels of carboxyhaemoglobin.'

Bannister switched on the microphone and turned back to the body. Pearson, though, wasn't listening any more. He was thinking about Carragher. Trapped inside the car. Smoke filling the interior, the upholstery beginning to burn. Panic rising. Starting to scream. The unimaginable agony of suddenly being engulfed in flames. That was something he didn't want to imagine. His mouth all at once dry, a cold sweat covering his skin. But anyway, that wasn't how it had happened with Carragher, was it? All the signs were that there was no panic, no frantic attempts to get out of the car. Why hadn't he made more of an effort to get away? The only reason could be that he had been physically restrained in some way. Incapacitated by drugs, maybe, or had suffered some kind of injury, an injury so debilitating that it prevented him from escaping.

Bannister went to the light box in the corner of the room and turned it on, then reached across and dimmed the overhead lighting a little. From the trolley underneath she took a manila cardboard folder, from which she slipped an A4-sized transparent sheet of film and clipped it to the light box. She stood for a moment studying the image. An X-ray of a human skull. Pearson noticed that same concentration, that same stillness in Bannister of a few moments ago.

'What's up?' he asked. He could barely stay awake now, his eyes raw and gritty. There would be an early start in the morning. Even if he managed to get away quite soon the most he could hope for was a couple of hours' sleep at best. So he added, 'In layman's terms.'

Bannister pointed at the illuminated image of the skull. 'Can you see these fracture lines above the temple?'

Pearson nodded. 'Yeah.' Although he couldn't. Not clearly, anyway. It was just that little bit too far away.

'Note how they radiate from a single point.' She traced each at a time with a finger. 'Notice how they cross these suture lines?'

Pearson nodded again. 'Yep.' He could sort of see what she was talking about. If he squinted a bit. And leaned forward as far as he could.

'Good. This is exactly what we would expect as the result of a fire.' She turned to him. 'What we would not expect would be this,' she turned again to point at another area of the skull, 'series of fracture lines radiating from a central, circular area.'

'OK,' he said, 'so what's that?'

'That,' said Bannister, 'and I will confirm this by examining the edges of the bone fragments under a scanning electron microscope, is an injury resulting from a severe blunt-force trauma.'

33

SATURDAY

Donna realised she had been walking all night. The sky had lightened without her noticing and she became gradually aware of her immediate surroundings, the aching in her legs. She turned on to the seafront and was confronted by a wall of almost impenetrable fog. It hung, twenty yards or so beyond the sea wall, along the tideline like a colossal white screen. She could just make out the spectral figure of something a little way out, bobbing on the unseen water. A ghost ship? Despite the fog, small points of moisture speckling her skin, the air was warm and humid; an invisible sun somewhere overhead. She could smell the sea, properly smell the sea, and it brought back a faint memory of a childhood trip to Cornwall. A week at the seaside for kids in care organised by some charity or other. You rarely smelled the sea here, despite the closeness of the brackish estuary and, further out, the North Sea. She came across an immense flock of gulls: silent, fogbound and immobile except for the shuffling of an occasional individual bird. A crowd of bald old men.

For once the seafront was quiet: the occasional cyclist or jogger, another huge flock of grounded birds. Even the usually ever-present growl of the traffic on the esplanade was muffled, sparser. She stopped for a minute to regard one of the palm trees that had been planted on the seafront. Some town planner's wet dream of the South of France. But the palm, like the town itself, was withering, its trunk covered in wind-scorched hair, stick-like offshoots forming imploring arms, its scant leaves either brown and dead or, where they were green, stunted. And even the ends of these leaves had started to singe and shrivel. Wind-blasted during the previous, severe, English winter. Somehow this dying plant made her feel incredibly sad. She put her face to the trunk, wrapped her arms around it. Then she began to cry. For the tree. For the boy on the motorbike – Patrick. For the policeman. Even for Mr Downey. For Alicia, who in death, like Daphne, had been transformed into a tree. 'Her soft body wrapped in a layer of bark/her hair turned into foliage/her arms into branches/her feet sunk into sluggish roots.' Donna caressed the tree and could feel its heart fluttering under the bark. So she pressed her lips to the wood and cried for Alicia. And for herself.

34

Pearson swung the Mondeo on to the seafront and Cat, glancing to her left, saw that the parking area was empty; the fire engines, the police vehicles, the forensic tent, the charred and gutted skeleton of the car, even the blue-and-white incident tape had all been removed. There was nothing to indicate that anything out of the ordinary had ever happened here, other than a yellow metal 'Police Notice' stating a date and approximate time and appealing for witnesses. And the outline of the car etched in the melted tarmac.

Pearson had picked her up outside her flat fifteen minutes ago, after an early-morning phone call: 'No point in using two cars when we'll be out together most of the day. Much more sensible to use one.' His, she thought, obviously. No leg room in hers, for one thing. And Pearson preferred to drive, for another. Now she realised it had been so that he could bring her up to speed on the results of Sean's post-mortem before she heard it from anywhere else. She had asked if they could drive along the seafront on the way into work. Not exactly because she wanted to visit the place.

The place where he had died. Brained. Set on fire. Burned alive. Not exactly, but because it was a habit she had fallen into. A last moment of relative peace, of quiet contemplation, before the stress and unpredictability of the day ahead. She liked to drive slowly and gaze at the water. Or, if the tide happened to be out, the mud flats; and, if the air was clear enough, the oil refinery on the other side of the estuary. Today, however, she couldn't see anything. Just a solid block of white fog which stopped abruptly at the sea wall. Cat leaned forward in her seat to peer out of the side window. Pearson said, 'It's like the end credits of *Scooby-Doo*.'

Cat turned to look at him, adopting the expression of the long-suffering, of someone who habitually dealt with the dim-witted and immature.

'You know,' he said, 'when the ghostly, claw-like hand comes out and makes a grab for them?' Pearson mimed the action. Cat pursed her lips and shook her head slightly. 'You must've seen *Scooby-Doo*?' he asked. Russell stared at him. 'It was a cartoon?' Pearson went on. 'A sixties thing. Four college kids and a dog in a camper van who went round solving crime? Shaggy, Velma, Daphne and Whatsisname? I can never remember him, blond, wore a sweater and a cravat. I always had my doubts about him. I mean, who wears a cravat? What was his name? What's that thing, when you know the word but you can't think of it? There's a word for it. But I can't think of that either.'

'Senility?' asked Cat. She turned back to look out of the side window. 'I didn't think people actually still did that,' she said. Pearson glanced out. There was a girl in a leather jacket and hoodie, hugging a tree. As they watched, she seemed to kiss the trunk and appeared to be talking to it.

'I think that tree's going to need more than the kiss of life,' said Pearson as he indicated right and they turned off the seafront.

'Onomatomania,' said Cat.

'What?'

'Onomatomania,' Cat repeated, 'It means "vexation at having difficulty in finding the right word".'

'And you think that's what I might be suffering from?'

'Among other things.' After a pause, she added, 'And the name you're looking for is Freddie.'

'Freddie? Are you sure?'

'Yep. Freddie. Freddie Jones. So, do I get a Scooby snack?'

'I thought you—'

'They made it into a film. Real people, CGI dog.'

'Russell! Pearson!' DCI Roberts bellowed as they passed the open, half-glazed door of his office.

When they went in Roberts was sitting behind his desk and two of the three other chairs in the room were occupied. Ferguson sat in one, and in the other was DCS Andy Curtis. Roberts nodded at Pearson. 'Shut the door.'

Pearson indicated that Cat should take the other chair, then weighed up whether to fetch another in before deciding there wasn't enough space. He shut the door and, hands in pockets, leaned back against the wall. Roberts picked up an elastic band from the desktop and wound it round his hand.

'As you know, there was another meeting of Gold last night,' he said. 'It's been decided that, due to his knowledge of DI Carragher's, uh ...' he paused, 'activities, it would be worthwhile bringing DI Ferguson into the investigation.'

Curtis leaned forward. 'I thought I should tag along in order to assess media strategy in light of any issues arising.'

Arse-covering, in other words, Cat thought. Roberts gave a curt nod in the DCS's direction. Not happy.

'Is that going to cause a problem?' he asked.

Cat felt all eyes turn to her. Am I going to cause a problem, that's what he really wants to know. Not if I want to stay on the investigation. Not if I don't want my reputation tarnished any more than it is already. Not if I want any kind of future in the Job.

Cat shook her head. 'No, guv.'

Roberts turned to the man from Professional Standards. 'DI Ferguson?'

Ferguson picked up his briefcase from the floor and placed it on his knees. He brushed away imaginary dust from its surface but made no move to open it. Without looking up he said:

'I'm sure you're wondering why, given that DI Carragher was only suspected of overclaiming expenses, Professional Standards took such a keen interest in him?' He glanced up briefly and then rubbed at the surface of his briefcase again. 'The truth is that DI Carragher has come to our attention before. When he was serving with the Merseyside force he was accused by a female officer of a serious sexual assault ...'

'That was all cleared up, wasn't it?' asked Roberts. 'The woman in question dropped the allegation.'

'That's true,' said Ferguson, 'but there was some implication that she may have been coerced.'

Cat frowned and shook her head. 'That's ridiculous.' As all eyes turned, once again, to look at her Cat continued shaking her head. 'It can't be true ...'

35

'**G**ay?'

Ferguson looked at the other men in the room for some kind of corroboration. As if one of them might offer first-hand knowledge one way or the other. Then he looked back at Cat.

'You're claiming that DI Carragher couldn't have sexually assaulted a female, because he told you he was gay?'

'He *was* gay,' Cat insisted.

'Or maybe you're coming up with something that you think might allay our suspicions for reasons of your own.'

'Look, sir,' said Cat, annoyed, 'if you're suggesting that we had a relationship, then I can assure you we did not. I've already told you that.'

Pearson had been shifting from foot to foot for the last few minutes. Desperately needing to piss. He took his hands out of his pockets and before Russell said anything else, something she would later regret, he cleared his throat.

'If DI Carragher told DC Russell he was gay, presumably in

confidence?' – a look to Cat, who nodded in corroboration – 'then I think we have no option but to take it at face value.'

'I'd still like to know where that gossip about us came from,' said Cat, not quite willing, even now, to let it go.

When she looked up and caught Pearson's eye he gave an almost imperceptible shake of his head. That look on his face. A gradual realisation. Then suddenly everything fell into place. Sean. Could it all have come from Sean? Even if Sean hadn't explicitly said there was something going on between them, she could imagine him not exactly going out of his way to deny it. Maybe even dropping a few hints of his own here and there. Enjoying the innuendo, joining in the banter. Taking pleasure in the fact that everyone in the nick had completely the wrong idea about him. And all at her expense. Bastard. The reluctant confession, all that shit about it being 'in confidence'. That he didn't want anyone else to know. That being gay wasn't exactly a thing you wanted to broadcast in the Job—

'I was just wondering,' said Curtis, 'how this might play with the public. I mean, I have nothing against gay people myself, you understand, but would the public be ready to see a gay policeman as, well, beyond reproach?' Once again, a look to the men in the room. As if she didn't exist. 'It's just, well, there's certain connotations associated with that sort of lifestyle, isn't there? One only has to study the literature on serial killers.'

Pearson recognised the imminent arrival of a hobby horse. Heard its squeaky, uneven wheels, saw its threadbare woollen mane, the dented and scuffed tin of its body, the scratches on its dappled paintwork. Gleefully Curtis grabbed the reins but before he could swing himself into the saddle, Pearson said:

'I think we're getting a little ahead of ourselves here—'

'Look,' Roberts cut in, 'speaking personally, I've got no

problem with him being a friend of Dorothy. So long as he wasn't a friend of Toto.'

Cat wondered whether, in DCI Roberts' case at least, the Equality and Diversity course they had all been made to attend hadn't been a complete waste of time.

'Can we just stick to what we actually know?' said Roberts.

'The point I was trying to make,' said Ferguson, 'was that if an officer is accused of one offence then a mistake could have been made. But if he is accused of two, or in the case of DI Carragher, three, then it warrants closer scrutiny.'

'Three?' asked Roberts. Then, his jaw muscles clenching and unclenching, he sat back in his chair. 'Go ahead,' he sighed.

'If I may,' said Ferguson, snapping the locks of his briefcase, opening it and taking out a sheet of paper. 'I believe, DC Russell, that both you and DI Carragher were involved in the investigation into the death of a sixteen-year-old girl called Alicia Goode?'

She glanced briefly at Roberts, who nodded at her to go ahead. 'Yes, sir.'

'DCI Roberts was the senior investigating officer on the case. DI Carragher was the deputy SIO?' asked Ferguson, looking between her and Roberts.

'That's correct,' said Roberts, nodding, 'I was the SIO. But it appeared to be a straightforward "unexplained" that would, more likely than not, turn out to be an accidental death. In these cases I generally remain in overall charge but the deputy would operate fairly autonomously.' Cat saw Roberts' gaze drift towards Curtis. The ranking officer. More arse-covering. 'In these circumstances,' Roberts continued, 'I just expect regular updates on progress and lines of enquiry. If at any stage it becomes apparent that the death might in any way be suspicious, there is an immediate escalation of allocated resources. In other words, it is treated as a potential homicide. But the Alicia Goode case never appeared to be anything other than an accidental death. So to all intents and purposes, DI Carragher remained in charge throughout.'

Ferguson nodded and turned back to Cat. 'So it's fair to say you might have a better grasp of the details than DCI Roberts?'

'I'd say that's probably fair, sir,' Cat admitted reluctantly. She shifted position: the plastic chair wasn't designed to be sat in for lengthy periods. Pearson's theory was that Roberts had chosen the chairs for exactly this reason. Cat cleared her throat. 'Alicia Goode, sixteen, was found on ground adjacent to the Queensway underpass. The body lay undiscovered for two to three days, even though the location is relatively busy, both with pedestrians using the footbridge and vehicular traffic using the road underneath. Due to a combination of factors – the positioning of the body, the heavily overgrown vegetation, a build-up of discarded refuse both in and out of sacks – she wouldn't have been immediately obvious to a casual passer-by, either on the overpass or in a car. The body was only discovered by council employees in the Parks Department, who had been asked to cut back the vegetation and clear up the rubbish. Toxicology results showed high levels of alcohol, cannabis and MDMA in her bloodstream. The post-mortem indicated that she had suffered a blow to the head consistent with a fall from the approximate height of the pedestrian footbridge. The pathologist stated that the probable cause of death was a puncture wound to the windpipe from the branch of a tree on which the deceased was impaled during the course of her fall.'

Cat took a breath. 'The underpass itself is not covered by CCTV but we collected and viewed CCTV footage from the immediate area in the period both before and after her estimated time of death. She was filmed in the town centre walking in an

214

erratic manner, which corresponded with the levels of alcohol and drugs indicated by the PM. No one was seen to be following her. We did an appeal for witnesses to her last known movements. Nothing was found to suggest anything other than a fall from the footbridge whilst intoxicated. So it was decided that her death should be ruled accidental.'

'And this was DI Carragher's decision?' asked Ferguson.

'He was the senior officer,' said Cat.

Ferguson nodded and looked down at the sheet of paper in his hand. As both his and Curtis' attention was elsewhere, Cat saw Roberts glance across at Pearson, his eyebrows raised, a slight shaking of his head.

'I hope there's some relevance to this?' Roberts asked, finally unwinding the elastic band from his hand and dropping it on the desk.

'There is,' said Ferguson, passing the piece of paper to Roberts. 'We've received an allegation regarding a serious physical assault.'

36

'Clive Townsend?'

DCI Roberts looked up from the piece of paper Ferguson had passed him and turned, first to the man from Professional Standards and then to Cat. 'Who's he?'

'A senior care assistant at the Abigail Burnett Children's Home,' said Cat.

'The Abigail Burnett? Wasn't that the place where our recent hanging suicide worked?' Roberts looked at Pearson.

'Sickert Downey,' Pearson supplied.

'Right,' Roberts nodded, 'Sickert Downey.'

'And Alicia Goode was a resident of the Abigail Burnett?' Ferguson asked Cat.

'She had been,' she said. 'She left the home some months before her death.'

Ferguson retrieved an A4 pad from the open briefcase which he still had balanced on his knees, shut the lid, took a pen from his breast pocket and clicked the top. As he made a note at the top of the page and underlined it, Roberts once again glanced across at Pearson and gave a slight shake of the head. Ferguson looked up expectantly. Roberts ran his hand over his face and sighed.

'OK,' he said, picking up the discarded rubber band again and winding it round his hand, 'during the investigation into Alicia Goode's death, certain concerns were raised regarding a lack of control exercised by staff over the kids' movement and behaviour. These concerns were passed on to Child Protection, who carried out an independent investigation in conjunction with Social Services.' He looked at Cat for confirmation.

Cat nodded. 'Guv.'

'As a result of which,' Roberts went on, 'it was decided that the Abigail Burnett was to be closed down and the then head, Sickert Downey, was given early retirement. Downey was subsequently found hanging from scaffolding in the town centre.'

'And this was judged a suicide?' asked Ferguson, looking up from his notes.

'In the face of any evidence to the contrary, yes,' said Roberts.

Ferguson nodded and looked back down at his pad. 'What happened to the residents and the rest of the staff?'

'The residents were found alternative accommodation,' said Cat, 'in other residential homes or, if they were old enough, offered support into independent living. As for the staff, you'd have to check with the other team. But because of the difficulty Social Services has in filling these posts, my guess is they would have been offered alternative positions.'

'In his account—'

'You took his statement?' Roberts asked.

'I did,' said Ferguson without looking up from his pad. 'In his account Mr Townsend states that he was "formerly employed" as a senior care assistant at the Abigail Burnett and he was forced to leave his post following suspicions raised about him during the investigation into Alicia Goode's death.'

Roberts unwound the elastic band from his hand and placed it on the desk. Then he put his hands on his head, closed his eyes and leaned back in his chair. 'Why don't you tell us exactly what it is that DI Carragher was accused of?'

Ferguson opened his briefcase again and took out another piece of paper. Cat saw the muscles in Roberts' jaw tighten and sensed Pearson, standing to her left, shift impatiently from one foot to the other.

'Mr Townsend's statement reads as follows,' said Ferguson. 'Quote: The interviewing officer, Detective Inspector Carragher, conducted the interview in a manner which directly contravened the Police and Criminal Evidence Act, Section C, Paragraph 11, Subsection 5, which states, "No interviewer may try to obtain answers or elicit a statement by the use of oppression," unquote.'

'Have you ever witnessed DI Carragher being overly aggressive when dealing with a suspect?' Ferguson had asked Cat in her third interview. She had known, or at least guessed, that this was what he was getting at. But the offhand manner in which the question had been asked, the abrupt change of tack, the hint of an allegation of sexual harassment from a female officer, and, let's face it, not having a fucking clue what Sean was up to, had all conspired to take her off guard. She had hesitated in her answer and Ferguson had sensed her hesitation. Then she had lied. And lied again. Since the interview she had dismissed any misgivings she might have had, had persuaded herself that there was nothing to worry about. If you just listened to the tapes then Sean would seem completely reasonable. In control. His voice level. Measured. If you were actually in the room with him it was another

219

matter. The body language was awry. Every movement, every gesture a precursor to violence. And the grey eyes, the flat tone of voice, only served to emphasise the discrepancy ...

'Do you enjoy working with young people, Clive? Young girls?' Carragher had leaned forward across the scarred Formica table in the interview room. Townsend blinked behind his metal-rimmed glasses, but said nothing. 'Come on, Clive. It's a fair question. Do you like young girls?'

Townsend again said nothing but this time reached up and flicked his shoulder-length brown hair away from his face.

'I mean, you must get a degree of, well, adulation? It's only natural. Young, impressionable girls. An older man. It must happen all the time. Even to someone who might find it difficult to attract a woman of his own age?'

Once again Townsend didn't answer. But his shoulders were tight and he glared back at Carragher.

'A man in your position must be able to get a neglected, unloved teenage girl to do pretty much what he wants, right?'

'Are we going to be much longer?' Townsend asked, looking between Carragher and Cat.

'We're investigating the death of a sixteen-year-old girl here, Clive.'

Townsend glanced up at the clock on the wall. 'I've been in here nearly two hours already.'

'If you're looking for sympathy, Clive, you'll find it in the dictionary – between "shit" and "syphilis".'

'And if you're waiting for me to admit to something I didn't do, you can go to hell.'

Carragher leaned back, rotating his shoulders in an effort to release the tension there. 'Been there, Clive,' he said, 'bought the

T-shirt. Got the keyring, the alarm clock, the pillowcases. Pressed the red button and seen the rare behind-the-scenes footage. Purchased the illustrated book that accompanies the series. Now I'm watching the repeats on Dave.' Carragher looked a little better now. Calmer. Cat watched his left hand slide across the table and entwine its fingers in the right. The left not trusting the right to behave itself.

Sean had been so certain, so convincing, that there was something wrong about the man they had been interviewing. So convincing, in fact, that at the time she had been positive he was right. Now, Cat couldn't be sure. Felt she couldn't be sure of anything any more. Not when it came to Sean, anyway. Then her mind went to the evidence boards. The pictures from the murder scene, the burnt-out shell of the Audi, the photographs, the grisly details in the post-mortem report.

37

DCI Roberts opened his eyes and took his hands off his head. He checked his watch.

'Why don't you just give us the gist, DI Ferguson, or we'll be here all fucking day.'

Ferguson looked down, his ears and the sides of his neck reddening, a tremor in the hand holding the sheet of paper. He cleared his throat again,

'Mr Townsend alleges he was subject to aggressive and pro-longed questioning, that DI Carragher parked his car on the street where he lived on a number of evenings, making no particular effort to hide his identity. In fact, Mr Townsend alleges that DI Carragher made it obvious that he was under surveillance, claiming, not without some justification, that this was meant to intimidate and unnerve him. Mr Townsend further claims that on more than one occasion DI Carragher followed him when he went out in his own car. Again parking in the same street and making his presence obvious. He claims that this persecution – his word –

culminated in DI Carragher forcing his way into his residence last Wednesday at around seven and subjecting him to a serious physical assault.'

If this was true, Cat thought, then the lies she had told up till now were the least of her problems. If it was true. Who was she kidding? It was more than likely, given what she had known already about Sean. What she had learned since then. More than *likely* – probable. Was this the first, the only, time Sean had done something like this? More than once Sean had asked her to say she was with him on a particular day at a particular time. To sign it into the log. When in reality she had no fucking idea where he was at all, or what he was up to. She had originally suspected he might be seeing someone. A man. A married man, perhaps, who wanted to keep it secret from his wife. Told herself, at various times, that it was a hangover. Or a long lunch. Or just plain skiving off. But it was never going to be anything as straightforward as that. Not when Sean was involved. She hadn't thought about it, not properly, or she would have just said no. Except he was her superior officer and he could, if he had wanted, have made things very difficult for her. Well, he'd certainly done that. It seemed completely ridiculous now. How could she have been so stupid? And she couldn't remember offhand the dates and times she had maintained she was with Sean when she wasn't. Not without going back and checking on the system. Sean had had it in his head that Clive Townsend was involved in some way. Where or how he had got this idea she wasn't sure, but it had been obvious in the interview. Maybe she could still salvage the situation. Maybe now was the time to come clean about her suspicions, tell the truth. Roberts was looking at her. As if he was waiting for a reply.

'Sorry, guv?'

'Did you have any idea that any of this might be going on?' Roberts asked.

Pearson glanced across at Cat. There had been a change in her body language. It was so subtle as to be almost unnoticeable. Unless you knew her. Unless you spent an appreciable amount of every day working alongside her. It wasn't something he could have readily explained to anyone else; no particular attitude of limb or attribute of movement. But it was there all the same. Guarded. On the defensive.

'DC Russell?' Roberts asked again.

Maybe she didn't care. Maybe now was the time to jack it all in. The Job. The career. The politics. The all-boys-together attitude that you were supposed to join in with, even if you were female. She was sick of the whole fucking lot. Finally she shook her head.

'No, guv. I had no idea.'

'Even if this Clive Townsend wasn't involved in the death of the girl,' said Pearson, 'the harassment, if it's true, might give us a motive for murder.'

'OK,' said Roberts, 'we'll make it a line of enquiry. Now, are we done? Only we're supposed to be having a meeting this morning?'

Curtis stood up. 'And I'm late for a meeting with the DCC.'

Ferguson snapped his briefcase shut and stood up. Curtis and Ferguson left the room and Pearson and Russell fell in behind.

'You two,' said Roberts. They turned and Roberts nodded at the door. 'Push that to for a minute.'

Pearson did as he asked and then turned back.

'By the way,' he said, 'we spoke to Carragher's neighbour last night. Name's Lorna Jeffries.'

'And? Get on with it, Pearson, I've already wasted enough fucking time with the other two.'

'She didn't know him that well. Just on nodding terms, according to her. But she's been having a bit of aggro with her ex. So Carragher comes in at the end of one particular row and sees him off. They have some kind of heart-to-heart. She says Carragher asked if she wanted to report it and she said no. We've checked on the system and there's no record of it.'

'Any previous contact between us and this Lorna Jeffries?' Roberts asked, looking between them.

'That,' admitted Pearson, 'we didn't check.'

Roberts sighed and made a face. 'So you think Carragher's leaned on this . . . '

'Raymond Walsh.' Pearson shrugged. 'It's possible. And maybe he's been leaned on a little too hard and taken exception to it. Decided to do something about it.'

Roberts considered it for a moment, then said, 'All right. After the meeting you can go and have a word. All right? Happy?'

The phone rang. Roberts picked it up and waved them back to the chairs.

'Hello, sir.' Roberts put his hand over the receiver, mouthed 'Dougie Ettrick' at Pearson and rolled his eyes. 'Assistant chief constable? You've done well for yourself, sir. Congratulations.' And then, 'Thank you, sir. Yes, a very sad business.' Roberts listened in silence for a minute, pushing a sheet of paper around his desk. Frowning now. Finally he said, 'That's correct, he was.' And then, 'A DI Ferguson. That's right.' Listening for half a minute, 'OK, yes, sir. Thanks again.'

When he put the phone down Pearson asked, 'Dougie Ettrick? What did he want?'

'Mostly wanted to rub it in that he's now an ACC. Offering condolences for the loss of a fellow officer.'

'And Ferguson?'

He rubbed his chin thoughtfully. 'It appears that him and Carragher might have had some previous,' he said, then moving on, 'OK,' picking up the sheet of paper from his desk, 'I didn't want to say anything in front of the Chuckle Brothers, but we've got a match back on the DNA from the dog-end at the murder scene.'

Pearson took the sheet of paper from him and scanned it.

Donna Freeman. Age sixteen. Three counts of shoplifting, two of criminal damage.

He passed it over to Russell.

'So, what? A witness?' asked Pearson.

Roberts shrugged. 'Fucked if I know. Probably got nothing to do with it. More than likely the dog-end's been there for days. But I've asked Uniform to bring her in anyway.'

38

'Where've you been?'
'Out.'

'Out where?' said Malcolm, sitting up and hooking his glasses over his ears, as if he'd actually been asleep. As if he wasn't really that bothered where she'd been. Although obviously he was. And obviously he hadn't been asleep.

He'd been asleep last night. After they had come back from the car park and she had lain on her bed with her eyes closed, trying not to think, and she might have fallen asleep herself for a little while but couldn't be sure. After she had lain there for what seemed like hours, just staring at the ceiling. After she'd got up and looked in the mirror and Alicia wasn't there. When she had decided she couldn't stand it a moment longer in the bedsit and had to get out. When she had stepped over his lifeless body lying on the floor under his parka. He'd been asleep when she had grabbed her keys and jacket and run down the stairs and out on to the street.

'Just out,' she said. 'Walking,' she said.

Crying, she didn't say. Hugging a tree, she didn't say. And also she didn't say this: Crying for all those dead people. Hugging a tree that wouldn't hug her back. Its stiff wooden arms held aloft, pointedly ignoring her. The rough rope of its outer husk scratching her face as she cried for all the people she had made die: Alicia, Mr Downey, Motorcycle Boy, the policeman. And for herself. Mostly for herself. Finally the tears had dried up and she had decided to come back. Where else could she go?

But it wasn't until a pigeon strutted defiantly into her path, its lone red eye blinking, the mutilated, empty socket where the other had been mushy and weeping, that she realised she had been on the move again. That she had left the tree on the seafront and been walking for the last ten minutes and was in the town centre. The pigeon cocked its head and regarded her balefully, challenging her to pass. A crimson wattle clung to its beak like the bloodied and clammy remnants of some partly digested carnivorous meal. A tatty feather hung from its breast, fluttering in a breeze she could not feel, before falling to the pavement. As she watched, more pigeons joined the first: swooping down from their perches on the ledges of the higher buildings, the rooftops and chimneypots of the shops. As if they too, like the flocks of gulls on the seafront, had been grounded, not by the fog, but by what she had done . . .

She wasn't telling him something, Malcolm knew. She was holding something back. Keeping more secrets. You couldn't really trust her. But she was pretty, sort of. Or she had been. Until she had ruined it by doing that thing to her hair; it looked crap now. He'd liked it when she had it long. When it was black and shoulder-length. But she had fucked it up and she didn't look as nice. She wasn't wearing make-up now, either. She used to. That made her look prettier too. More, like, grown-up or something. Except for when she had all that white paint on. That had just been fucking weird. Now her face was just scrubbed clean. He liked the clothes she used to wear better as well. She still wore black. He liked her in black. But she wore that motorcycle jacket all the time now. It was much too big for her. Plus some boy had obviously given it to her. It wasn't new, it had all scuff marks down one side. So she'd obviously got it off some bloke or other.

After the row at the playground, Malcolm had gone back home. Angry. Hurt. Decided he didn't want anything to do with her any more. After a day or so, though, he had changed his mind. Still angry and hurt, but wanting to see her. He hadn't been quite ready to come back properly, unless she apologised. And he knew she wouldn't do that. So, earlier the previous night, he had waited on the other side of the road in that little alleyway until she came out. Trailing her from a safe distance. He had seen her walk along the seafront and follow the car into the car park. He had gone down on to the beach for a few minutes. Unsure what he should do. Not knowing if he really wanted to find out what she was up to. On the beach he had found a big stone. A pebble. Like the egg of a dinosaur, he thought, as he picked it up. But as he turned it over in his hands he realised it was more sort of pointed at one end. More triangular. Like a huge, petrified tear-drop.

There were more and more of them, the birds. Scrofulous and moulting – everything in this town seemed sickly and dying, or already dead – twitching their heads to and fro. Making that weird sound. Staring at her reproachfully. Their red claws fidgeting on the shit-strewn paving stones. Waiting for something. For her to say something. To explain herself. For her to do something, something about Alicia.

He had stood in the shadows between the beach huts and watched. Had watched her as she exposed herself to that bloke. It was obvious what she was up to now. It was what he had thought. What he had known; what he hadn't wanted to think about. Having sex with men. For money. He had seen the bloke take money out of his wallet and give it to her. He couldn't look. Although at the same time he wanted to. Wanted to see what happened, like some old pervert, like one of those blokes who liked to watch their girlfriends or wives fuck someone else. But he didn't watch. He felt sick. He turned away and back into the shadows between the beach huts. Felt the heavy stone in his hand. Felt how the sea had made it all smooth. Felt the grains of sand beneath his fingers rasping across its surface. He was going to do something. He was going to make it stop.

The noise of the shuffling, restless birds – cooing, chirring, gargling – was getting louder now. It was so loud that she could barely hear herself think. Feathers worked their way out of the breasts of the birds, each one shivering and dropping to the pavement where immediately another dishevelled, diseased bird sprang up in its place. Donna wanted to scream, felt the scream forming in her chest, felt the panic rise through the back of her skull. She clapped her hands. Stamped her feet. Shouted at the top of her voice. The flock of pigeons wheeled skywards in an explosion of wings.

But when he turned back Donna was getting out of the car. Looking upset. Looking ready to run. So he had changed his mind.

Changed his mind and dropped the big stone in the shape of a teardrop. Dropped it and stepped back into the shadows.

She had decided to go back. Back to the bedsit. Where else could she go? Back to the bedsit and Malcolm. Malcolm lying on the floor under his parka, his hand balled into a fist near his mouth as if he had wanted to suck his thumb while he was asleep but had resisted the temptation. Malcolm and his sweaty feet. Malcolm who yesterday had washed her face clean of the white paint, the black lips, the eyeliner. Who had sat by her and read to her out of his library book of Greek myths. Who had made her a cup of sweet tea. Who had told her to drink it, even though she didn't much like tea, because he said it was what you were supposed to do if you had had a shock. But also Malcolm who, when he thought she was asleep, had put his hand on the outside of her knickers. A reverent pilgrim touching a sacred, mystical artefact. Or at least she thought he might have put his hand on the outside of her knickers. He had definitely put his hand up inside the big, baggy T-shirt she wore for bed and felt up her tits. She turned back to Malcolm, who had pretended he was asleep, and who now asked her:

'Where've you been?'

'Out.'

'Out where?' said Malcolm, sitting up and hooking his glasses over his ears.

'Just out,' she said. 'Walking.'

'I was worried about you.'

'Yeah? Why?'

It was a stupid question. She knew it was a stupid question. Knew even before she saw the look on his face. The look that said he thought it was a stupid question. He shrugged as if he didn't need to explain and she sat down on the bed.

Malcolm said, 'The Old Bill have been here.'

'Fuck! The police? What did they want?'

'They wanted to talk to you.'

'Me?'

'Yeah.'

'What did you tell them?'

'Nothing,' Malcolm said. 'I didn't answer the door.'

'So how do you know it was the Old Bill then?'

'They did that thing, you know, where they knock and ring the bell at the same time? You always know it's them. So I didn't answer the door.'

'So you don't know it was them?'

'It was,' he said. 'I saw the car. And I heard them talking on their radios. They knocked again and shouted your name through the letterbox. Must've thought you were asleep or something. Or pretending to be out.'

'And they just went?' she asked.

'After a while. But they're bound to come back.'

'Fuck.' Donna ran her hands through her hair. Thinking. Or trying to. Trying to work out what to do. Not really coming up with anything.

'Fuck!' she said again.

Malcolm, looking down, running his finger along in the thread-bare carpet, said, 'You could always come and stay with me. At my nan's.'

His nan's? Funny, she'd never asked him where he lived when he wasn't dossing on her floor. She only knew that he went away somewhere. And then came back again. She had never thought about where he actually went. Never thought about him at all when he wasn't there. His nan's? Well, they couldn't stay here: Malc was right, the police would be back. All the tears, the

234

walking hadn't helped. It couldn't stop what had happened with the policeman – with Sean – couldn't stop what had happened with Sean going round and round in her head. She had fucked up again. She had stabbed him. Stabbed him. The worst thing was, she hadn't meant to. Not really. But she had got angry. Angry with Sean for laughing at her. Because he hadn't done anything. Because he hadn't arrested the person she knew had killed Alicia. Or caused her to be killed. Or was involved in some way.

39

'Uh, Lorna Jeffries ...' Cat said as Pearson arrived back at his desk.

'What about her?'

'When she said she hadn't made any official complaint? It isn't strictly true.'

'OK,' said Pearson scooping up his mobile and keys from the desk. 'C'mon, let's go. You can fill me in on the way.'

In the car, at the third set of traffic lights. The lights changing from green to amber to red as they approached. Pearson applying the brake, depressing the clutch and popping the gearstick into neutral before coming to a stop and putting the car into first. Riding the clutch, looking across to Russell, who sat staring out of the side window. Not saying anything. She'd been quiet for most of the day. Withdrawn. The lights changing from red to red-and-amber to green. Pearson pulling away before, finally, he said:

'So? Lorna Jeffries?'

'There's a couple of 999 calls logged on the system,' Russell said, turning from the window but not quite looking at him. Preferring, instead, to stare out of the windscreen. Her voice flat, mechanical. 'In the first one she claims someone had been in the back garden. That she'd heard the patio furniture being moved, a chair being overturned. She thought she might have seen someone looking in through the patio doors. Might have heard a sound like metal on the glass, as if a ring had been tapped on it. Two uniforms attended, the male PC checked out the garden, back door and windows while a WPC sat with Miss Jeffries and took a statement.'

'Did you speak to either of them?' Pearson asked.

'Yeah, the female PC. She said that Lorna was pretty shook up. Told her that she thought it might be her ex.'

'Ray Walsh?'

'Yep. She told her they'd been having some aggro over access visits with the son.'

'And?'

'Well, the male PC said they'd make a point of dropping by her way in the panda every so often, gave her some advice on making the house more secure. And that was about it. On the same night, an hour or so later, Lorna's Facebook status was changed to "You won't frighten me . . . if that's what you're trying to do. I'll always do what's best for Jack."'

'OK.' Pearson nodded.

'So it means she lied to us,' Russell said, 'when she said she didn't want to get Walsh in trouble? When Sean asked if she wanted to make an official complaint?'

Pearson flicked the indicator, waited for a break in the flow of traffic, then took a left turn. 'Well, if you want to split hairs, technically she didn't. Unless there's an official complaint on the system made after Sean's visit?' Russell shook her head. 'And I take it there's no record entered by Sean about the conversation?'

'No.'

Pearson nodded. 'So she didn't technically lie. Just didn't tell us about all this previous stuff.' After a few minutes he asked, 'You said there were a couple of calls?'

'Yeah. About a week later, she made another emergency call. Two uniforms again. But this one, the brigade attended as well. When the first-responders turned up the fire was already out. A rubbish bin outside the back door that had been pushed up against the house. Different pair of officers, but the same set-up as the previous time: the male PC did a search of the back garden, checked the fencing was secure, tried to ascertain a possible point of access, made sure the patio doors and all the windows hadn't been tampered with.'

'And?'

'Nothing. Meanwhile she's telling the female PC about her domestic agg with an ex-boyfriend again.' She nodded, pre-empting his question. 'Ray Walsh. But she stops short of actually accusing him of setting the fire. When the male PC pushes her, asks if she wants them to go round and have a word with Walsh, she starts to backtrack. Doesn't want to get Ray into trouble, she might have accidentally started the fire herself, she can't really be sure now. But then she changes her Facebook status a couple of hours later: "What the f-star-star-star are you doing starting a fire? How f-star-star-star-ing stupid can you get? You're putting our son's life at risk". Three exclamation marks.'

'Mmmm, the fire thing's interesting. If it was Walsh,' Pearson said, coming to a stop, applying the handbrake, turning off the engine. 'This is it.'

*

Pearson knocked and tried the bell of Ray Walsh's house for the third time, even though the house was in darkness and it was pretty obvious no one was home. He turned away from the door and scanned the street.

'So,' said Russell, 'd'you think Sean might really have put the frighteners on this Walsh?'

'Seems likely.'

'Even if he did, though, Walsh isn't likely to say anything.'

'He might not need to,' Pearson said, nodding across at one of the houses opposite, slipping his mobile out of his pocket and putting it to his ear. 'We've got CCTV.'

40

SUNDAY

Cat had always loved this view. Every time she looked at it, it seemed different somehow. The light subtly changed and altered from the time before. The sky could be reflected a thousand different ways in the pools of water left by the retreating tide; silver pearls of mercury mirroring a white sky in the strange light of dusk, an orange sunset scattering puddles of blood. Or the night might be clear, black and silent, the tide full. The still, grey surface of the water barely moving except for the occasional mild disturbance from a gentle breeze. Or the tide out, the air misty over the great expanse of silt, so that the silver tanks of the oil refinery on the far shore were obscured from sight. Today, though, the sky was a dull slate grey, featureless and monotonous. The water of the estuary spread out below it in a listless, murky brown expanse that seemed to match exactly her mood, a profound sense of depression she had carried with her since the meeting in Roberts' office two days before.

*

'How did it go with Gold this morning?' Pearson had asked.

Roberts' glance went briefly to Cat: in that moment making a calculation, weighing up whether she could be trusted, whether he could talk freely in front of her, then returning to Pearson. 'As you'd expect. A complete fucking waste of time.'

He had taken the piece of paper from his desk and passed it across. While Pearson had scanned it, she had felt absurdly grateful for being included. Then Pearson had given that short, dismissive grunt and passed the paper across and she had instantly felt a wave of shame for feeling that way. That desperate need to belong. The perennial outsider. The white sheep of the family. Too serious and too scared of doing the wrong thing. She remembered lying awake in the evening as a little girl, listening to the muffled sound of the television downstairs. Terrified that something was about to go wrong. Vaguely aware that her family, her father in particular, was up to something they shouldn't be. Always expecting that knock on the door, that insistent ringing of the bell. The late-night visit from a policeman. How ironic was it then that she should join the very organisation of which she had been so petrified? And, having joined it, immediately, and for the first time in her life, broken its rules?

Out in the estuary, it looked like someone was swimming. A woman. A dark head bobbing now and then into view among the swell and ebb of the brackish water. Who in their right mind would swim out there? It was the fucking North Sea, for God's sake! Even on a day like today, after weeks of hot weather, the temperature must still be bone-chillingly cold. Watching for a few minutes, Cat became aware that she hadn't seen any sign of a limb breaking the surface. No hint of a body's tell-tale wake. Surely she would have seen the occasional leg or arm? Unless the figure had just been drifting lethargically on the tide. Unless she had been standing here for the last five minutes staring stupidly at the body of a drowned, or drowning, woman . . .

The dark head, or whatever it was, was suddenly lost to view among the waves. Panic rising in her chest, afraid to blink, Cat stared at the place she had last seen the object. Holding her breath. Not daring to look away. Reaching blindly for the mobile phone in her handbag. As her fingers closed around it the dark object broke the surface. Closer to shore. She saw the friendly, handsome face of a Labrador and realised that she had been watching a seal.

That was another thing about the fucking Job. It sucked all the joy, all the trust from you. Made you see the bad, the darkness in everybody and everything. So that now, looking out across the mud flats, the estuary and the shore of Kent beyond, instead of being able to appreciate, as she did most mornings, the shifting cloud formations, the play of light on the water, the sanderlings, turnstones and ringed plovers at the water's edge, all she could think of were the dangers of the foreshore. The treacherous tides that had dragged so many unsuspecting people away. Areas of sucking mud that could hold you in their implacable grip, the gusting wind snatching away your cries for help, the unexploded munitions on board the wreck of the SS *Richard Montgomery* broken up on a sandbar during the Second World War. And the danger posed by human predators: pickpockets, junkies, rapists, paedophiles. And, of course, murderers.

Each part of the beach, each inlet between the breakwaters had its own identity. A different gradation of top layer, from large pebbles at the mouth of the river to a kind of coarse grit further downstream. She dug the toe of her shoe in. Here it was mostly a mixture of sand and tiny shingle.

The worst of it was, she had given her trust to Sean. Had allowed herself to be swayed by his conviction that Clive Townsend had played some part in the death of Alicia Goode. Had thought of him as something more than a colleague. As a friend. A close friend. Only to find now that everything she knew about him, or thought she knew about him, was a lie.

She bent over and picked up a handful of the sand. She squeezed the tiny stones in her palm before letting them fall between her fingers and back on to the beach. Sean had faults. Well, that was a fucking understatement. The more they uncovered about him, the less she realised she actually knew about him. The less she liked him, if she was being honest. But did that excuse the way his death – his murder – was being treated by his fellow officers? 'I was just wondering,' Curtis had said, 'how this might play with the public. I mean, I have nothing against gay people myself, you understand, but would the public be ready to see a gay policeman as, well, beyond reproach?'

It typified the attitude of some parts of the Job; to gays, to minorities, to women. As in every other walk of life, attitudes were changing. It just seemed that within the police force they were changing that little bit slower. At least with some people. Andy Curtis was not exceptional. His kind were becoming all too common. A political cop who spoke almost exclusively in management jargon, who used phrases like 'media strategy', 'public perception' and 'damage limitation'. This political manoeuvring, she supposed, was a function of the middle management of any institution, any large organisation, in the country. Well, maybe. But in other institutions and organisations it wouldn't revolve around a colleague's murder, would it? It was sickening that Sean's murder should come down to this: nothing more than an exercise in PR.

Could you wonder at the snide, behind-their-backs comments, the sly shared looks, the smirking schoolboy conspiracy, the contempt felt by front-line officers like Roberts and Pearson: 'another prick who's spent half his life fucking around at university', with the look to her – 'No offence.' Was that how they saw her? How they talked about her behind her back? Was she to be forever lumped in with the Dougie Ettricks and Andy Curtises of this world simply because she had a qualification, a university education? Sometimes she felt that she didn't belong wherever she was. But wasn't this desperate attempt to fit in, to be accepted, to be part of the all-boys-together club that was the Job, the reason why she was in this position in the first place? Under suspicion from Professional Standards for something that Sean might have involved her in. Though what it was, or rather how serious it might yet become, she could only guess at. The subject of innuendo from her workmates regarding a non-existent sexual liaison with a now-deceased superior officer. And was it her imagination or, since being interviewed by Professional Standards, was everyone in the nick more wary in her presence? A little less friendly than they had been before? Some of them, she was convinced, were certain she had been talking to Ferguson. If not dropping them personally, then at the very least dropping Sean in the shit.

'Is that going to cause a problem?' Roberts had asked. Cat had felt all eyes turn to her. And had thought at that moment: Am *I* going to cause a problem – that's what he really wants to know. Not if I want to stay on the investigation. Not if I don't want my reputation tarnished any more than it is already. What a fucking joke that was. Not if I want any kind of future in the Job. But standing here this morning, looking out over the mud flats, she wasn't sure that she did want a future in the Job. Wasn't sure she wanted any part of it any more.

41

Donna woke in a strange bed. She could tell right away it wasn't hers. Before she opened her eyes even; it smelled clean for one thing. And the pillowcase and sheets were much softer than the ones on her bed. When she bothered with them. Most of the time she just slept on the bare mattress. Her eyes came suddenly open. She lay there for a minute or so, too nervous, too scared to move. She could hear the sound of breathing. Air drawn in through wet nostrils then expelled noisily through an open mouth. She could feel the hot, rank breath of someone, some thing, on the back of her neck. At the same time she became aware of a rustling noise. There was something in the bed with her. Without turning, as slowly, as carefully as she could, she reached out behind her . . .

Empty. Just the feeling of a blanket under her fingers. She was alone, in a single bed that had been pushed up against a wall. As she took deep breaths, as her heart slowed, she realised the rustling was just the sound of the foam chips moving in the pillow underneath her ear. The noisy inhalations and exhalations only the sound of her own respiration. The hot, rank breath on the back of her neck had merely pursued her from the dream, the nightmare, she had just woken from. All the same she turned to check, to see with her own eyes, that she was alone in the bed. She was in Malcolm's house, she remembered. His nan's house. He was sleeping on the settee. His nan had insisted on it, and Donna had been more than happy with that. Malcolm's nan said she would let Donna stay. But only if Malcolm slept on the settee. Only if he washed his bedclothes, only if he tidied and cleaned his room. It was nice to sleep in a clean room. Her own place was filthy. Had been filthy for as long as she had lived there. It had been filthy when she had moved in and she couldn't be arsed to do anything about it. This room was much nicer. Proper furniture and everything. Only cheap stuff, but a proper wardrobe, a bed-side cabinet, a desk and a chair. It hadn't been decorated for a while; the wallpaper was looking tired, the paintwork faded. But it wasn't that bad. Not compared to her room. No mirror though. She had wanted to bring the mirror, even though it was broken. But Malcolm had said his nan would kick off, would make him chuck it away, and Donna hadn't wanted to take the chance. From where she lay she could see that there were blobs of Blu-Tack on the walls, areas of lighter-coloured wallpaper where posters had been hastily removed: something embarrassing Malcolm hadn't wanted her to see. His models were still there though. Badly con-structed plastic replicas of World War II aeroplanes on shelving units along two walls. She had studied them the previous night before getting into bed. Reading the name of each model in turn from the ridged and smudged transparent label on its little stand. Malc was crap at making models. Even she could see that. It was sweet. The loose and lopsided propeller on a Hawker Hurricane. Lumps of green and brown camouflage paint messily daubed on the fuselage of a Spitfire. The misaligned transfers of aircraft insignia on a Messerschmitt. The whorls and ridges of Malcolm's fingerprints fixed in glue across the windshield of a Dornier.

Donna yawned. She hadn't slept well. Malcolm's nan had had her telly or radio on all night. She had been able to hear people talking. Too low for her to make out what they were saying properly, but loud enough to keep her awake. She swung her legs over the side of the bed and sat up. Ran a hand through her hair. Malc had found a charger from somewhere for her clippers and had tidied it up at her place before they left. Worried, again, about what his nan might think. Donna could smell her own breath. Could taste it. Drawing it in over her furry tongue, letting it out over her manky teeth. When was the last time she had brushed her teeth? She couldn't remember. She had to make a special effort to remember things like that these days. Washing. Brushing her teeth. Eating. That sort of thing. She leaned down and picked up the two-litre plastic bottle of Diet Coke from beside the bed, unscrewed the top and took a swig. It was disgusting. Warm, flat. Sugary water. She picked up her leather jacket from the end of the bed and found her fags and matches in the pockets. Checked her phone: no missed calls, no messages. She put a cigarette in her mouth and struck a match, lit her cigarette. Watching the red-headed figure twist and writhe in the match's flame. Watching as it blackened and turn to ash. There had been ash in her dream, she remembered.

Ash fell like snow from a night sky. A blizzard of grey flakes disintegrating into dust as they settled. The hot air burning her skin. Scorching her nostrils. The whole world seemed as if it was on fire. An inhuman, high-pitched, ululating screaming like the wailing of a siren. Or a car alarm—

*

Donna jumped as the match burned down to her fingertips. She shook it out and put it in the plastic cup on the bedside cabinet along with the other dead matches, the incinerated remains of cigarettes, the ash.

Her mobile rang. Her stomach clenching, she checked the call display and pressed the button to connect.

'Yeah?'

'Donna?'

The signal was bad. Sez's voice fading in and out. The sound of the wind hitting the mouthpiece at the other end.

'You're up early,' Donna said.

Sez laughed. 'I'm not up early, you silly cow. It's Saturday night, I'm on my way home.' She said something else but it was lost in the bad signal and the wind. 'I've talked to Clive,' she said, her voice fading in again, 'and he wants to meet you.'

'Yeah?' Donna's voice small. Her throat suddenly dry. 'When?'

'Tonight.'

'OK.' Donna cleared her throat. 'Where?'

Sez told her and then asked, 'You know the place, right?'

Donna disconnected. And found she was shivering. Her hands shaking. She knew the place. She had been there before.

42

'**M**orning.'

Cat turned only now, at his greeting. Though she must have heard his approach across the shingle, must have sensed his presence at her shoulder, she hadn't moved. Staring instead out across the estuary, lost in her own thoughts. Pearson gestured vaguely in the direction of the road.

'I recognised the car. Thought you might be down here.'

Cat said nothing, turning back to look out across the water. After a minute she stepped on to the beach. Pearson hesitated for a moment and then followed, falling into step beside her. Half expecting her to turn on him, ask him what the fuck he was doing here, tell him to leave her alone. When she didn't, hadn't said anything in fact for a few minutes, he knew half the battle was won. They walked in silence, Russell staring down at the beach, scanning the sand.

'Do you think this thing with Sean is down to me?' Not really a question. At least not a question to which she expected an answer. She bent over, picked something up from the sand, examined it briefly and put it in her pocket. Pearson held his tongue. Something he had learned from years of interviewing people. Years of hearing other people's confessions. Once someone had shown the inclination to start talking, the slightest interruption, the briefest of diversions, could kill the momentum. Once they had stopped, more than likely you wouldn't get them started again. So, let them talk, see where it took you. Only speak when absolutely necessary. Use 'minimal encouragers': positive body language, a nod, a well-placed 'Uh-huh' or 'I see'.

'Sean asked me to reconcile the team's expenses.'

Pearson didn't bother too much with expenses. Back in the day you got a flat subsistence allowance, didn't need receipts and received your expenses in cash in a little envelope. Nowadays things were a lot tighter, everything had to be accounted for. So he filled in his car-mileage log. Got reimbursed for petrol. But claiming back the few quid he spent on sandwiches? Some things were more trouble than they were worth.

'I tried to get out of it. But it was either me or Gilbert. So ...' She shrugged. 'To be honest, I found anything else I could do to avoid it. You know what a fucking fuss everyone makes about things like that. I knew what it'd be like. They can't find this or that receipt, it'd be all "Can't you just let this one go?" Then getting the hump with me, like it was my job in the first place. Eventually I had to do something. So I'm on the system and Roberts comes in and sees me. Wants to know what I'm up to, looking through the receipts I've got on my desk, Sean's receipts, and I'm coming up with excuses, making myself look an idiot in the process. Anyway, he's obviously not satisfied. He takes everything off me. Next thing I know, Professional Standards are called in.'

They came to a wooden breakwater and Pearson clambered awkwardly over. He sat for a moment astride it. Noted the ache in the base of his back, the full bladder, the desperate need to pee. He waited while Russell climbed lithely over. One step up on to the breakwater. One step off.

'I don't see that you could have done anything different,' Pearson prompted, worried that the interruption, their negotiation of the breakwater, would cause the momentum of their conversation to leak away.

'Maybe not,' she sighed. 'But that's not all of it.' Pearson slipped his hands in his pockets and fell into step beside her again. 'I think Sean had a gambling problem,' she said. 'There was nothing I could put my finger on specifically. No concrete proof. But he had that kind of personality, right?' She glanced across at him and Pearson nodded. 'Like, I used to get in the car and he'd end a call abruptly. I got the impression they weren't personal calls.' When Pearson looked across, she shrugged. 'I don't know, tone of voice? I caught the odd word, the odd sentence here and there. Plus one week he'd be flush, throwing his money around. Next he'd be skint, borrowing off you. I mean, we all get strapped now and then coming up to pay-day. But this was at random times in the month . . .'

'OK,' said Pearson, 'even if you had proof, as long as he could explain where he was getting the money to gamble, it's not a criminal offence. He'd have been offered counselling with Occupational Health. Advised that a gambling habit might leave him open to corruption, offered help to get his finances in order, manage his habit.'

Cat bent down once again and picked up something from the sand. She looked at it, rubbing the sand away with a thumb, then casually pitched it back on to the beach.

'Except there was something else. Wasn't there?' Pearson asked. 'Drugs, right?' She looked at him and this time it was his turn to shrug. 'You didn't look that surprised at his flat. When we found the razor blade with coke on it. Disappointed, maybe. Concerned. But not surprised.'

'No,' she agreed. 'One night we were on a surveillance op together. He gets in the car and he's obviously high. Sniffing. Paranoid. Hyper, even for him. He sees me looking at him and he gets all defensive: he does the occasional recreational line, he was called at short notice on his day off, he didn't expect to be working . . . ' She shook her head. 'So I let it go. There were other times, it wasn't so obvious, but I got the impression he'd been taking something. OK, maybe I should've told someone, but I counted him as a friend, I didn't want to drop him in it. Plus he was my superior officer. I would've had to be pretty sure of my facts, right? If I wanted to take it further?'

Pearson could just imagine Carragher's reaction. Turning up at the nick one morning, being asked to provide a sample without prior warning, being followed into the bog by a member of PSD, likely as not Ferguson. Pissing into a little plastic pot as someone looked over his shoulder. A positive test meant suspension and probably instant dismissal. As did a refusal. He couldn't imagine Carragher taking kindly to any of that. Or to the person who put him in that position in the first place.

'I don't know,' Cat said, 'maybe I was just too much of a coward.'

When she stooped once again to pick something up, his curiosity got the better of him. 'What are you doing?'

'Sea glass,' she said, rubbing the sand from something and then holding it out for him. She dropped it into his hand.

'Looks like a stone to me.'

'Hold it up to the light.'

He held it up and looked through it. It reminded him of the

frosted glass you used to get on the door of the saloon bar in a pub. When he said so, she studied his face, wondering whether he was trying to wind her up. He held it out for her and said, 'What do you do with it?'

'Some people make jewellery out of it. You don't actually "do" anything with it. It's to look at.' She took it back off him. She didn't tell him she put hers in a glass jar by the window because she liked the way the light shone through it. The way its colours changed with the time of day.

'So it's bits of old broken glass?' Pearson asked.

'Yeah,' she agreed, 'bits of broken glass.'

Bits of broken glass, she thought, that have been tumbled around in the sea for decades. In some cases a hundred years. Each one, like any animate object, any living thing, had a past, its own back story. She shook her head. 'Were you born a cynic?'

'They say a cynic's just a disillusioned romantic.'

'"They"? Or you?' She pursed her lips and shook her head again. 'Somehow, I just can't see you as ever being a romantic.'

They began to walk again, Cat's eyes sweeping across the surface of the sand. But it was obvious her heart wasn't in it any more. Worried he might miss his chance, might have already missed his chance, to get her to say everything that was on her mind, he asked:

'So what's the story with Carragher and this Clive Townsend?'

She shot him a look. 'You don't miss much, do you?' They walked in silence again for a while, then Russell sighed. 'Sean thought Townsend had something to do with Alicia Goode's death. He was convinced of it. Don't ask me why. "Information received" is my guess. He never actually told me. But he was so convinced, so adamant, that I believed it. Or I let him convince me. It didn't take a lot. Not after we'd interviewed Townsend.

255

He was so full of himself. A nasty piece of work. One of those people who make your skin crawl.' She glanced across quickly, then looked away. 'Anyway, I knew Sean was up to something. Guessed really. What Ferguson said: parking on his street, making it obvious that he was following him. It was just so typically Sean.'

Typically Sean? When, Pearson wondered, did surveillance become witness intimidation? Again, a criminal offence. The officer arrested, his desk, his house searched, treated like any other person charged with intimidation of a witness. And, by rights, something that should have been reported.

'And giving Townsend a beating?'

'I didn't know, not for sure.'

'But you suspected he might be capable of it?'

'Sean?' Cat gave a bitter laugh. 'I'm beginning to think that Sean was capable of anything.'

'Not what you told Ferguson.'

'No,' she agreed. 'Like I said, I wasn't sure. But if I had been sure? Would I have cared?' Russell sighed again. 'I don't honestly know. I'm not sure of anything any more. I told you I thought this whole thing might be down to me. I'm thinking now that maybe I wanted Sean investigated. That maybe I didn't try very hard to hide from Roberts the fact I was doing the expenses for Sean. That I needn't have had Sean's expense claims in plain view like that where they could be easily seen. Maybe I thought that way Roberts would find out about him, what he was up to, and it wouldn't have been my responsibility, I wouldn't have turned him in. Fuck, I don't know.'

They stopped walking, staring out across the water, neither of them taking in the view. Finally, hands in pockets, scraping the beach with the heel of his shoe, Pearson said:

'You're thinking maybe if you'd said something earlier, Sean might be alive?'

Cat looked down, shrugged again.

'Whatever this is about,' Pearson said, 'it isn't expenses. Whatever Carragher was involved in, it was his choice. His responsibility. Not yours. Or anybody else's. If you want my advice, don't go making any rash decisions. In fact, don't do anything for the time being. Let's just see how this all pans out.'

43

The front door opened.

Cat had been wrong. After they had interviewed Dave Cowans – toothpaste on his chin, a bloated drinker's face, the heavy brow, the misshapen forehead and port-wine stain – she had said that his was a face that had been hit by a bus. But she had been wrong. *This*, Pearson thought, was a face that had been hit by a bus and, having hit it, in a last-stop lay-over at the end of the line, the bus had reversed, gears crunching, tyres slipping on the mulching leaves and discarded cigarette ends in the gutter, and hit it again. And maybe a few more times after that. All that was missing was the cartoon treadmark of a tyre down his shirt. But who knew? Ray Walsh, standing in the shadow behind the half-open door, was wearing only a dressing gown and slippers. Warily eyeing Pearson's brandished warrant card.

Walsh sighed. 'What do you want?'

Pearson indicated the interior of the flat with the warrant card – 'Do you mind if we have a word, Mr Walsh?' – before slipping it back into his inside pocket.

'About what?'

'It might be better if we talk inside?'

Walsh seemed momentarily undecided, then swung the door wide. The hallway was spacious and similar in decoration to Lorna Jeffries' house: stripped and sanded floorboards, yellow emulsion for the walls, woodwork taken back to the original timber. It could almost be the same place. Except for the motorbike on its stand along the opposite wall.

'I used to leave it outside in the square,' Walsh said, looking over at it, 'but the kids fuck around with it, sitting on it, sticking keys in the ignition trying to start it up, rocking it off its stand . . .'

They followed him into the living room; light-blue emulsion for the walls, stripped and varnished floorboards again, a grey three-piece suite, a home cinema, a teak coffee table, a magazine rack. Magazines, broadsheet newspapers, neatly folded and put away. Walsh sat down in one of the armchairs and indicated the sofa with his chin.

'What happened to your face?' Pearson asked, taking a seat.

'An accident.'

'Did you come off your bike?'

'I fell down the stairs.'

Looking away. Pulling his dressing gown across his lap. Taking a tobacco tin out of one of the pockets. Opening it and taking out a pre-made roll-up. Closing the tin again. Cigarette and lighter in one hand, he hesitated. 'D'you mind?'

'Your house,' said Pearson.

'Yeah, right,' putting the cigarette in his mouth, sparking up his lighter, 'as if that fucking matters nowadays.' He lit his cigarette and drew in a breath. 'So, what's this all about?'

'Do you know a Miss Lorna Jeffries?' Pearson asked.

Walsh sighed again. 'I might have known it would be about her.'

As he picked up the ceramic ashtray from the coffee table and put it on his knee, Cat tried to see past the busted nose, the swollen and blackened eyes, the nasty bruise on his forehead. He looked his age, an old fifty even, with his slightly protruding ears, the auricles pink and curling in on themselves, the sort of ears that put you in mind of a bat. Dangly silver cross in the right lobe. Hair receding at the temples, thinning to a downy fluff on top of his head. But at least he had resisted the urge to shave it close to his skull, the usual response to male-pattern baldness. His teeth were uneven. Straight, but noticeably shorter on one side of his mouth than the other. As if he had had them smashed at one point and had enough money to have them fixed and filed but not quite enough money, or maybe just lacked the inclination, to have them capped.

Walsh tapped the ash from his cigarette into the ashtray. 'What's she been saying now?'

'Miss Jeffries claims that you've been harassing her.'

'Oh yeah?' Unimpressed. 'What is it I'm supposed to have done this time?'

'She's made allegations before?'

'Not to the police, no. Just to everybody fucking else in the world.'

'Such as?'

'Her family, that shrew of a mother of hers, her friends – our friends, at least they used to be. Posting stuff on social media, Facebook, that sort of thing.'

Walsh, irritated, took a drag of his cigarette and ground it out in the ashtray, put the ashtray back on the coffee table.

'So, you haven't been pestering Miss Jeffries about access to your son, Jack? Demanding to see him, pick him up from nursery? Asking to have him stay over?'

'"Demanding"?' He shook his head. 'Asking. Asking to see my son. Asking very nicely.'

'You haven't parked across the street from her place?'

Walsh looked down, picked something off his dressing gown. 'All right,' meeting Pearson's gaze, 'a couple of times maybe. I'd just wanted to see Jack. I didn't approach them, didn't even try to talk to him … Look, she won't let me have any access at all. How is that fair? I could have got a solicitor, gone through the courts, but I figured it would just get petty and spiteful. I've been trying to be reasonable. Fat lot of fucking good that's done me.'

'OK, Mr Walsh,' said Pearson, 'I can understand how upsetting this all is. Especially given your history.'

'What? What "history"?'

'Your daughter?'

Walsh shook his head. 'She's not started all that again?' He opened his tobacco tin again and took out another roll-up. 'Look, I haven't got a daughter. Never have had.' He lit his cigarette, shut the tin and put it on the coffee table. 'It's just something she's made up. It's … I don't know, I mean, why make up something like that?' He picked up the ashtray, took another drag on his cigarette. Finally he looked up. 'Thing is, like, every time she tells it to someone it's different, right? My daughter was eight, snatched by some paedo. She was eleven and died at a zebra crossing outside her school. She was thirteen and died on one of those unmanned railway crossings. It's like whatever she sees on the telly at the time, that's what happened.' He shook his head. 'Funny thing is, I didn't even know she was doing it. Not right away. I was getting all these, like, sympathetic looks, everyone being really nice to me. But too nice, d'you know what I mean? Like they're frightened to say the wrong thing around you?'

He ran his fingers gently over his bruised forehead, traced either side of his swollen nose with a thumb and forefinger. 'She comes across as all understanding, you know? What did she say to you? "It's not his fault"? "He's just terrified it might happen again"? "He wouldn't let me out of his sight"? It's just not true. It's all a fantasy.' He shook his head again. As if even now he couldn't quite believe it all.

'When I first met her, I couldn't believe my luck, had no idea what she saw in me. But, something like that happens, you're not going to turn it down, are you? Even if it does seem too good to be true. So I spoiled her. Who wouldn't? Bought a house. Did it up. Bought her nice things. Took her on expensive holidays. I didn't mind the money. I was happy to have someone to spend my money on. It wasn't until later that I realised there was something wrong. Something wrong with her. That she's wrong in the head. Not until after the kid was born. She wouldn't let me have anything to do with Jack. Wouldn't let me change his nappy, feed him, give him a bath. Nothing. Then she starts with all these stories, right? Like I'm the one who's not right in the head. Like I'm over-possessive, jealous, whatever. All this shit about my non-existent daughter . . .'

As Walsh took another slow drag of his cigarette, lost in thought, Pearson glanced across, a 'What the fuck's all this?' expression on his face. Cat shook her head. Pearson indicated the door with his chin, then stood up. Walsh looked up.

'I think we're done for now,' Pearson said.

Walsh, looking relieved, ground out his cigarette, put the ash-tray back on the coffee table and stood to see them out.

In the hallway Pearson turned. 'Miss Jeffries tells us you had some kind of altercation on her doorstep?'

'Once,' Walsh said. 'That was once. And then that fucking psycho next-door neighbour turns up.'

'And then what?'

'Then nothing. I left. I realised I wasn't going to get anywhere. And I certainly didn't want to get into anything with that neighbour of hers.'

'The psycho.' Pearson paused. 'Did you know he was a serving police officer, Mr Walsh?'

'Not at the time,' Walsh said, 'but I saw his picture in the paper. He's the one in the car park, right? The one that got burned?'

'Correct, Mr Walsh,' said Pearson. 'Let me see if I've got this right: you have this "bit of a shouting match", her words, then your ex-partner has a heart-to-heart with her next-door neighbour. All of a sudden you stop bothering her. Then, we come round to see you and you look like that.' Pearson nodded at Walsh's face.

'An accident. How many fuckin—'

'Meanwhile your ex's "psycho" next-door neighbour turns up dead.'

Walsh's gaze slid away from Pearson, along the hall, and stopped on a toolbox behind the front door. On top of which sat a lump hammer with a wooden handle, something on the metal head. Something that had dried. Something that shouldn't, by rights, be there. Something reddish in colour. Cat noticed the subtle change in Pearson's posture, the sudden additional wariness, and she let the straps of her handbag slide through her fingers until it rested on the floor. Just in case.

'I use it for work,' Walsh said. Pushing past him, Walsh opened the toolbox and put the hammer inside. He shut the lid and stood up.

Pearson said, 'I think you need to come with us, Mr Walsh.'

Walsh shook his head. 'You're not seriously saying I've got anything to do with that copper's death?' He looked from Pearson to Cat. 'What? Because of ...' He gestured at the toolbox. 'You've got to be fucking joking, right?' When neither of them said anything, he asked again, 'Because of that?' He banged the side of his fist on the wall, 'I don't fucking believe it! This is all down to her. That fucking bitch ...'

Fair enough, Cat thought, Walsh already had a busted-up face. And he was wearing just a dressing gown and slippers. But it didn't mean he wouldn't do something stupid. For a few seconds no one moved. Finally, Walsh relaxed.

'All right, all right.' He held up his hands. 'I'm not going to cause any trouble.' He sighed. 'I suppose I've got time to put my trousers on, have I?'

44

When they re-entered the incident room, Pearson's desk was occupied.

Flustered, Neil Ferguson looked up. 'I hope you don't mind,' he said. 'There was nowhere else to sit.'

Pearson looked around the crowded room. He was right, there *was* nowhere else to sit. But all the same, he did mind. Instinctively Ferguson reached out and pulled the briefcase on top of the desk an inch or two closer to him. Momentarily putting Pearson in mind of a seventies B-movie: on an internal Trans American flight, the would-be blackmailer, a nondescript lab technician in round steel-rimmed spectacles, sweat dappling his top lip, clutches the metal briefcase containing the deadly stolen pathogen to his chest . . .

'Is that the CCTV footage I requested? From outside Raymond Walsh's flat last Wednesday?' Pearson asked, bending forward to take a closer look. Still not quite sure why he was the one having to stand.

Last Wednesday. Cat remembered that night. Cleaning the

flat. Going for a run. Taking a shower. Settling down in front of the telly with a glass or two of Chardonnay. All the while trying repeatedly to contact Sean on his mobile and having no luck. Wondering what the fuck he was up to. Well, it seemed now she might be about to find out.

Exterior view of a square. Seen from a high angle looking down. Shot in black and white. The image slightly grainy. An Audi A8 clearly visible among a row of parked cars. The early-evening light reflected from the windscreen, making it impossible to see who was inside.

'Same make and model driven by DI Carragher,' Pearson said, tapping the image of the car on the screen. 'Pity we can't make out the colour or index plate. Any idea how long it's been there?'

'By this time,' Ferguson said, 'the car's already been stationary for seventy-seven minutes.'

'How much more is there?' asked Pearson.

'I haven't seen it yet.'

'Why don't you run it on a bit?' The cursor hovered over the digits in the left-hand corner of the screen. The knuckles of Ferguson's right index and middle fingers blanching as he depressed the right mouse button. The time ticking rapidly through, first the seconds, then the minutes. The image on the screen remained static. A subtle variation in light the only clue to the passing of time. The whiteness faded from Ferguson's knuckles and the digits on the time counter slowed again.

19:04. The driver's door of the Audi opened. A man got out. White T-shirt. Blue jeans. A pair of sunglasses removed, placed on top of the dashboard. The driver's door slammed shut. A look left and right up the street. A roll of the shoulders. The man walked off, disappearing out of shot at the bottom of the screen.

'Can you run that back?' Pearson asked. Ferguson clicked

the mouse and the man reappeared at the bottom of the screen. Walked backwards. The roll of the shoulders. The look right and left along the street. The driver's-side door sprang open and went to his hand as if magnetised.

'Stop,' Pearson said. The image froze and he nodded. 'Yep. That's Carragher. Do we have the view from the other side of the square?'

Ferguson typed something and the screen split in two.

19:04. Cat felt a transitory dislocation as the two figures, the two Seans, emerged at the same time from the car. The Sean on the top half of the screen with his back to the camera. The Sean on the bottom half of the screen seen from the front. The removal of the sunglasses. The placing of them on the dashboard. The slamming of the car door. The look left and right up the street. The roll of the shoulders. The two Seans walked off, the top Sean away from the camera, the bottom Sean towards it. Cat experienced an instant of unreality. A passing light-headedness allied with an anticipatory queasiness, an absurd feeling that the two Seans might collide, or become momentarily superimposed before merging together . . .

The view changed to a full-screen image of Sean walking away from the camera. He stopped outside a house, knocking insistently, leaning on the doorbell. After a few seconds the door opened and Sean pushed through, his head jerking forward, his momentum carrying him inside. The door shut behind him.

The exterior view of Ray Walsh's house. The half-glazed front door with stained-glass insets. The bay window with wooden slatted blinds. The dwarf conifer in a pot in the front drive. The oil stain on the gravel. In the left-hand bottom corner, the seconds ticked slowly by. The view of the front of Walsh's place unchanging. The half-glazed front door with stained-glass insets. The bay window with wooden slatted blinds. The dwarf conifer in a pot in the front drive. The oil stain on the gravel . . .

Five billion years ago, Pearson thought, a star was formed. In the darkness and coldness of space, clouds of gas and dust condensed. Grew hotter as their mass increased. Hydrogen nuclei fused together to become atoms of helium. The released energy heated the core of the proto-star. The rotation of this stellar object produced a protoplanetary disc. Within this disc material clumped together through the process of accretion to become a planet. On this planet an atmosphere developed. Lower forms of life appeared. These unicellular organisms evolved into more complex structures. These more complex arrangements of molecules eventually became higher forms of intelligent life. And these higher forms of intelligent life on that planet now stood around wasting their fucking time in front of a computer monitor waiting for a door to open.

'D'you mind if I sit down?' he asked. 'My knees are killing me.' His knees cracked in confirmation as he straightened up. He and Ferguson exchanged places. When he had sat down Pearson asked, 'Can you run it forward a bit?' Ferguson leaned across and clicked the mouse.

19:11. Cat watched the door open and Sean emerge, pulling the door closed behind him.

'In the house about six minutes,' Pearson noted. Sean strode across the square. About ten yards from the Audi the sun broke through the clouds and for a few seconds Sean was caught in bright sunlight.

'What's that on his shirt?' Pearson asked, squinting at the screen.

Ferguson leaned forward. Stared at the screen. Shook his head.

'Can you stop it?' Pearson asked. Ferguson clicked the mouse and froze the image. 'Blood maybe?' Ferguson ventured reluctantly.

'Could be,' Pearson agreed, 'it's the same shade as the car,' tapping the image of the Audi again. He swivelled in the chair to face them, said to Ferguson, 'According to the statement you took from Clive Townsend, he claims he was assaulted by Carragher last Wednesday. At around seven in the evening, right?'

'Correct.'

'So, obviously he was lying.' Pearson flipped a thumb at the screen behind him. 'Because at seven o'clock last Wednesday, Carragher was busy beating the shit out of Ray Walsh.'

He looked across at Cat and gave her what he obviously thought was a meaningful look. Well, perhaps this did get her off the hook. To a certain extent. She couldn't be tied to this. This was something else, something personal. But staring at the frozen image of Sean on the screen, his shirt splattered with what was undoubtedly Ray Walsh's blood, somehow it didn't make her feel any better.

45

'Someone burned to death here.'

The creature, something bovine, some or other breed of cattle – but half human at the same time, a Minotaur maybe – scratched ruminatively at a large flap of jowl with a hoof and nodded out through the car's windscreen into the car park. Donna struck a match, the flame reflecting in the Minotaur's red eye. The smell of something acerbic, some accelerant, briefly stung her nostrils. She watched the red-headed figure twist and writhe in the match's flame. Watched as it blackened and turn to ash. Tinnitus a high-pitched screaming in her ear. The wail of a siren. A ululating, insistent car alarm. She lit her cigarette, shook out the match and flicked the shrivelled corpse of the matchstick away through the open side window.

'Deliberately set alight as he sat in his car,' the creature said. Donna could smell his last meal – meat, fat, gristle on his hot, sour breath. She put a foot up on the seat but, as it followed the movement, immediately put it down again. Donna looked away. Took a drag on her cigarette, looking down at the rubbish in the footwell. Takeaway burger containers. Screwed-up paper wrappers. A crushed Styrofoam cup. A tray containing pieces of wrinkled and whiskery chicken skins and the remnants of gnawed bones.

'A copper, I heard,' it said. 'I think we might be parked in the exact place it happened. Don't you think that's pretty cool?'

The car was alight. Sean sitting behind the wheel. His hair on fire. His body writhing in agony. The sound of high-pitched screaming. The smell of burning flesh . . .

After a minute, studying the glowing tip of her cigarette, lost in her own thoughts, she realised that the thing, the creature, the Minotaur or whatever it was, was looking at her.

'You're not squeamish – are you, Donna? This isn't going to work if you're squeamish.'

'Nah, I'm just,' she shrugged, 'a bit nervous, I suppose.'

It laughed to itself. 'Of me?'

She shrugged a reply, slipped her hand into the pocket of her leather jacket. Brushed her fingers along the handle of the knife, the metal scabbard, comforted by its weight, its presence. She took another drag on the cigarette. The Minotaur's huge wet nostrils twitched as she exhaled a cloud of blue smoke through which she saw two figures. Slightly indistinct. A blurring at the edges, an overlay of two images. Then the two images merged with an almost audible click and the Minotaur retreated.

'You're not exactly what I was expecting,' said Clive Townsend.

'Why? What were you expecting? Someone a bit more like Sez?'

274

Neither was he quite what she had been expecting. His appearance had changed since the Abigail Burnett. He had grown one of those stupid goatee beards and he wore black-rimmed glasses. Though Donna wasn't sure he actually needed them. She had seen him wear steel-rimmed spectacles when he worked at the home, but she had always suspected that the lenses might be plain glass. And he didn't wear them all the time. Maybe he wore contacts. He had shaved his head, too. It was completely bald. He ran his hand over it now and conceded, 'I suppose so.'

Looking her up and down, he said, 'Your hair's a bit short. Do you always wear it like that?'

Donna looked away, gave a slight shrug, took a drag of her cigarette and pitched it out of the window. He reached across and grabbed her chin, turning her head from one side to the other. He studied her face for a moment.

'How old are you?'

'Sixteen.'

He let his hand drop, his knuckles grazing her right breast. 'You look younger,' he said appreciatively. 'You could maybe pass for twelve. And with that short hair, no make-up ... you've got a bit of a boy thing going on.'

Once again she found herself the subject of his appraisal, livestock being assayed for value. Merchandise mentally matched to a list of potential buyers.

'Are you clean?'

'Clean? What d'you mean? I wash, yeah, course.'

Townsend laughed. Out loud this time. He ran his hand over his bald head again and said, 'Kneel up on the seat and face into the back of the car.' Donna hesitated. 'I thought you wanted to do this,' Townsend said. 'Sez told me you were up for anything.'

Donna's fingers closed around the handle of the knife,

squeezed it quickly. Then she took her hand out of her pocket, knelt up on the seat and faced the rear windscreen. Trying not to think. Behind her she heard the sound of him repositioning himself in his seat, felt the suspension shift slightly. She waited for his hands to move inside her skirt, yank down her knickers. She stiffened. Anticipating his touch. Trying to steel herself not to cry out. She felt his hot, meaty breath on the back of her thighs. Felt her body begin to tremble. Trying not to think. Trying not to wet herself. Trying not to cry. She gritted her teeth, blinked back the tears. Trying not to think, but thinking all the same: You dirty bastard, you dirty bastard, you dirty bastard . . .

She felt his hand on her left ankle. He pulled her leg out straight and she felt him run his fingertips across the skin behind her knee, up the back of her leg, down her calf. He did the same for her right leg. The sound of movement behind her. Again the slight shift of the car's suspension. He said, 'OK, you can sit round.' When she sat back down he said, 'Lift your T-shirt up and pull the waistband of your skirt down.'

She looked at him, determined not to be afraid. Biting her bottom lip, she did what he said. Pulling the T-shirt up, exposing her small breasts. For a moment the red eyes were back, the smell of animal arousal. Wet nostrils scented the air. The sound of muffled, confused conversations that may have come from somewhere beyond the open window. But when she looked out there were no passers-by, the parking area was empty. But as the creature leaned down, his hot breath on her belly, his fingers combing the edge of her pubic hair, the noise grew louder. The horns were yellowed, gouged and scratched. At the base of each there was some kind of growth, a moss, or a fungus. The top of his head was furrowed. The hide, worn in patches, a greasy, threadbare suede. An overpowering scent of animal musk filled the interior of the car. Now, she thought, was the time to do what she had come for. She slipped a hand into her pocket again, fingering the knife. As her hand closed around the handle she imagined plunging it into the beast's exposed neck. Drawing it through the veins and muscles there. Feeling the hot blood run across her fingers, over her hand . . .

Looking down, though, she became aware of how frightened, how truly terrified she was. The neck looked far too broad, far too powerful for her to puncture with the feeble blade she clung to in her pocket. The voices, up to now a background hiss of several poorly tuned radios, became a racket of competing, insistent opinions, all clamouring at once for her attention, and she froze, unable to move. Abruptly he sat up. As if a radio had unexpectedly been switched off, the voices were gone.

'OK, pull your T-shirt down and take off your socks and boots.' Suddenly she felt weak, all strength, all resistance sucked out of her, and she recognised that the opportunity had gone. Taking her hand out of her jacket pocket, she did what she was told. Again she felt his fingers move over her skin as he leaned down and examined each of her feet in turn. Her hand moved towards the pocket, the knife. But the movement was unconvincing, even to her, the muscles in her arm weak and shaky, as if exhausted by the repeated lifting of some far too heavy weight. Townsend sat up again. 'OK you can put them back on.'

Donna barely had the strength to pull her socks back on. She just wanted to leave now. Just wanted this to be over.

'Take your jacket off.'

'I don't do needles,' she said.

'Take your jacket off,' he said again.

Donna struggled in the confines of the car to shrug off the leather jacket. Townsend took her right wrist, turned her arm over, ran his fingertips into the crook of her elbow, studying it. Then he did the same with her left.

'OK,' he said, finally satisfied. 'Do you smoke?' Before she could say anything, anything stupid, he said, 'Not fags. Anything else?'

'Weed. When I can afford it.'

'Nothing else? Meth? Crack?'

Donna shook her head. 'No.'

'And you're a virgin, right?'

Donna nodded.

'So you've got no STIs?'

'No.'

'Ever had any?'

'No.'

'All right. Because the sort of people I'll be introducing you to ... well, let's just say it wouldn't be in my interest to upset them.' He ran his hand along her leg, a little too far along her leg, left it there a little too long. When she looked at him he was smiling, enjoying her discomfort. Then he gave her leg a little pat and took his hand away. 'Don't worry. We're going to make a lot of money, you and me.'

Donna didn't say anything, just hung her head, unable to meet his gaze.

'Sez will give you a ring when I've sorted things out.' After a minute he said, 'Well, what are you waiting for? You can go now.'

On the street, watching the tail-lights of the car disappear into the night, she started to cry. Fucking crying again. It's all you ever do, is cry, she thought. You are fucking useless. All this time. All this effort. And when it came to it what did you do? Absolutely fucking nothing, that's what.

46

MONDAY

No offer of mints today, Pearson noticed, extra-strong or other-wise. No chance of sitting down either, the three plastic visitors' chairs in Roberts' office having been taken by Curtis, Ferguson and Russell. Forced to stand again, leaning against the wall by the door, arms folded across his chest. He was feeling a little more comfortable at least. No urgent need for the bathroom. At the moment. Just the ache in his knees making him shift his weight occasionally from foot to foot. Cat Russell had adopted a studiedly neutral expression, hands folded in her lap. Ferguson, head down as usual, was fingering the leather of his briefcase. Curtis was talking, had been talking for the best part of the last ten minutes. Roberts, tired and irritable, more irritable than usual, was rubbing at the corner of his right eye, looking like he was rapidly losing patience.

'It's been three days, Martin,' Curtis was saying. 'Please tell me you've got something I can give to the media? Something beyond the usual "pursuing a number of lines of enquiry". I'm the public face of this investigation, Martin, the one who has to stand up in front of the cameras and explain our perceived lack of progress.'

Despite his best, or worst, intentions – it depended after all on your particular point of view – Pearson found himself having some sympathy for Curtis. Although Curtis had been only too eager to put himself forward, and undoubtedly saw a successful outcome in terms of any personal benefit that could be gained, at the moment Pearson didn't envy him. After the initial from-the-scene reporting – glimpses of police activity; the comings and goings of SOCOs, shot from behind the cordon; film taken from a hovering helicopter; pieces to camera from their crime correspondents taking a gratuitous delight in the more graphic details of the death; speculation substituted for the absence of hard facts; statistics quoted to provide a scientific gravitas – the initial good will of the media had, as always, started to be eroded by the sense of a lack of progress, a perceived scarcity of any hard information, the suspicion that the force was holding out on them in some way, and the mood of the reporting had subtly changed. There was now an insinuation of failure, the hint of police incompetence. The twenty-four-hour news channels would soon start rolling out their own string of so-called experts. A lecturer in criminology from this or that university. An author plugging a book on another case that bore some vague similarities. Someone who was ex-Job, someone introduced as having 'worked in the Metropolitan Police for over thirty years', who would give his opinion on how the investigation was being carried out. Its shortcomings. How, in his opinion, it should be carried out. Some arsehole who didn't have the first idea how to run a large-scale inquiry. Someone like Dougie Ettrick. Most worrying of all, they might choose to pursue the human-interest angle. A detailed consideration of the background of the victim. The last thing anyone wanted.

'I understand there was an arrest yesterday in connection with the case,' Curtis asked.

'An arrest,' said Roberts, 'but we're not even close to charging him as yet.'

'A weapon was taken away?' Curtis asked. 'Is that right? A hammer?'

Pearson wondered where he had got his information from. Because, judging by the look on the DCI's face, it wasn't from Roberts.

'A search of the house,' Curtis went on, 'found that the suspect, Raymond Walsh, was registered as a director of a number of different companies, all providing decorating services? I understand that one or more of these has been flagged previously in connection with a string of suspected arson cases.'

'Suspected, yes,' said Roberts. 'A series of fires that we considered could be arson. Carragher looked into them, but was unable to find a connection. Or any real evidence that they were started deliberately.

'A lump hammer,' he continued, searching through the papers on the desk, 'was recovered from Walsh's address and sent to Forensics for examination,' picking up an A4 sheet, 'A "dry, reddish-brown material" was observed on the face of the head of the hammer. Tests, however, were unable to identify any trace of blood, residual DNA or human tissue not belonging to Raymond Walsh on any part of the hammer.' He passed the paper across to Curtis. 'What they did find,' looking pointedly at Pearson, the tone of voice suggesting that Pearson had gone out of his way solely to waste his valuable time, 'was brick-dust, plaster, glue, paint. The usual kind of shit you'd expect from his job.'

'So without this,' Curtis flapped the sheet of paper before

passing it back to Roberts, 'what sort of case can we make for Walsh being responsible for DI Carragher's death?'

'Circumstantial, at best. Walsh is in a dispute with Carragher's neighbour over visitation rights to their son. The neighbour, Lorna Jeffries, has made two previous complaints against Walsh for harassment. Trespass, overturning garden furniture, setting a fire in one of the bins ...'

Pearson moved from one foot to the other.

'Yes?' Roberts asked. 'You got something to add?'

'Sir. There's no proof that Walsh was in her garden,' Pearson said. 'According to the officers attending. Plus, she didn't actually make specific allegations against Walsh. In fact, she went out of her way to say she thought it might not be him.'

'Are you saying he might not have done any of it?' Ferguson asked.

Pearson shrugged. 'She posted stuff on Facebook to make it seem that way. She had a row with Walsh on her doorstep. They both admit to that. On the other hand, Walsh claims she'd told all their friends that they'd split up on account of him being over-possessive because he'd lost his daughter.' He looked to Russell. 'She told us the same thing, right?'

Russell nodded to Roberts. 'Guv.'

'There's no record of a daughter,' Pearson said. 'So if she can make up something like that, maybe the whole thing's a fabrication. The harassment, the fire, even the scene on the doorstep could have been engineered. She sees Carragher pull up and creates a drama for his benefit. OK, she claims she asked Carragher not to make it official. Even if she did, maybe she knew him a bit better than she's letting on and she gambled on him going round and giving Walsh a pasting.'

'If she suspected Walsh *was* involved with these arson cases in

282

some way, the fire in the dustbin and the posting on Facebook would be a good way to flag it up for us.'

'Or,' Pearson said, 'a warning to him that she knew, and to lay off.'

After a minute or so during which no one else spoke, Curtis said, 'In the meantime, Raymond Walsh has a very strong case if he wants to bring a lawsuit against us.'

'Which kind of makes you wonder,' said Ferguson, 'why he hasn't already.'

'So,' said Roberts, turning to Curtis, 'what do you suggest, sir?'

'Bail him. For the time being. And in the meantime we need to do some digging into these arson cases. Just in case he decides to sue us for assault.'

Pearson sighed. 'Well, there goes our main line of enquiry. So where does that leave us?'

Roberts, who had been looking for some time for something to keep his hands busy, finally settled on a biro. He rolled it under his fingertips across the desktop. 'All suggestions welcomed.'

'Clive Townsend,' Pearson said. 'Why haven't we brought him in yet?' When no one answered, Roberts looked at Curtis.

'Up until last night,' Curtis said, 'as far as we were aware, he'd simply made an allegation of physical assault against DI Carragher. So it was thought a little politically sensitive to have him brought in for questioning.'

'But we know now,' said Pearson, 'from the CCTV outside Raymond Walsh's flat, that DI Carragher couldn't have committed the assault on Clive Townsend. Losing your job. The subject of sustained harassment, a physical assault. It could all add up to a motive for murder.'

'Except,' Curtis pointed out, 'he wasn't assaulted.'

'OK,' said Pearson, 'so he's made a false allegation. Against an officer who is later found dead. That's suspect in itself.'

Curtis thought for a moment. Then he turned to Roberts and nodded. 'Agreed. I think we've got enough.'

'There's a slight problem,' said Ferguson. 'Mr Townsend hasn't been seen at the address he gave on his statement for nearly a week.'

Roberts stared at Ferguson as if he held him personally to blame. Then, shaking his head, he dropped the pen on to the desk, put his hands on his head and shut his eyes. Pearson caught Cat's eye. The prospect of a very long, very tedious day in the incident room lay ahead. The sighing. The muttering under the breath. The tapping of fingernails on the desktop. And that was just her. Answering calls. Logging them on the system. Lawrence's bald patch as he turned away from the room to take another personal call. Gilbert strumming his bottom lip and staring indecisively at his screen. Chasing up calls already logged. The most interesting already prioritised and allocated. So they would be left now with only the most unpromising, the most unlikely, and long hours of frustration, inertia. Eye strain. Arseache.

He cleared his throat. 'Any news on the girl? The DNA on the cigarette at the murder scene?'

'Donna Freeman?' Roberts supplied without opening his eyes. 'No. As yet no trace of her either.'

47

Malcolm knocked softly on his bedroom door and listened. There was no answer. He'd knock once more and then go in. That way he'd been polite and given Donna the opportunity to wake up. That way it wouldn't be his fault if she'd kicked the covers off again. It wouldn't be his fault if the big T-shirt she wore for bed had ridden up around her waist like it usually did during the night. It wouldn't be his fault if he saw her underwear. Maybe last night, he thought, she hadn't bothered to put any on. After the thing at the car park, when she had slept, he had put his hand up her T-shirt. Even managed to get a feel of her tits. Then he had put his hand on her knickers. Just the outside. Since then he hadn't thought about anything else. Had made himself not think about anything else. Not about the car park. Not about anything. He hadn't tried it on again. He'd been too scared. Even while he had put his hand up Donna's T-shirt and especially when he had put his hand on the outside of her knickers he had been terrified that she would wake up and catch him at it.

Malcolm knocked softly again, and when there was no answer

he turned the handle and went in. The bed was empty. Just a mess of covers. She must have sneaked out early this morning without him hearing as he slept on the settee. He might have guessed she'd do something like that. There was something she wasn't telling him, something she was holding back, keeping secrets. You couldn't really trust her, he'd known that even before the car park. Before he'd seen her exposing herself to that bloke, taking money off him. It probably wasn't the first time she'd met him in that car park, she probably had sex there with him all the time. That motorcycle jacket she wore all the time wasn't new, it had scuff marks all down one side and it was miles too big for her. She'd probably got that from him. That was probably where she'd been last night. Not with him, of course, some other bloke she was having sex with for money. Coming back late, after his nan had gone to bed and he had fallen asleep on the settee. Tapping on the window to be let in, upset, crying. She cried a lot, cried all the time for no reason. There was something wrong with her, he'd known that since the day he'd met her in the café.

But last night she had been worse than usual, totally off her head, like she'd taken something. Terrified. As if something really bad had happened. But Malcolm couldn't get any sense out of her, couldn't find out what had happened, whether she'd been beaten up or raped or anything. She just kept on talking really fast and saying a lot of stuff that didn't make any sense. And crying. All the time he'd worried that she was making too much noise and would wake his nan, so he'd managed to persuade her to go into the bedroom and had shut the door behind them. By this time she was nearly hysterical and when he held her because he didn't know what else to do, talking quietly to her, stroking her hair, she was shaking so much her teeth were chattering. Finally he'd calmed her down and helped her into the T-shirt she wore for bed and stayed with her until she'd fallen asleep. He hadn't tried to touch her or anything, not even to put his hand inside her T-shirt, just gone back to the settee and lain there for a long while not able to sleep. Wishing then that he had had a feel of her tits again, or maybe even put his hand inside her knickers this time, but by then it was too late and somehow he must have fallen asleep and she'd crept out again. Malcolm sat down on the bed. Donna was going to do something stupid. He didn't know exactly what. But something stupid. Something *else* stupid. Something even more stupid. She'd kept on about doing something about Alicia since the day they had met in the café but he had managed, up to now, to stop her. Now she was going to do something stupid, something that would ruin everything.

He thought back to the previous night. Tried to think about what Donna had said. Mostly it had been crap. The sort of mad stuff that people always said when they'd had too much to drink or taken something. But maybe there was something in what she had said that would give him a clue to where she had gone.

48

Déjà vu all over again, Terry Milton thought. Sitting in his office at the club, staring at the closed door, nursing a glass of Scotch. Thinking back on all the minor evasions, the half-truths, the outright lies. Looking down at his glass now, Milton ran his finger around the rim.

'Truth is, Frank, I wasn't insured. Had my public liability, all that. All the stuff I needed to run the club. But the rest?'

Truth is. Funny how you reached for that phrase. Or something similar. 'Truth is ...' 'Trust me.' 'To be honest ...' How they came automatically to your lips just before you were about to tell a lie. Like a big fucking flashing neon warning sign. He had held his hands up then in apparent surrender. 'What can I say? I forgot to do it. I fucked up. Like you've always said, Frank. I'm a fuck-up.'

Pearson didn't dispute this. But he knew he wouldn't. He knew exactly what Pearson thought of him. It was there, on his face. It was always on his fucking face. 'Always have been. Always will be, probably.' He picked up his glass. Drained it. Put it back on the desk. 'What's the matter, Frank? Really, you should be pleased. You've been proved right after all.'

Not the complete truth, Milton had thought after Pearson had left and he'd sat alone in his office, staring at the closed door. When Ray Walsh had approached him about torching the club again – putting in an inflated estimate (three inflated estimates from his three different companies so it would look as if Milton had made the effort to find the best price), offering to split the profits – it had seemed a good idea. Maybe they were pushing their luck a bit, setting fire to the club for a second time so soon after the first. But they had got away with it once. Besides, his options had run out. It was either that or lose the club. Or . . . there was a second alternative. Except even the thought of doing that again had made him feel sick.

He had sat in his office that night too. After a while. After too fucking long. After he had realised that the night wasn't going to be quite as much fun as he had initially thought it would. He had stayed behind the bar at first. To look after the place, he told himself. Even though they had provided, had insisted on, their own bar and waiting staff. He had wanted to make sure it all ran smoothly. That's all. That was what he told himself. But really as much as anything he wanted to see what was going on. Join in the fun. At first it had seemed just that, just a bit of fun. So, maybe some of the girls had looked a little young. Hard to tell with the lights down low like that. But who knew? It was difficult to know these days anyway. And the older you got, the trickier it got. During the night, the music ratcheted up, the lights lower still, the club gradually filling up, he began to notice that the girls, boys too by this time, were beginning to look younger. Way too young. No way to pretend any of these were anything but underage.

Drunk. Stoned. Looking scared and confused. The punters, too, had changed. Louder. More raucous. The atmosphere suddenly uglier, threatening. Later still, kids stumbling round dazed, barely clothed. A naked girl, scarcely a teenager, at one of the tables on the lap of some much older man. In one of the darker recesses of the club, a group of older punters gathered around a kneeling figure ...

At some point in the night, before he had grabbed a bottle of Scotch from behind the bar and retreated to the sanctuary of his office, too late, too fucking late, a buzz of excited anticipation had swept the room. A swell in the crowd as someone new entered the club.

'Sissy's here!' he heard someone say. Shouted greetings. Scattered applause. Then Milton had seen her. Blue dress. Little white apron. Bad blonde wig. False lashes. Scarlet lipstick. An obscene Alice in Wonderland downing in one the offered drinks. Some too-old drag queen who, long since, should have packed it in. Lapping up all the attention. Clambering awkwardly onto a table in too-high heels. Wolf whistles. Coarse catcalling. A licentious thrusting of his pelvis. 'Go on, Sissy love,' someone yelled, 'show us your cock!'

The skirt lifted to expose the nakedness underneath. Wild applause. Then, high-kicking, losing his balance on some spilled drink on the table's surface, stumbling momentarily, the wig had slipped to one side. And Milton had recognised the person underneath. Or rather, later he had seen the same face on the television news and in the papers. Defending the staff at the children's home. Justifying his own position as director. And been able to put a name to it. Afterwards the same man would be found hanging from the scaffolding outside his club. Sickert Downey.

49

The automatic doors opened and Donna stepped into the café area. A franchise of a nationwide chain, each outlet so unvarying, so nearly identical that she could have stepped into any one of a thousand on any high street in the country. Except for the dead air. The solid mass of stale heat. The line of sick and old people. The misbuttoned pyjamas, the precariously gaping nightdresses. The ratty dressing gowns. The crumpled tissues clutched in tremulous hands. The underlying smell of human waste that a layer of antiseptic could not mask. The light levels shifted ...

Time-lapse footage: the shadows of clouds moving across the tops of rolling hills.

Donna found that she had moved forward in time; though by seconds or by minutes she wasn't sure. She had moved in space, joined the end of the shuffling, disorderly queue for the hospital shop. The nearly deceased and the soon to be departed waiting to buy tabloid newspapers, celebrity gossip mags, puzzle books, bags of jelly babies. Donna's hand went to her head and she ran her fingers through the bristles on the top. Malcolm had managed to find a mains charger from somewhere that fitted her clippers and had offered to tidy up her hair. Just clippered it really, the top a little bit longer than the sides. It had been sweet of him. Even though when he had finished he had looked at her and said in a sulky, disapproving way, 'You look like a boy.'

'With that short hair,' Townsend had said appreciatively, 'no make-up . . . you've got a bit of a boy thing going on.'

The way he looked at her made her skin crawl. As if something slimy was slithering over her. She could almost see the silvery, glittering slug-trail that his eyes had left. When he smiled it reminded her of Sez, when she had met her in the playground. Not a nice smile. There was something nasty in it. Something cruel. She wondered if Sez had deliberately mimicked the expression, spending hours in front of a mirror in order to achieve just the right set of her features. He ran his hand over his bald head again and said, 'Kneel up on the seat and face into the back of the car.'

Kneeling on the seat, looking out of the back windscreen. She could see the lights of passing cars on the main road. The yellow streetlamps. The light pollution in the night sky above the pub opposite. She realised later that even if someone had come along and seen her like that they would probably just think they were a couple of pervs, that they were putting on some kind of show. It might have drawn a crowd. Trying not to think about what was happening, staring into the footwell behind the driver's seat: trodden-in crisps, an empty plastic bottle of lemonade. Some loose change. The back seat. Trying not to cry. What looked like some sort of nylon overalls. A Nike trainer. Balled-up black socks. A pair of crumpled jeans. An empty, broken CD case. Trying not to think about the thing behind her. But in the middle of the back seat Clive Townsend's face stared unblinkingly back at her from behind the laminated plastic of an NHS security pass.

She told herself now that, even as she had stood on the street and watched the tail-lights of the car disappear into the night, even as she had felt her frustration, her uselessness, even as she cried in anger and shame, she had started to form the idea.

Donna got a can of Diet Coke and, as an afterthought, picked up some celebrity gossip magazine or other. You couldn't really sit at a table and do nothing. Or, worse, stare at the other people. Not for long. That sort of thing drew attention. It wouldn't be long before the counter staff would start wondering what you were doing there. And not much longer than that before they were getting Security to move you on. Better to keep your head down and pretend you were just killing time. Pretend you were waiting for someone who had an appointment somewhere in the hospital. Better still to look at your watch every now and then, or check your phone to make it look like you were waiting on a call or a text. Maybe he wouldn't come through here. Maybe she was wrong. But it was the best idea she had. She'd sit at a table where she could see the entrance to the lifts and staircase. Among the nearly dead, the soon to be dead and, by the looks of it, the recently dead. Even if they hadn't quite realised it yet. On the way from the counter several of the newly passed passed her. Trailing in their wake the odour of need. The whiff of desperation. The hum of anticipation. B & H. Menthol Superkings. Golden Virginia. Amber Leaf. On their way outside to join the cluster of fellow nicotine addicts huddled by the main entrance. Her hand went to her pocket and she fingered her cigarettes and matches. Thought about joining them. What if he didn't come through the main entrance? What if he came a different way and she missed him? She felt the knife in her pocket. She was here now. Had decided on a course of action. Donna put down her Coke and magazine. She couldn't risk it.

She sat down at the table. Ready to kill time among the dead.

50

Terry Milton had sat in his office that night. Unscrewed the lid of the bottle. Poured himself a Scotch. Drained it. Poured himself another. Downing one after another without really tasting anything. Even that was a lie: he'd had a nasty taste in his mouth. And no matter how much he drank it wouldn't go away. At some time in the early hours he had, finally and thankfully, passed out. He had woken the next morning with a banging headache, telling himself that he still had the club. Kept on telling himself. Somehow it wasn't enough. Somehow it didn't matter that he'd cleared his debt and made a few quid on top as well.

The money had gone soon enough. And more too. Spent recklessly. Like he'd wanted it off his hands. Like deep down he wanted to lose the club. Soon enough he was in debt again. So when Ray Walsh had approached him for the second time, it wasn't just the opportunity of clearing his debts that had made it seem like such a good idea. It felt like an opportunity to cleanse the club, to free it from the taint of what he had allowed to happen there. To make another fresh start.

Then, of course, he had cocked up the insurance. Had had to borrow money again from the same people. No option but to agree to their extortionate rates of interest. So now he was back in exactly the same position as before. If he didn't keep up the repayments he was going to lose the club or . . . He felt the weight of the bottle of Scotch in his hand. He considered gripping it by its neck, hurling it at the far wall, seeing it explode into a thousand shards. Watching the amber liquid slide down the oak panelling. Then the moment, the flash of anger, was gone and he thought better of it. What would be the point of that? A waste of a decent Scotch. The office stinking of booze, his fingertips finding unexpected splinters of glass for months afterwards. Instead, he unscrewed the lid. Poured himself another drink. Sipped it slowly, savouring the flavour on his tongue, the warming feeling in his throat as it went down. He placed the glass back on the desktop. Ran his finger around the rim.

He had known it was coming, of course. The 'And now, Terry, your name's come up again . . . ' Had known as soon as Carragher had stopped in the corridor and tapped the half-full containers with his foot, made the little crack about accidents, about the club burning down. So, he didn't have to listen. Not really. Just sit and watch Carragher's lips moving. He knew what Carragher was going to say. Knew where this was going . . .

Except he hadn't. Hadn't known at all. Hadn't had a fucking clue.

'Insurance fraud, Terry?' Carragher had shaken his head. Disappointed. Saddened by this unseemly behaviour. 'Mind you, overclaiming from a multinational whose first reaction, whose company policy, when one of their clients phones with a legitimate claim, is to immediately reject it? Who drag their heels in the hope they can get away without paying out what is rightly due? Some might say that *that's* morally wrong. So where's the harm in putting in an exaggerated estimate for redecoration? How much do they waste on sponsorship, advertising, entertaining and business trips? It just gets passed on to the customer through higher premiums anyway. Am I right? In the end,' he shrugged, 'who cares? Everybody's at it, right? So nobody's really bothered.'

Milton took the bottle out of the drawer again. Unscrewed the lid. Poured himself another drink. Screwed the lid back on the bottle. Put the bottle back in the drawer. Took a sip of his drink. Waiting for Carragher to get around to asking for the money. Waiting to see how much he would ask for. How long he would give him to come up with it. Carragher hadn't spoken for a while. Just stared. The grey eyes unsettling. Bereft of any real colour. Too cold. The eyes of a psychopath.

'But kiddie-fiddling, Terry? That's a different matter.'

Milton froze. The glass halfway to his lips. Swallowed. Swallowed again. Looked at the glass in his hand. Put it back on the desk. There was a disconcerting stillness about Carragher. Stony-faced, his eyes studied Milton's movements.

'As I told you,' Carragher said, 'the original source wasn't the most reliable. The information was a bit sketchy. So maybe I didn't set too much store by it. But then I thought, What the hell, maybe it's worth looking into. Doing a bit of digging. Calling in a few favours. Spending a bit of money. It's amazing what you can find out if you know who to ask. And how much it will cost.'

He had laid it all out then. He knew about the debt Milton couldn't pay back. Knew who had approached him about the 'little favour'. The staging of a minor 'entertainment', just a small 'private party'. Their usual venue had been compromised, the house linked to the investigation of Alicia Goode's death.

So, somewhere a little more secluded, a little more discreet, was needed. He knew the time and date the party had taken place at the club. Even knew who had been there – knew absolutely fucking everything. And then, Milton had realised he was going to be arrested. For insurance fraud. For arson. For involvement in a paedophile ring. He had known then that, despite everything he had done to prevent it, he was going to lose the club. So when Carragher had said, 'Must be an expensive business, doing up a club? Sandblasting the outside, stripping all the old paint, sanding down the wood, repainting. Not to mention the new dance floor, lighting, sound system ... You must've had to borrow quite a bit to do that, right? The interest on that kind of loan must be crippling. So the last thing you would want right now, I'm guessing, would be to lose all your income, right? For the club to be closed for any length of time. So, say, detailed, time-consuming, forensic examinations can take place? I mean, who knows how long that would take?' When Carragher had said that, he had felt relieved. Childishly grateful. To the point of tears. Tears had actually fucking sprung to his eyes. And he had known at that moment, known he had a way out, a way of staying out of jail, a way to keep the club. He had reached into the drawer again. Taken out the bottle. Putting the bottle back in the drawer after every drink was his way of discouraging himself from drinking. Slowing himself down a bit. It didn't, of course, make the slightest difference. He still drank the same. And all that putting the bottle in and taking it out of the drawer did was piss him off. He poured himself a drink. A little celebration. He asked, 'How much?'

When Carragher told him, he had known something else. He had known that he could never pay it. He had known he couldn't find that kind of money. Not in the short time Carragher had given him. He couldn't find that kind of money however long he was given. He had known, even as they arranged a time and place to meet. And even if, by some miracle, he did find the money, could he trust Carragher not to act on the information he had anyway? Or, more importantly, to leave Milton out of it somehow? His eye had strayed to the heavy iron door-stop. Was he willing to do something like that? Was he *capable* of doing something like that? There was another way, of course, there was always another way. A way where he wouldn't have to deal with it directly himself. A way, though, that would leave him even more in the debt of the people he owed money to. Whom he had let use his club. Whom he would probably have to let use his club again. He took out his mobile and laid it on the desk. His eye moving between it and the door-stop. He hadn't known then. Hadn't known what to do for the best. Hadn't known after he had had another drink. Hadn't known as he sat at the bar pretending to read the paper. Still hadn't known when Frank Pearson had turned up and asked to have a word.

51

She was in the hospital café. Sitting next to her at the table. Alicia had on a T-shirt, over which she wore a jacket. Some designer-name thing. Both black, naturally. Donna didn't like the jacket much, too old-fashioned. And not in a retro way. Alicia had had her hair cut. Clippered close to the skull. It didn't suit her. She wondered if Alicia was trying to look like her. Motorcycle Boy was wearing a leather jacket with lots of zips and those sew-on badges. He had contrived to rip it somehow in exactly the same place as her own. Had scuffed the leather of the arm to match the scuffing on her own jacket. He took off his crash helmet and put it on the table. Running his fingers over the dents and scratches on its surface. Pale and shaky, he put his hand to his forehead and slowly closed his eyes as if the light from the overhead fluorescents was too harsh. The policeman, Sean, was wearing a soot-stained white T-shirt. Wisps of smoke rose from his body and his hair smouldered. But his flat, grey eyes registered neither pain or surprise. Donna noticed the light level shift again. Dipping then brightening. Looking up, she became aware of the slow, stroboscopic cycling of the fluorescent tubes. A persistent, irritating hum. A fat bluebottle hanging suspended in the air, its wings moving in ultra-slow motion. Alicia was trying to gain her attention.

Donna turned to her. 'What?'

'Tell me again what we're doing here?' Alicia asked.

'You know why I'm here.'

Alicia shook her head. 'It doesn't matter.'

'You keep saying that. It matters to me, Alicia. I've got to do this.'

'It doesn't matter.'

'It does matter. If it hadn't happened ... things might have been different.'

'Everyone has arguments, hun. It's just one of those things. And even if we hadn't had a row, there's no saying things wouldn't have turned out exactly the same.'

'If we hadn't had a row,' Donna said, 'you might not have gone to that house, to that party. Or I might have gone with you. I might have been with you and I might have been able to stop it happening.'

Alicia looked away. 'Maybe,' she mumbled.

'Instead, the last thing I said to you was ...' She shook her head. 'I can't remember what it was. Something horrible though. That's the worst of it, I can't even remember what the fucking row was about.' Donna realised she was crying. Fucking crying again. She swiped away the tears with the arm of her leather jacket.

Alicia looked back at her. 'It doesn't matter, hun. Really. It doesn't.' Alicia was about to reach out and put her hand on Donna's arm when Donna suddenly stood up. She had seen him. Moving across the lobby. Towards the lifts.

*

Pearson jabbed the call button again and stared up at the illuminated numbers above the lift. They hadn't changed now for at least five or six minutes. He felt an almost overwhelming lethargy, a stiffness in his joints, the beginnings of a migraine ticking behind his left eye, arseache from sitting at his desk all day. He checked his watch. Half an hour of visiting time left. Half an hour of struggling to think of things to say. Half an hour of stilted conversation. Half an hour of sitting in that overly hot ward. Somewhere in his progress from the main entrance through the hospital's café area to the lift lobby, his attention had been snagged by something. Something he couldn't quite put his finger on. An itch somewhere you couldn't quite reach, between the shoulderblades, maybe. The mental equivalent of catching a sleeve on a barbed-wire fence. You had to stop and deal with it or you couldn't move on. A detail his subconscious had registered in passing but was only now making his conscious mind aware of. The café, he decided. In-patients in pyjamas and dressing gowns queuing at the counter. A teenage mum sitting at a table, wiping the nose of a toddler in a pushchair. An elderly couple in matching anoraks, the woman struggling to open a vacuum-packed sandwich. A man busily tapping on his iPhone. A porter with tattooed forearms sipping from a coffee and marking up horses in a newspaper. And, hunched over a magazine, someone in a leather biker's jacket and hoodie. A girl, he was certain, even though the hair was no more than a dark stubble. There was something vaguely familiar about her. He had seen that leather jacket, that hoodie, in the last couple of days. Something familiar, too, about the girl. Her size? Her shape? But so what? Lots of kids wore hoodies. Lots of kids wore leather jackets.

The tree hugger. But if it was her, if she was the girl they had seen on the seafront hugging the palm tree – so what? Her frailty, her lack of hair, the circles under her eyes, the general air of exhaustion, the fact that she was in the hospital, suggested that she might be undergoing chemo or radiotherapy. The lift arrived and the doors opened. Having placed her, having scratched the itch and unsnagged the barbed wire, he stepped into the lift. And felt someone step in behind him. He turned to face the other occupant. Pearson experienced another brief failure of recall. Then recognition dawned.

'Evening. Colin, isn't it?'

Colin had his head on upside-down. A shaved skull. A clipped goatee beard. A diamond stud in one ear. The only thing that gave his face some kind of orientation was the black-rimmed glasses. Colin, who had brought his mum back from her physiotherapy. Even then there had been something about Colin that Pearson didn't like. Something that just hadn't quite rung true. Something fake. And his eyes were brown, he noticed, and not, as his mother had insisted, blue.

'Clive,' the other man corrected.

'Clive? Really? My mum always calls you Colin.'

'Yeah,' he said coldly. 'Well, she got it wrong.'

Donna watched Clive Townsend disappear into the lift, the doors close behind him. Watched as the numbers above the lift lit up and the lift ascended. The light stopped on *4* for a few minutes and then started down again. As the doors opened on the empty lift Donna turned away and took the stairs. Not down, but up into the Labyrinth.

A minute later, Malcolm followed her up.

PART THREE

52

TUESDAY

'Do you know why you're here, Donna?' Cat asked.

The girl looked down and ran her fingers around the can of Diet Coke on the table in front of her, seeking reassurance, and Cat saw the white scalp through the black stubble of her hair. Cat had placed the drink in front of her when she had entered the room. There had been an initial confusion. Then, like a diver in muddy water, a fingertip search conducted in zero visibility, a tentative recognition. Once identified, her hand now seemed obsessively drawn to the solidity, the familiarity of the aluminium can. Donna flicked the open ring-pull with an index finger.

'Because of what happened at the hospital?'

The hospital. Cat found it hard to reconcile the girl opposite with the frenzied knife attack that had left one man requiring over thirty stitches and another fighting for his life in intensive care. Her vulnerability, the deep circles under her eyes, the scattering of nascent pimples on her chin, the bitten fingernails, the grubby black T-shirt all seemed at odds with that level of violence.

'That's right,' Cat said. 'Do you remember what happened at the hospital, Donna?'

'Yeah.' Donna frowned. Briefly stopped flicking the can's ring-pull. 'Sort of.' She turned the Coke can on the table. Traced the red lettering on its side with a fingertip. Took a sip of the drink and, putting the can back on the table, started flicking the ring-pull again. Her eyes moved across the tabletop, taking in the pads, the pens, the box of tissues, the tape recorder. 'I . . . I had a knife . . . I remember . . . I wanted to stab him. I tried before . . . I wanted to before but I couldn't do it . . . '

When the girl had stopped talking, the urgent rush of words finally subsiding into an uneasy silence, punctuated by the sound of the ring-pull being flicked, Cat asked:

'And this thing? The thing in the car at Ness Road car park . . . '

'A minotaur. It was a minotaur. I saw one in Malc's encyclopedia of Greek myths.'

'OK,' Cat said doubtfully, 'this minotaur, this was Clive Townsend?' She looked up briefly from the notes she had been making on her pad, to see the girl shrug. 'We need to hear your answer, Donna.'

The girl looked up. Not at Cat, exactly. But sort of through her. Or around her. As if Cat was obscuring something of more interest. Donna moved her head slowly. Frowning. Putting her head first on one side then the other. Turning to one side like she might catch a glimpse of something from the corner of her eye. Cat resisted the urge to look over her own shoulder, to turn and check behind her. Instead she nodded at the recorder.

'For the tape recorder, Donna?'

'Yes,' Donna said, then, clearing her throat, she repeated, 'yes.'

Cat looked down at her notepad. Then to get it right in her

mind, to put the girl's words in some kind of order, to make some sense of what she had said, she asked:

'You were in the car with him, with Clive Townsend, and you had the knife, the same knife, and you wanted to stab him then but you were too frightened? Have I got that right?'

Donna, looking down at the tabletop, shrugged again.

'Is that "yes", Donna?' Cat asked.

Donna looked at the tape recorder and cleared her throat again. 'Yes.'

'Why did you want to stab Clive Townsend, Donna?'

'To kill him,' she said matter-of-factly.

'OK,' Cat said slowly. 'Why did you want to kill Clive Townsend?'

'Because of what he did to Alicia.'

'Alicia?' Cat asked. 'Alicia Goode, do you mean? She was at the Abigail Burnett with you?'

Donna nodded at the table. Then remembering, her eyes going to the tape recorder, she mumbled, 'Yes.'

'She was your friend?'

Donna was crying. Fucking crying again. All of a sudden she couldn't help it. Couldn't stop it either. The woman police officer took a paper tissue from the box on the table and handed it to her. Donna took it and wiped her eyes. Then she blew her nose.

'Are you OK, Donna?' the woman asked. Cat, she had said her name was. When they had started. After they had all spoken into the tape recorder. Cat. She seemed nice. Pretty. 'Are you OK to carry on?' Cat asked.

'Yeah.' She nodded, squeezed the balled-up tissue in her fist, reached out and gripped the metal can.

*

'What did he do to Alicia?' Cat asked. 'Clive Townsend. What did he do to Alicia?'

'He killed her.' Her voice hoarse, she cleared her throat again. 'He killed her. Everyone says he didn't. Everyone. But I know he did,' she started to nod, 'I know. He killed her. Or he made it happen. Somehow. He made it happen.'

'Why do you think that?'

'He used to pay some of the girls to have sex with him.'

'At the Abigail Burnett?'

Donna nodded.

'And Alicia? Did he pay Alicia to have sex with him?'

Donna stopped nodding. Looked down at the table, uncertainly shaking her head. Her hand left the Coke can and went to the bare arm under the T-shirt. Cat saw her grab some skin between a thumb and two fingers. Twist. She glanced across at Pearson, who shook his head, mouthed, 'Move on.'

'You thought that Clive Townsend was responsible for your friend's death. And that's why you wanted to kill him?'

Donna nodded and said in a small voice, 'Yes.'

'So you went to the hospital. And you saw Clive Townsend. Do you remember what happened then?'

The girl's eyes flittered around nervously. As if they were tracing the flight of an agitated fly, a fat bluebottle which moved around the desktop but settled repeatedly on the spots of blood that had appeared on the bandages covering Pearson's hands.

53

Pearson noticed the girl looking at his hands again. Unsettled, threatened, by their presence. Trying to work out whether they had any significance, any relevance to why she was here. He slid them slowly across, then under, the table. The movement pulling at the stitches in his palms. Making the bruising on the back of his skull and the right side of his neck throb, despite the heavy-duty painkillers he had swallowed. The girl stared for a moment at the space where his hands had been. To Donna Freeman's left sat the social worker. Introducing himself as her personal adviser, and acting as her 'appropriate adult'. Leaning back, up to now, on two legs of his chair but sitting forward when the girl had started crying. Now taking a keener interest in proceedings. Shaven-headed, wearing round, steel-framed glasses and a grey hoodie, he had arrived on an expensive-looking racing bike and had the shaved legs and lean muscles of someone who obviously took his cycling seriously. Pearson was grateful for the sudden change in position, sparing them all as it did the unexpurgated view of his anatomy that had been on show inside his Lycra shorts. To the girl's right sat the female duty solicitor. Not much bigger than the girl herself. Slightly heavier, though this wasn't too hard to achieve. Older, but not by that much. A mop of sandy curls over a pale complexion. A jacket a size or two too big for her. Fidgeting uneasily, repeatedly and unnecessarily shifting the A4 pad on the table in front of her. Tapping her pen on her teeth. Obviously more used to dealing with petty theft and criminal damage than a case of attempted murder. By the time the preliminaries had been dispensed with, by the time they had introduced themselves for the tape, Pearson had already forgotten their names.

'You saw Clive Townsend,' Russell said again. 'Do you remember what happened then, Donna?'

Pearson remembered. He had been sitting in the visitor's chair talking to his mother. Or rather, not talking. She was sitting in the brown leatherette armchair by her bed. Had been telling him about some or other neighbour whom he didn't remember, but whom she had insisted he did. Telling him that she had heard that the woman had died. Though how she had managed to come across this nugget of information while in the hospital and having, as she had insisted anyway, no visitors apart from him, he was at a loss to comprehend. They had been sitting awkwardly, having not spoken for a few minutes, Pearson asking again, 'So you're all right then? There's nothing I can bring you?', when he noticed his mother's attention was elsewhere. He had turned to see the girl. The girl he had seen earlier in the cafeteria, the girl they had seen on the seafront hugging a tree, in her hoodie and leather biker's jacket. Standing stock-still, staring at someone across the ward. Pearson followed her gaze.

Colin – Clive – looked as if he had seen a ghost. The girl took something out of her pocket then. Something that glinted in the reflected light of the overhead fluorescents. Pearson was pushing his chair back, turning, moving towards her. But too slowly. She had already moved across the ward and, taking the man he now knew to be Clive Townsend completely by surprise, stuck the knife in his chest. By the time he had reached them she had delivered another blow, maybe two. Pearson had managed to wrestle her off him, thought he had the situation under control, that he might get away with only a few superficial cuts from the knife blade, when something heavy had landed on his back and knocked them all to the floor. Desperately trying to wrestle the knife from the girl's grip, the boy clinging to his back, punching him repeatedly on the neck and the back of the head. Blood, his own blood, pooling beneath him. He became aware of his mother's voice. Shouting his name repeatedly. Not in anxiety, or fear for his life. But in embarrassment. When he had finally gained control of the knife, had his arms tightly around the girl so that she could no longer pummel him, when some unseen hand had dragged the boy off him, he glanced over his shoulder to see his mother sitting in the armchair next to her bed, looking up and down the ward to check if anyone had noticed the undignified spectacle her son had been involved in. She sighed loudly and said in a tone of complete exasperation, 'Frank!'

Russell was saying, 'The boy who was with you at the hospital—'

'Malc,' Donna said.

'Right. Malc. Malcolm Mitchell. Is he your boyfriend?'

Donna was about to deny it, was just starting to shake her head, when she thought better of it and started to smile. 'Yeah,' she said, 'I suppose he is.'

After a minute, Russell said, 'It wasn't the first time you'd been in that car park, was it?'

Donna looked down at the table, shook her head. 'No.'

The duty solicitor looked up from her notes.

'Last Friday,' Pearson said, 'the body of Detective Inspector Sean Carragher was found in a burned-out vehicle in Ness Road car park. A cigarette end with DNA identified as belonging to Donna was recovered from the scene.'

The solicitor considered this for a moment, then sighed, 'Go ahead.'

Russell nodded and turned back to the girl. 'Had you been in that car park before, Donna?'

54

'Had you been in that car park before, Donna?' the woman asked.

Donna had forgotten her name. She'd said it. Donna thought she'd said it. When they'd introduced themselves into the tape recorder. She had said what her name was when she had given her the Coke but Donna couldn't think what it was now. Donna reached out and touched the can again. Flicked the ring-pull.

'Yes,' she said. She said yes because the woman had asked her not to mumble and to talk clearly so that the tape recorder could hear what she said.

'With who?'

Donna didn't answer.

'Who were you with, Donna?' the woman asked. 'We know you were there. We've got your DNA.'

Had somebody said something about that? A cigarette or something?

'With the policeman.' Donna cleared her throat. 'With the policeman.'

'With a policeman? Do you know his name?'

The woman seemed to be asking all the questions. The man with the bandages on his hands hadn't said anything. She didn't think he'd said anything. She couldn't remember properly. It was all so confusing. She was starting to forget who had said what. It was all getting jumbled together.

'Yes,' Donna said, 'Sean.'

'Sean,' the woman repeated. 'Do you know his last name?'

Donna thought. Had he told her his last name? Maybe he had and she'd forgotten it. Anyway she didn't know it now. So she said, 'No.'

'OK,' the woman said. 'What were you doing in the car park with Sean?'

'I wasn't having sex or anything,' Donna said. That was what she thought Donna was doing. That was what everybody always thought everyone else was doing. She'd done it. She wasn't a virgin or anything. Even though she'd told Clive Townsend she was. Let Sez think she was. She'd done it. She hadn't got much out of it. Didn't even like the boy very much. She'd only done it because everyone else was doing it and she'd wanted to see what it was like. Now she'd done it she couldn't see what all the fuss was about.

'OK,' the woman said, 'you weren't having sex. So what were you doing in the car park with Sean?'

'He was one of the policemen who came and spoke to us when Alicia died.' She looked at the woman. Had she been there too? Maybe. She couldn't remember.

'So you knew him from then?'

'Yes.'

'Not before?'

Donna shook her head. 'No. I told him then about Clive

318

Townsend.' She touched the Coke can. It was warm. 'Told him that Clive killed Alicia.' She took a sip of the Coke. Flat. Tepid. The can almost empty. She was still thirsty but if she asked for another drink they would probably get angry with her and she would probably get into trouble.

'And he didn't believe you?'

'No.' Donna shook her head again. 'No one believed me. Everyone just kept saying it was an accident, that Alicia had just fell off the bridge, but I knew it wasn't, I knew she'd been killed.'

'By Clive Townsend?'

'Yes.'

'But Sean didn't believe you?'

'No. I told him what was going on at the Abigail Burnett. Told him what Clive Townsend was up to. That he paid some of the girls to have sex with him. That he set them up with other men for money and stuff, presents . . .'

Donna ran her hand up her arm. Found the skin under the T-shirt. Pinched. Twisted. To stop herself saying too much.

'And what did Sean say?'

'He said the information wasn't good enough. He said that he wouldn't be able to arrest him just with what I'd told him. He told me to see if I could find out anything else.'

'And did you?'

Donna shook her head. 'He gave me some money and told me it was finished.'

'This was in the car park?' the woman asked.

'Yes.'

'So he'd given you money before?'

Donna nodded. 'I used to meet him in the car park and tell him what I'd found out and he'd give me some money.'

'But he told you that what you'd found out wasn't any good?'

319

the woman asked. 'This was the last time you met him? In the car park?'

Donna nodded.

'We need to hear your voice,' the man said, 'for the tape?'

Donna looked at him then. She had tried not to. Because he ... it was confusing. She could see ... like before, two faces which were sort of blurred at the edges, like what she had seen before with Mr Downey, in the car with the other policeman, with Clive Townsend. Two images overlaid one on top of the other but as they moved apart ... the two images, the two faces were the same.

Donna looked away quickly. Stared at the tape recorder and then said, 'Yes.'

'So what happened then?' The woman again.

'When he gave me the money I got out of the car but then I changed my mind and went back.'

'Why did you do that, Donna? Did you want to hurt him?'

'I – I wanted to make him do something, I wanted him to take it seriously!'

Donna was shouting. Sort of. Being a bit too loud anyway. She hadn't meant to shout, to raise her voice like that, so she said, 'Sorry.' Then, worried that she had said it too quietly and the tape recorder hadn't heard, she said again, a bit louder, 'Sorry.' She looked over at the tape recorder. It made her nervous. It was scary having that thing sitting there listening to everything you said.

'It's OK,' the woman said. 'So you got back into the car. What happened then?'

'I just wanted him to stop laughing at me,' Donna said. 'I was angry, I didn't mean to do it. It just sort of happened.'

'What did? What just sort of happened?'

'I stabbed him.'

The woman looked across at the man with the bandaged hands, wrote something on her pad and then asked, 'And then what did you do?'

'I got out of the car.'

'And you didn't do anything else?'

'Like what?'

'I don't know,' the woman said, 'anything.'

'No.'

'Did you kill him, Donna? Did you kill Sean?'

Donna started shaking her head.

'Did you hit him over the head with something?'

Donna kept shaking her head.

'A stone or something? A brick maybe? A hammer?'

Donna kept shaking her head.

'Did you set the car on fire, Donna?'

Donna shook her head. 'No. No. No. No . . .' She wanted to say it. Wanted to keep on saying it, keep on saying it and shaking her head until the woman stopped asking her about it.

The woman held up her hand. 'OK,' she said. 'OK. It's all right.' Before Donna couldn't stop saying it and would just go on saying it for ever. The woman said, 'But you were there? When he died.'

Not really a question. Donna wanted to shake her head. Wanted to do anything so that the woman would stop asking her questions. So that she wouldn't have to think about it any more.

'You were there, Donna,' the woman said softly. 'What happened?'

'I can't remember,' Donna said.

And she wanted to say this now. And shake her head. Keep on saying she couldn't remember and shaking her head. She

321

couldn't. She couldn't remember. Not all of it. Some of it. But even that she didn't want to remember. Didn't want to think about. Didn't want to tell anyone.

Standing. In the deeper shadows between the beach huts. The hot air burning her skin. Scorching her nostrils. The car alight. Sean behind the wheel. His hair on fire, his body writhing in agony. There was the smell of burning flesh, the sound of a high-pitched screaming. And beside her, hopping from foot to foot. The burning car reflected in its pink eyes. A large white rabbit in a fake parka.

'Look at him burn!' it shouted excitedly. 'Look at him fucking burn!'

55

'What did you make of that?' Cat asked.

They were by the vending machine, in the corridor outside the custody suite. Pearson wasn't sure what he made of it. The girl veering between rambling and incoherent or else uncommunicative and monosyllabic. Cat having to go back at times over and over the same question, trying to make some sense of her answers. He still wasn't quite sure he had followed it all. It hadn't helped that the interview room had been so hot. That he hadn't eaten this morning because the wounds on the palms of his hands had been so uncomfortable. That the codeine-based painkillers he had been prescribed left him light-headed and queasy. Now, despite putting his cup inside another, the heat of the liquid through the plastic was making the stitches in his palm sting. When he lifted the drink to his mouth he felt a pain along his arm and into the shoulder that made him feel sick.

'"... So, Minos, moved/to cover his disgrace, resolved to hide/ the monster in a prison,"' Cat said, staring distractedly down into her coffee. She upturned the cup, swallowed. '"In this the Minotaur was long concealed/and there devoured Athenian victims sent/three seasons, nine years each ..."'

'What?'

'The Minotaur.' She dropped her empty cup into the bin. 'It's from Ovid. *Metamorphoses*.'

'Oh, yeah.' Pearson nodded sagely. As if he was familiar with it. As if he had a copy open on his bedside table at this very moment. 'Half man, half bull, wasn't it?' he said, to show he wasn't a complete ignoramus. He finished his own drink, swivelling the plastic cup, watching one droplet of tea chase another around the bottom. 'Didn't it eat children or something?'

'A devourer of innocents,' said Cat.

'Yeah. Best not say anything like that in front of Roberts, eh?' Pearson pitched his empty cup into the bin, then winced, wishing he hadn't.

'Are you OK?'

'Yeah. I'm fine.'

Having asked the question, DCI Roberts nodded once. Already moving on. Pearson hadn't expected too much in the way of sympathy. He hadn't been disappointed.

'So,' Roberts asked, 'how did it go?'

'She's admitted to the attempted murder of Clive Townsend.'

'Yeah, well, it would be a bit hard to deny it. Seeing as we've got about a thousand fucking witnesses, right?' He looked between Pearson and Russell as if they were a couple of imbeciles intent on trying his patience.

'What about the Carragher crime scene?' Curtis asked. 'Did you ask her about the DNA on the cigarette?' He was sitting in the chair furthest from the door, Russell between them. Ferguson had offered Pearson his chair, which he had accepted gratefully, and now stood in Pearson's customary position against the wall. Roberts looked back from Curtis to Pearson.

'Well . . .' Pearson hesitated, wondering how best to put it.

'You must have something?' Roberts asked. 'You've been interviewing her for the last couple of fucking hours.'

'She's got a few . . .' Pearson cleared his throat, an echo of the girl's behaviour, 'mental-health issues.'

'"Mental-health issues",' Roberts repeated. 'What exactly does that mean?' He turned to Cat. 'This is your area, isn't it? You did a degree in psychology or something, didn't you?'

'Guv,' she nodded.

'So then?'

'She really needs a full psychiatric evaluation by a qualified professional—'

'I'm not asking for your diagnosis, DC Russell,' said Roberts, leaning back in his chair, closing his eyes and putting his hands on his head, 'just your observations.'

'Auditory and visual hallucinations. Difficulty in determining what is real. Lack of personal hygie—'

'Which leaves us where?' interrupted Curtis. 'Have you got anything at all I can give the media?' He looked slowly around the room. Annoyed, shaking his head. 'There has, after all, been the death of a serving police officer. The public will be expecting a quick arrest.'

Roberts finally opened his eyes, rubbed a hand over his face, said to Pearson, 'Did you manage to get anything from her?'

'She admits to stabbing Carragher,' said Pearson.

'Stabbing?' Curtis asked. 'I don't remember seeing anything about that on the post-mortem report.'

'It didn't show up at the PM,' said Pearson, 'too much damage around the abdominal area due to the expansion and splitting of the intestines during the fire.'

Curtis swallowed. A little green around the gills.

Ferguson said, 'If her mental-health issues are as severe as you seem to be suggesting, any evidence she gives may well be deemed by the court as unreliable. If it does go to court, and she is convicted, her defence will push for a secure hospital rather than prison. More than likely, though, she will be considered unfit to stand trial.'

After a few moments Pearson said, filling the silence, 'I think it would be worth talking to Malcolm Mitchell.'

'About the events at the car park?' Roberts asked.

'Malcolm Mitchell,' said Curtis. 'He's the boy who was with her at the hospital, during the attack on Clive Townsend?'

'That's him,' said Roberts.

'Which sort of points to them being pretty close,' Pearson said.

'So let's talk to him,' Curtis said.

'OK,' Roberts agreed. 'We'll need someone to act as an appropriate adult. He lives with his disabled gran. When an officer went round to inform her of Mitchell's arrest she was taken poorly. She's being looked after by a neighbour.'

'What about the girl's social worker?'

'Is he still in the building?'

'Might be,' Pearson said, 'I'm not sure.'

Roberts picked up his phone. 'I'll get the front desk to stop him.'

'What about the duty solicitor?' Pearson asked.

'Her too.'

56

'If someone does something,' the boy asked, 'and it's an accident, it's not really their fault, is it?'

The same interview room. The same people. Cat. Pearson. The duty solicitor, Chloe. The social worker, Ben. First names. All very polite. All very friendly. So as not to spook the interviewee. Malcolm Mitchell. His can of Coke unacknowledged. Ignored. Unopened. Looking down, running his finger along the edge of the table. Then studying its tip. Confirming the diligence of the cleaning staff. An unsuccessful attempt to style his fine, blond hair into spikes. A dried stain on the right lens of his steel-rimmed, round spectacles. The ghosts of effaced piercings. Thin shoulders under a grey school shirt. Malcolm unhooked his glasses and held them up to the light. Green eyes. Weak. The right following behind the left as if in deference. He breathed on the lenses, cleaned them on his shirt and hooked his glasses back over his ears. Looking down again, he started flicking the edge of the table with his thumb.

'If it's an accident?' Malcolm insisted. 'You can't really get in trouble for that? Can you?'

'Why don't you tell us what happened,' Cat said softly, 'then we'll have a think about it. Is that OK, Malcolm?' Malcolm shrugged. Sniffed. Nodded at the tabletop. Cat waited. The boy said nothing. 'You were with Donna at Ness Road car park last Thursday night, Malcolm. Can you tell us what happened?'

Malcolm stood in the little alleyway on the other side of the road. In the shadows. Looking up at the window of Donna's bedsit. Not sure what to do. He was still angry, hurt by what she had said at the playground, but he wanted to see her. He had already been standing there for an hour or more. Not quite having enough nerve to go across and ring the bell. Not wanting to go home. The light went out in Donna's room. A minute later the front door opened and Donna came out, slamming the door behind her, wearing the leather biker's jacket. The one that was too big for her, the one that had been given to her by some bloke. She hesitated for a moment on the pavement. She'd done something to her hair. Cut it all off, shaved the sides. The top a mess. And her face was made up all weird. Painted white. Donna turned towards the seafront. He decided to tag along, see what she was up to. Following from a safe distance. On the other side of the road. Putting a car between them. Ducking into doorways. Staying in the shadows. At the seafront she stood by the sea wall for a long time looking out, although it was too dark to see anything. She wasn't going anywhere in particular, wasn't doing anything interesting, and Malcolm was bored, thinking about going home after all, when a car passed. Slowed down and turned into the car park. Donna watched it as if she recognised it. Then followed.

Malcolm went down on to the beach. Not sure what to do

328

next. If he went into the car park, he would be seen straight away. Donna had recognised the car. And she had been waiting by the sea wall for a long time. Maybe she had arranged to meet someone? He wasn't sure he really wanted to know. He could only think of two reasons why you would meet someone in a car park at night. Drugs or sex. Hands in the pockets of his parka, he kicked around the shingle, scattering the stones, listening to the sound it made. Listening to the sound of the waves, though it was too dark to see that far across the water. He came across a big stone. Felt it under the sole of his trainer. Nearly slipped. He bent down and picked it up. A pebble. Like the egg of a dinosaur, he thought. No. More sort of pointed at one end. More triangular. Like a huge, petrified teardrop. Turning it over in his hands, running his fingers over its unbroken surface. It was no good, he wanted to know what she was up to. Had to know what she was up to. Whether she was meeting whoever it was that was in that car. Someone older. Someone with money.

Seconds later he was standing in the shadows between the beach huts and watching. Watching as she exposed herself. Watching as the man took some notes out of his wallet and gave them to her. It was what he had thought. What he had known. What he hadn't wanted to think about. Having sex with men. For money. He couldn't look. But at the same time he wanted to. Wanted to see what happened. Like some old pervert. Like one of those blokes who liked to watch their girlfriends or wives fuck someone else. He couldn't watch. Instead, feeling sick, he turned away and moved back into the shadows. In his pocket he felt the heavy stone in his hand, the grains of sand beneath his fingers rasping across its smooth surface. He was going to do something. He was going to make it stop. But when he turned back Donna was getting out of the car. Looking upset. Looking ready to run.

So he changed his mind and dropped the big stone and stepped back into the shadows again.

Donna walked a few paces. Away from the dim light cast by the streetlamps. Into an area where it was a little darker, where it was more difficult to see what was going on. He saw her stop and look at something in her hand, stuff it in her pocket. Then take it out again. She might have taken it out again. Or taken something else out of her pocket. She looked at it for a moment; from where he was he couldn't tell what it was. Then Donna turned back and got into the car.

Malcolm looked around for the stone. He wished he hadn't dropped it now. He wanted the weight of it in his pocket. He wanted to feel its shape. Wanted to run his fingers over it. The grains of sand scouring its surface beneath his fingers. He found the stone half under one of the huts. He picked it up and turned to see that, inside the car, they were arguing. The driver's-side window was open. But the distance, the wind coming off the estuary, made it impossible to hear what they were saying. They started to struggle. The man gripping Donna's wrists. Laughing at her. Malcolm moving forward, the stone clenched in his hand inside his pocket. Donna broke free, or the man let her go, and she sort of lunged at him, striking him in the stomach. Malcolm's trainer squeaking on the tarmac of the car park. The man turning. Donna getting out of the car. But it was too late. The stone already swinging. Connecting. A sickening reverberation running up Malcolm's arm. The man's eyes rolling up into the top of his head . . .

Malcolm stared at the stone in his hand. Not quite believing what had happened. As if, somehow, it was to blame. As if the stone had willed it to happen and Malcolm had had no choice but to do what the stone had wanted.

Donna came running around the car. Panicked. Frightened by what she had done. Stopped. Looked at Malcolm. At the stone in his hand. Looked into the car. Shocked. Her face unmoving. Impassive beneath the white mask.

'Fucking hell, Malc,' she said, at his side now, 'what have you done?'

The man sat slumped in his seat. His head back against the headrest. His eyes rolled back into the top of his head. The whites showing. Not making a sound. Not moving.

'Is he dead?'

Malcolm shrugged, 'Dunno,' not taking his eyes from the man in the car. He couldn't take his eyes off the man in the car.

'Shouldn't we check or something?' Donna asked. 'I dunno, take his pulse or something. Like on the telly?'

He gestured at the car. 'Go on then.'

Malcolm saw Donna swallow, look into the car, shake her head.

'D'you think he's dead?' she asked.

Malcolm nodded, 'Yeah,' and then after a pause, 'I think so.' They stared at the body again.

'What are we going to do, Malc?'

'Dunno.' Then, quickly, 'Leave him.'

'We can't just leave him.'

'Why not?'

Donna stared into the car. Swallowed. Malcolm turned to leave but Donna grabbed the sleeve of his parka. 'Malc?' He turned back to her. The eyes in the white face frightened. 'What about fingerprints and that? DNA and stuff?'

'What?'

'I've been in the car,' she said. 'Won't it have, like, my DNA and stuff in it? They'll be able to tell, won't they? That I was in the car?' Malcolm looked back into the car. 'I'll go to prison, Malc. They'll find my fingerprints and my DNA an' all that and I'll go to prison.'

Donna started to cry. Softly at first. Then the tears were running down her face. Her nose streaming. She swiped at it with the sleeve of her leather jacket. The white make-up, blotches of her own skin, black lines of mascara, snot, fused in the light from the streetlamps.

'What are you doing?' Donna asked as he moved towards the back of the car.

He opened the boot, pushing aside the toolbox, the jack, a pair of overalls. Searching through the oilcans and rags. 'Have you got matches?'

'Yeah. Why? What are you going to do?'

Malcolm took out the plastic container of petrol and held out his hand. 'Let me have them.'

Then they were standing in the shadows between the beach huts. After he had doused the car in the petrol. Put the plastic container back and slammed the boot. Lit one match after another and dropped them on to the man's body. Watched them all gutter briefly and then go out. Until, with only a few left, one had finally caught. A halo of blue flame creeping along the car's paintwork. The car was properly alight now. Then the screaming started. And they ran. Pulling Donna with him down on to the beach. Stumbling. Losing their footing in the sand. Scrambling up again. Dragging Donna by the elbow. Running along the beach. The whoompf! as the car went up. Donna grabbing his arm. Gasping for breath. Saying she couldn't run any more. Throwing up on the shingle. Crying again. Finally he collapsed. Realising the stone was still in his pocket, he threw it away. Threw it as far as his strength would allow. He heard the plop in the dark as it hit the water.

Malcolm had finished talking. There was a stillness in the room. A silence. Even the clicking of the duty solicitor's pen had ceased, though Cat couldn't be sure when. There was a tightness in her chest and she realised she had been holding her breath. She released it in a slow exhalation. Seconds stretched into a minute. When she looked up nobody would meet her eye, both the social worker and the solicitor taking an unnatural interest in their pads. Neither actually writing anything. Malcolm was running his fingers along the edge of the tabletop again. Checking for dust. Cat glanced across at Pearson, who raised his eyebrows and reached to turn off the tape.

57

'I waited for her.'

Cat saw Pearson hesitate, his bandaged hand hovering over the tape recorder's off button. Then it retreated and disappeared once more beneath the table. Cat glanced across at him. He gave an almost imperceptible nod that said, *Let's see where this is going.*

'I used to leave my house early, and she always left it to the last minute, so most mornings I could walk with her to school.'

'This was when she was at the Abigail Burnett?' Cat asked.

Malcolm nodded. 'There was a big crowd of us. After school we went to the café . . .'

'You just sort of hung out together?'

Malcolm shrugged.

'A big crowd,' Cat said, 'so, she was popular?' She looked across at Pearson again and raised an eyebrow. This didn't seem at all like the girl they had interviewed that morning.

Malcolm shrugged.

'We need to hear your answers, Malcolm.' When he looked at her she pointed at the tape recorder with her pen. 'For the tape?'

Malcolm fidgeted in his seat and then said, 'People liked her. Boys.' Disapproval. A slight wrinkling of the nose when he said this.

'What were you doing in the car park with Sean?'
    'I wasn't having sex or anything.'

Had that been a strange first reaction? Or not? Donna hadn't known that Carragher was gay. And if you were in a car with someone at night in a car park, wouldn't that be your first intuition? But maybe the response had been so quick, so insistent, because at school she had slept around. That would certainly make you 'popular'. No matter how odd you might seem otherwise.

'You didn't like it?' Cat asked. 'That she was popular with other boys?'

'S'pose.' Malcolm shrugged.

'She had other boyfriends?'

Malcolm didn't say anything.

'But now she's your girlfriend?' Cat asked.

Malcolm stopped doing his thing with the table edge and looked at her. Confused.

'Donna? She's your girlfriend,' Cat said again.

'Donna?' A frown. A negligible curl of the lip as if he was ever so slightly appalled by the idea. 'No.' Looking down at the table, shaking his head. Even a slight shudder.

Another glance across at Pearson. Her turn to be confused. 'She seems to think you're her boyfriend,' she insisted.

'Donna?' Then, conceding, 'I like her, I suppose ... ' At least, thought Malcolm, he used to like her. When he had met her in the café. When she had her hair long and black. Wearing that black jacket. When she used to wear make-up. When she used to look like Alicia. Or tried to. But she wasn't her. She would never

336

be Alicia. No matter how much she pretended to be. Donna would never be what Alicia was.

'So why hang around Donna?' Cat asked.

'She reminded me of Alicia. Sort of . . . ' Another shrug. 'A bit, anyway . . . '

Pearson, who had been compulsively running one bandaged hand over the other under the table, worrying at the edges of the gauze dressings, picking at the surgical tape that secured their ends, suddenly twigged what – *who* – this was really about and leaned forward.

The boy glanced down at Pearson's hands on the tabletop. Pearson noticed how grubby the bandages were. The tape on the right already loose. Dried blood spotting the palm.

'You asked if something was an accident whether you could get in trouble?' Pearson prompted.

Malcolm swallowed and gave a nod.

'You weren't asking about what happened in the car park, were you?'

Malcolm shook his head.

'For the tape, Malcolm,' Pearson said gently.

'No.'

'OK, Malcolm,' Pearson said slowly. 'Do you want to tell us what happened?'

Malcolm stood in the little alleyway on the other side of the road. In the shadows. Looking up at the window of Donna's bedsit. The front door opened and Alicia came out. Looking angry. Slamming the door behind her. Looking up and down the street, then storming off in the direction of town. Malcolm looked up. Donna was silhouetted in the window frame, backlit by the bedside lamp

337

on her floor, watching the street. He waited until she turned back into the room and then followed Alicia . . .

Malcolm trailed off. Cat looked over to Pearson, who nodded for her to carry on.

'Did you see where Alicia went?' she asked.

A nod. Three fingers rubbing the top of the table now. 'She went to a big house. I don't know where it was. But there was sort of a park opposite. A green or something with a bench in it. So I sat on the bench and waited.'

'Did you see anyone else go in the house?'

Malcolm rubbed the side of his nose, sniffed, nodded. 'Some people turned up in cars.'

'People?'

'Men. Older men.'

'Anyone else?'

'Some girls.'

'Girls?' Cat asked. 'How old were these girls?'

A shrug, then he shifted his position in the seat. 'About Alicia's age? Sixteen? Older maybe, some of them.'

'Not younger?' Cat glanced over to Pearson. But his attention was on the boy.

Malcolm shook his head, shifted in his seat again. 'No.'

'OK, Malcolm. What happened then?'

Malcolm sniffed again, shook his head. 'Nothing. She came out.'

'How long did you wait outside, do you think?'

'Dunno. Couple of hours? More maybe.'

'Did anyone else come out?'

'Suppose so. I was waiting for Alicia.'

'There were still people in the house? The lights were on?

338

Music playing?' Malcolm shrugged. Cat glanced across at Pearson, who shook his head. 'OK, Malcolm,' Cat said, 'Alicia came out. What happened next? Did you follow her again?'

'Sort of.'

'Sort of?'

'After a while, I knew which direction she was going. But I didn't want to walk through town, it's too bright, too many windows.'

'You thought she might see you? You didn't think she'd be happy about you following her?'

'What are you doing here? Why do you have to keep fucking following me around all the time?' Alicia had turned on him. Until a few minutes ago, he had been trailing a hundred yards or so behind her. Not noticing that her pace had slowed. Not realising that he was now that close. Close enough to touch her. Becoming suddenly aware that they were on the overpass across the dual carriageway. The abruptness, the violence of her anger, had shocked him. 'I've told you before. Leave me alone. You're like a fucking little puppy or something, always following behind me like that.' Why was she so angry? He hadn't done anything. Wouldn't do anything. He just liked to be near her. Liked to look at her. That was all. She was so beautiful. So cool. 'Why are you always following me around?' Alicia asked, shouted, still angry. Why did she have to ask that? It was obvious, wasn't it? He lov—

'You're a fucking weirdo,' Alicia said.

'But you ...' *But you smiled at me*, he wanted to say. She'd smiled at him. On the stairs. Hadn't she?

Malcolm turning that corner on the stairs in school. The little landing where the girls gathered to comb their hair and do their make-up. Alicia standing in front of the long mirror, staring at her

339

reflection, pulling a brush through her hair. The strands falling through the bristles like silk. Glossy, even in the poor overhead lighting. Noticing him, she smiled. Or he thought she smiled. For a moment it took his breath away, standing transfixed as a tide of noisy schoolboys broke around him. Not daring to move, as he was buffeted and jostled. Finally she broke from his gaze, turning away with that knowing look on her face. Eyes down, he forced himself onwards up the stairs. It wasn't the first time he had noticed her. But it was the first time she had noticed him. Noticed him enough to smile. It was a smile. He was sure of it. The more he thought of it, the more sure he became. He could still remember that moment, just by closing his eyes.

'What are you doing?' She sounded scared, and faintly disgusted.

Opening his eyes, 'I thought you liked me,' he said. Pleading. Beginning to whine.

'You?' A sneer. 'No. I don't like you – what is your name anyway? Mervyn or something, isn't it?'

'Malcolm.' Quietly. Shamed. Looking down at the pavement.

She laughed. 'Malcolm! Well, no, Malcolm,' like he was some kind of retard or something, 'I don't like you, you stupid little prick. Why would I like someone like you? Why would I even bother with someone like you?'

'You got more interesting friends?' he asked.

'Well, yeah.' *Stupid.* She didn't say. Didn't have to say. She looked out into the night. The yellow sodium lamps. The motorway. Followed the lights of a passing car twenty or so feet below.

'I mean, let's face it, Malcolm, who wouldn't be more interesting than you?'

'Like at that place you went to? That house?'

340

'Have you been following me all night?' Less angry now. More sort of scared; and Malcolm was glad.

'"Interesting" there, was it? Did you meet "interesting" people there? Do "interesting" things?'

'Yeah, that's right,' she said. 'I met some interesting people. And I fucked them. Loads of them. Grown-up, interesting men. And I fucked every single one of them.'

Why did she have to be like that? Using that word. Why did she have to keep on saying that word? Suddenly, he didn't like her. She wasn't cool or anything. He didn't even think she was beautiful any more. She was ugly. Using ugly words. Her eyes all red like that. Mascara running down her face. A bubble of snot at one nostril. Alicia saw him looking and took a tissue out of her pocket and wiped her face. Studying the balled-up paper. The black smudges her make-up had left on it. Taking a few shuddering breaths. She looked at him. 'Tell you what, Malcolm, if you've got the money, I'll fuck you too.'

She was ugly. Dirty. Had a filthy mouth. How could he ever have liked her? Let alone think that he lov—

'You got any money, Malcy?' Taking a step towards him. 'You want to fuck me, don't you?'

He lost it. Shouted. Or growled. Or maybe he screamed. Looking back now, he wasn't sure what sort of noise he'd made. Or whether he'd made a noise at all. He rushed at her. Pushed her. Pushed her because he wanted to get her away from him. Pushed her in the chest. Too hard.

He didn't realise what had happened. Not until she wasn't there any more. He looked around for a second. As if she might be playing a trick on him. As if, at any moment, she might suddenly reappear. Then he looked over the edge. Alicia was lying at the bottom. Lying all funny. Her legs all tangled up behind her and in the brambles or whatever they were. He couldn't make her out clearly. But it looked like she had landed on some bushes. Or a tree or something. She was making a strange sound. Like she was trying to say something. Or trying to cough or catch her breath. Like a gargling. Like her mouth was full of water. Then he saw that there was ... like a branch or something like that ... and it was sticking in her neck. Sticking right through her neck. Right through and out the other side. Malcolm stood there. Staring. Not knowing what to do. Then he did. Then he ran.

'But when you do something,' Malcolm said, looking up at Pearson, appeal in his eyes, 'and it's, like, an accident? It's not really your fault, is it?'

58

THURSDAY

'Bollocks!' said Cat, having turned away from the phone and covered the mouthpiece with her hand.

'What's up?' asked Pearson, looking over, taking a bite out of a toasted egg sandwich he had just bought from the canteen.

'Hospital,' she said waving the phone in both her hands. 'I rang up to check on the status of Clive Townsend.'

'And?'

She took her hand from the mouthpiece for a moment and spoke into the phone: 'Could you hold the line a minute please?' Putting her hand back over the receiver she said, 'Some kind of balls-up. They had the shift handover between the nursing staff this morning and when they went to check on him—'

'He wasn't there.'

'You don't sound surprised.'

'It had a certain air of inevitability about it, given what else has gone on in this case,' he said, taking another bite of his sandwich.

'He was supposed to be seriously ill. I thought that was what Acute Admissions Unit meant. It's in the name.'

'I thought he was in intensive care.'

'They moved him yesterday. They judged he was out of immediate danger.'

'Obviously,' Pearson said, washing down the mouthful of bread and egg with some tea, 'he wasn't quite as serious as he led everyone to believe.'

'Has anyone ever told you you have a talent for stating the fucking obvious?'

Pearson took another sip of his tea and smiled to himself behind the cup. Then he said, 'Even if he hadn't given us the slip, what have we really got on Clive Townsend? An allegation that he may have been grooming teenage girls for sex. And really that comes down to his word against that of a severely disturbed girl.'

'Unless any of the others back up her story. If several people come forward and say the same thing? Then the weight of the accusations may be enough. One person says something you can write it off, right? But if a few say the same thing? Then it becomes difficult to ignore.'

Pearson didn't have an answer. Not one that she would have liked. Instead he had a question. 'Has he had any visitors? Any phone calls?'

While Cat relayed the question down the phone, Pearson picked up the last of his sandwich and put it in his mouth, screwed up the paper bag it had come in and pitched it into the bin under his desk.

Cat was saying, 'Yes, that would be very useful. If you could, yes, it is very important. Thank you. OK.' When she had put the phone down she said to Pearson, 'None of the night shift

344

are in. They're going to ring them at home. They'll get back to us.'

Roberts' office. The three of them in the visitors' chairs. Pearson nearest the door. Cat Russell furthest away. Between them Neil Ferguson, briefcase on his lap.

'I thought I'd have the three of you in here,' Roberts said, 'while DCS Curtis is busy downstairs with the media briefing. The other two know, but just so you are aware, DI Ferguson, Clive Townsend has absconded from the hospital.' He put his hands behind his head, laced the fingers, applied pressure, trying to relieve some of the tension in his neck and shoulders. Said, to no one in particular, 'One of the things that has always bothered me about this case was, why did Clive Townsend make the allegation about the physical assault by Carragher being on that particular day, at that particular time? When it was so easily disproved? Why not pick a date and time he knew Carragher was sitting around in his car in his street?'

Roberts, top button undone, tie at half-mast, was unbuttoning the cuffs of his shirt, rolling up the sleeves. First it's Philip Marlowe, thought Pearson, then *Scooby-Doo*, and now *Columbo*.

'Unless someone else chose the date and time,' Roberts said, addressing the top of Ferguson's head as he did his habitual caressing of the briefcase on his lap. 'Chose a day when they knew Carragher wouldn't be at work. A time when he had been known to hang around outside Townsend's house. OK, you couldn't know for sure who he was with. But, with his phone already tapped, you would have a good idea who he wasn't with.' A look towards Cat, who held his gaze momentarily before breaking away and staring down at the floor. 'And DC Russell tells me that you had already asked her about a physical assault in the interview you conducted with her on the same Wednesday afternoon? *Before* the incident with Townsend was even supposed to have happened.' Roberts scratched an armpit. 'I had a call,' a look to Pearson this time, 'from Dougie Ettrick, you remember?'

Pearson nodded. 'Guv.'

Turning back to Ferguson: 'So I know you and Carragher had previous. I gave him another ring earlier – if there's anything Dougie likes it's a bit of gossip. He told me that the woman who brought the sexual-assault charge was a PC at the nick where both you and Carragher worked. The assault was investigated and it came out that you and her were having a relationship. Long-term thing. Keeping it quiet. Low key. Rumours, nothing official, but you know what nicks are like . . . '

Pearson glanced across at Russell. Received a sour look in return.

'Seems she developed a bit of a thing for Carragher though. Obsessed, according to Dougie. Made a big play for him. Made it obvious that she was interested in him. Made a bit of a fool of herself, so the story goes. But he knocked her back. We now know why. According to Dougie, she didn't take it so well.' Roberts took a breath. 'She started pestering him. Notes left in the office. Telephone calls, emails, texts. Finally she makes up this story about a sexual assault.'

Roberts started tapping the biro on the desk. 'Anyway, as you said, she changed her statement. The case was dropped. Carragher asks for a transfer to a different force. Then, a couple of months later, you manage to get one of your mates who's retiring to get you a temporary secondment to the same force . . . ' Roberts scratched his neck with the blunt end of the pen. 'When Clive Townsend makes an allegation against Carragher – maybe it's a bit vague on the details, maybe you already think it's bullshit –

you think, Here's my chance to nail him. You pick a time and day when it's pretty certain he won't have an alibi. Unfortunately for you, the day after Clive Townsend's complaint is filed DI Carragher is found dead. All of a sudden you've got a problem. Townsend's statement is already on record. The harassment, the intimidation, the allegation of physical assault, you realise that would make him a suspect in Carragher's murder. You can't take the chance of us bringing him in. What if he denies he even made the allegations, puts you in the frame instead? So you manage to insinuate yourself on to the investigation, convince Curtis that you might be useful. Maybe part of you still wants to discredit Carragher, maybe even then you can't leave it alone. In any case you manage to persuade Curtis not to bring Clive Townsend in. That it wouldn't be in the force's interest.'

Ferguson was still looking down at his lap. Hadn't looked up since Roberts had started talking. But his shoulders were that little more hunched. His fingers applying just a little more pressure across the briefcase's surface. Pearson's arse was starting to ache, his right cheek going to sleep. Surreptitiously he shifted position. Roberts was rolling the biro across the desktop again.

'Then,' Roberts continued, 'you've got another problem. How were you to know that you would pick the exact same time that Carragher would choose to give Ray Walsh a doing?'

It might also explain, Pearson thought, Ferguson being at my desk. Maybe he'd just been nosing around? Had come across the CCTV footage by chance? Maybe he had known that Pearson had requested it, that it would have been sent through directly to his computer. Might explain his flustered demeanour. Ferguson hadn't been expecting him and Russell back, so he'd taken the chance to look at it, to find out exactly how damaging it might be.

347

'Now we're going to start wondering why Townsend would make a false allegation. Best all round, best for you, if Townsend disappears. Only he's attacked, by Donna Freeman. Laid up in hospital. So you've got no choice but to go and see him, tell him that we're going to have a word about these allegations of sexual abuse of minors. Trouble is, you were seen. The description's vague: around five-ten or six foot, dark hair, moustache. Not much to go on, granted. But enough to make me, us' – a look to Pearson again – 'start wondering.'

Roberts stared at Ferguson, the top of Ferguson's head. 'The upshot of all this,' Roberts said. 'DI Ferguson? Look at me.'

Reluctantly, Ferguson looked up.

'The upshot,' Roberts repeated, pointing the pen at Ferguson, 'of your fucking pride being hurt, and the subsequent ridiculous, pathetic personal vendetta you waged against a fellow officer, is that a man we suspect of grooming young children for sex is now out there on the loose somewhere.'

Epilogue

Pearson sat in the waiting room, fretful, restless and doing just that. Waiting. There was nothing else to do but wait. There were none of the usual distractions. No muted television broadcasting programmes about property development. (Although it seemed to him that these went out at a time in the morning when the main audience would be the unemployed, who couldn't afford to buy houses for cash at auction. And property developers who would already be out, one presumed, developing property.) No radio quietly playing the latest incarnation of a bland, insipid boy band. Indistinguishable, to his ears, from all the other bland, insipid boy bands. There were no tatty old copies of the *Reader's Digest* or *Country Life*, not even a dog-eared copy of a crossword or wordsearch magazine, most of whose puzzles would have already been incorrectly filled in in heavy biro. The seating wasn't exactly conducive to a long wait either. Half a dozen orange moulded-plastic chairs with metal legs. But then the 'Oncology Department' in which he sat was, essentially, a Portakabin in the hospital car park.

Waiting. Waiting on the result of another blood test: 'Yeah, I know it won't hurt, I'll just feel a bit of a prick.'

Now, though, the jokes had dried up. Along with every drop of saliva in his mouth. His nerve faltering, the bravado crumbling. He stood up. Needing to stretch his legs. Slipped his hands, bandages replaced by plasters, stitches removed from all but the deepest cuts on his palms, into his trouser pockets. The sound of his footsteps too loud on the lino, the wooden boards beneath. The grit under the soles of his shoes. The empty room.

This morning before he left for work – two hours in front of a computer, unable to concentrate on anything – he had stood by the open driver's door when the Hat Lady had passed by the house, trailing her wheeled shopping basket. He had given his customary salute and received a nod in acknowledgement. Staring at her hat. Trying to unscramble the cyphers and codes concealed within the arrangement of silk flowers on its brim. Hoping for some pointer to the result of the blood test. But it had, as usual, told him nothing.

On a shelf fixed to one of the partitions that had been erected to make offices, someone had left a newspaper. When Pearson unfolded the tabloid he found himself staring at the now too-familiar photographs on the front cover. Somehow the media had managed to get hold of pictures of Donna Freeman and Malcolm Mitchell that made them appear deranged and evil. Grainy. Blurred. Staring straight at the camera. The expressions on their faces cold, devoid of emotion. These would have been snapped from a distance through a telephoto lens and if the images had been clearer, Pearson guessed, the expressions on their faces would probably have shown a kind of numb shock. Unimaginatively, and inaccurately, they had already been dubbed 'a modern-day Bonnie and Clyde'. There had been a concerted effort to smear the reputations of the two. A gleeful disclosure of their troubled backgrounds: junkie mothers, absent fathers, life in care or with an elderly grandmother. And in the case of Donna Freeman, her record of petty crime, her association with the Abigail Burnett children's home. The implication that she would probably never stand trial and therefore escape justice because of her mental condition.

Malcolm Mitchell was now on remand, awaiting trial for the murder of Sean Carragher and the manslaughter of Alicia Goode.

'Erotomania,' Russell had said, as they stood in the corridor having just interviewed the boy.

'What's that? A new board game?'

'Erotomania, or de Clérambault's syndrome, is a psychological disorder. The mistaken belief that somebody is secretly in love with you. Him,' Russell said, seeing his confused look, nodding towards the door of the interview room, 'Malcolm. It's an obsession, a fixation on someone who the sufferer believes is of higher status. Like a television presenter, a pop star or some other kind of celebrity. They can pick up some kind of private sign from the person they believe is in love with them. It's called a "delusion of reference" ...'

She trailed off, realising that he wasn't convinced.

'It would explain why he stalked Alicia Goode,' she said. 'The smile on the staircase? Something as seemingly insignificant as that can be enough.'

'Maybe,' Pearson said doubtfully, 'or maybe he's just a lonely kid who fancied someone out of his league.'

'Speaking from experience, are you?'

*

Carragher, on the other hand, was portrayed as a selfless and courageous law-enforcement officer. Newspaper articles made mention of a commendation, a complete surprise to Pearson, for his part in an undercover operation in Toxteth, during which he had sustained a shotgun wound to the stomach, and resulting in the arrest and conviction of a major drugs ring.

DCS Andy Curtis had appeared at a subsequent media briefing in which he described the arrest of the two teenagers as 'a satisfactory outcome to a tragic case where a public servant sacrificed his life in pursuit of his duty'.

The death of Sickert Downey had been reinvestigated in light of the death of Alicia Goode and the attack by Donna Freeman on Clive Townsend. No significant link was established between the suicide of the director of the Abigail Burnett children's home and the two former residents and former care worker. Nothing was found to contradict the original finding of suicide, and in the absence of a note the exact motivation for his actions remained unclear. Although the loss of his job and the circumstances surrounding it, along with the possibility that he may have been aware that he was suffering from cancer, could conceivably have been contributory factors.

Detective Inspector Neil Ferguson had been suspended while the Independent Police Complaints Commission were looking into what potential charges he might face.

Clive Townsend was still at large, whereabouts unknown.

Pearson hoped the anger, the indignation, the desire to bring Clive Townsend to justice that Cat Russell so evidently felt would outweigh the resentment, the new-found cynicism and antagonism towards the Job that she had recently voiced. Hoped that this would be enough for her to decide to stay with it, at least for a little while. Hoped that, after a time, she would have a change of heart, now that they had been interviewed by Professional Standards. Cat had decided to come clean about her suspicions regarding Carragher's drug-taking, his gambling habit and, most importantly, his intimidation of Clive Townsend, and to take whatever consequences came her way.

'Probably the best thing to do,' Pearson had told her.

'Probably?'

'Definitely. You'll be all right. There'll be no appetite to air any more dirty laundry in public.'

Pearson had predicted correctly, as it turned out. Russell's actions might not be wholly forgotten, however. Even if no official record were kept. Even if in time it became only some vague memory of a past indiscretion that would be brought to light at a future promotions board.

As for himself, he had decided to say nothing. By rights he should have reported what he had discovered about Carragher from their conversation on the beach, but hadn't. He'd had the opportunity to rectify that in his interview with Professional Standards but had decided, once again, to keep quiet. (And in so doing hadn't he too, just like Carragher, crossed the line? Maybe not to the same extent. But once that line had been crossed, that principle abandoned ... even if he had convinced himself at the time that he had done so with the best of intentions. Wouldn't Carragher, at some point, have convinced himself of the same?) He could tell himself that it had been to save the career of a promising young officer. But were his motives that clear-cut? That noble? That selfless? He had always imagined there was a line over which he would not step. Now it seemed that that particular line was anything but indelible. That it had been drawn in nothing more lasting or permanent than chalk. Now that chalk line – or, more aptly considering where they were when he had told her to keep Carragher's indiscretions to herself for the time being, that mark in the sand – had been blurred and redrawn a little further out.

There was also the question of his brother-in-law. Terry Milton was involved in this somehow. Up to his nuts in it. He had lied to Pearson. Lied to his face, and more than once during the course of this investigation. But he had let it slide. So maybe he had managed not only to overstep the line, but to take a running jump across and over to the other side. Not for his sake, certainly not for Milton's, but for Ruth. Whatever Milton was involved in, it would inevitably come back to hurt Ruth. The only question was this: would Pearson's intervention, or lack of it, make the damage, the fall-out, better or worse?

Just then, his name was called.

When Pearson slipped behind the wheel of the Mondeo, having been given the all-clear, it had begun to rain. He rested his head on the steering wheel. Feeling relieved. And foolish. Tears pricking his eyes. He heaved in a few breaths, exhaling slowly, tamping down his emotions. He had convinced himself, almost convinced himself, that if he did have cancer he wouldn't have the treatment. Would forgo the chemo, the radiotherapy. Would rather avoid the horrendous side effects: the pain, the vomiting, the diarrhoea, the fatigue. All of it. He had asked himself what he had to live for. And come up wanting. So he had convinced himself that he wasn't afraid of dying. He wasn't that concerned. Until it really came down to it. And then he was. Finally he let out a shuddering sigh. He sat up and rubbed his face, looked at his reflection in the rear-view mirror, shook his head.

'You stupid old sod.'

He took some deep breaths, turned on the windscreen wipers,

watched them for a minute or two. Up in the main part of the building, on one of the wards was his mother. He considered for a moment whether he should go and see her. He shot a cuff and checked his watch. Nearly visiting time. Or he could probably go back to the nick and put in a few hours, if he really wanted to. He looked, once again, at the main part of the hospital. Then he turned the key in the ignition and started the car. For once, just for today, both his colleagues and his family would have to get along without him.

Acknowledgements

I would like to thank the following people not only for their invaluable assistance during the editing process but also for their generosity, kindness and, above all, patience.

Sarah Armstrong, a long-term mentor, good friend and trusted reader. The first person who made me believe that I might actually be able to write and could have something worthwhile to say.

Phil Tucker, another good friend and trusted reader who allowed me to brazenly steal his experiences while offering indispensable counsel regarding police procedure, terminology and attitudes. Any inaccuracies in respect to these, whether deliberate (for the furtherance of the story) or due to my ignorance or misinterpretation, remain completely my responsibility.

Juliet Mahony and Sarah Lutyens from the Lutyens & Rubinstein Literary Agency, who saw something in my first failed attempt at novel-writing and stuck with me when others didn't. Juliet, additionally, for her continuing support and advice.

Jade Chandler at Sphere for her enthusiasm, encouragement and guidance. One can only admire her stamina for having gone through multiple versions of this novel in what must have been excruciating detail.

The team at Sphere: Catherine Burke, Katherine Armstrong, Thalia Proctor, Emma Williams and Kirsteen Astor, for getting this book out into the world.

Debbie, without whom nothing would be possible.

Q&A with the author

You turned to writing after completely losing your eyesight in 2002. Why did you choose something so visual as your next challenge, or have you always written?

When I lost my sight I was working in the City as a self-employed computer consultant contracting out my services to investment banks and stockbrokers. This was suddenly taken away from me. So I was forced to look at doing something else. Initially I didn't regard writing as a career choice, just as something I might be interested in doing. I really liked writing when I was at school, I suppose in common with a lot of other people, but somehow the idea of pursuing it as a career never entered into it. I was encouraged by the tutor on my creative writing courses to believe that it was something I had a talent for.

You received a distinction in creative writing from the advanced Open University course. There's been a lot of debate about creative writing courses in the media and how useful they are to writers. What did you get out of the experience and how was it helpful to you?

I think it is not overstating the case to say it was life-changing for me. My tutor was brilliant and I received a distinction in every piece of work I submitted. Whether this was merited or not it certainly encouraged me to believe that I had some talent for writing. Having said that I think there is a danger in staying in the 'academic' environment too long. At some stage you need to step out of it and join the 'real' world of publishing, which can be very bruising in terms of your ego.

What is your writing process?

I'm not sure I've ever understood this question. Maybe because I don't necessarily believe I have a defined process. I'm only now at the final editing stage of my second book; I'm still learning my chops. In terms of how I work: I sit at a desk in front of a computer and keep office hours Monday to Friday. I do believe you have flashes of inspiration but these usually come, for me at least, when I have been thinking solidly about a piece of work. It is only when you step away that the subconscious, which has continued to turn the problem over, presents you with a solution or new direction.

If, on the other hand, you are asking how an idea is developed into a novel, *Burned and Broken* grew out of writing exercises I had completed for my creative writing course. I generally think in terms of 'set pieces'. That is, I 'see' a scene in my mind's eye – that visual thing again – like a small loop of film which is repeated with alternate dialogue and actions but always in the same setting with the same characters. I had a scene in my mind, viewed through the eyes of a sixteen-year-old girl who was talking to someone about abuse going on at a children's home. At some stage the man she is talking to lights a match to smoke a cigarette and she sees the flare of the match reflected in the red eye of a minotaur. During the rest of the conversation this minotaur image reappears intermittently, overlaying the face of the man. This later morphed into the scene between Donna and Clive Townsend in the car. The second set piece was of the young girl sitting in a car seen through the eyes of a policeman. Her hair is shaved at the sides and the top is ragged and uneven, her face is heavily made-up, the choice of Pierrot in this case was quite deliberate. The third scene was developed from a radio play featuring a police interview between a female officer and a Scottish detective from the professional standards department. It was set in a claustrophobic room. It is hot and raining outside – I wanted to convey the claustrophobic feeling of the jury room in the film *Twelve Angry Men*, an image which has always stuck in my mind. This piece of writing was really the seed from which the whole book grew.

Why crime fiction in particular?

A good question. I don't really know. Most of the pieces on my creative writing course were more supernatural in nature. I suppose, though, I have always read crime fiction but generally alternate a book at a time between crime and literary fiction. My aim was to write something with the sensibilities and characterisation of literary fiction and the strong plotting of crime novels. It is up to the reader to decide how successful I have been.

How did you come up with the idea for *Burned and Broken*? Did you have the plot in mind first, or the idea of Frank and Cat's partnership?

Definitely the characters. I had previously written a book with Cat, Pearson and Roberts as the main characters. Although this attempt was rejected I knew the characters were strong and worked well together. Plot for me usually 'grows organically'. Which is another way of saying I have completely no idea how to plot in the conventional sense. I formulate the characters and create settings and set piece scenarios first and then hope that the plot will somehow fall out as I go along. If I have a good start and I roughly know where I'm headed that is enough. The ending I have in mind when I start is usually not the ending that I finish up with when the writing has stopped and the dust has settled.

Various police forces have been widely criticised recently, especially in relation to their failure to protect young and vulnerable people. Was this something you were aware of when you started writing and, if so, did it influence your narrative?

The book is not meant to criticise the police's handling of vulnerable people and I hope it doesn't come across that way. Cat and Pearson are decent, compassionate people who are trying to do the right thing despite the conflicts arising from their personal lives and the operational constraints faced by the modern police force. I also wanted to write something more 'realistic' than the usual serial killer storyline. The police are on the front line every day dealing with people on the margins of society and many of those have mental health issues. I wanted to give a voice to the marginalised; those who are born into situations where they have very little choice or chance to do anything with their lives.

Where did your characters come from? Are any of them based on yourself, or others?

Most are amalgams of several different people – a mannerism here, a turn-of-phrase there. Someone's eyes added to someone else's hair. Real people mixed with people off the telly, in films. But ultimately the characters can only come out of the writer. The writer can imagine himself as a particular character, inhabit that person, but ultimately you will bring your own experiences, your own baggage. If you are successful you will write something that will hit a nerve with your reader who, luckily, will bring their own life experience and this will have a bearing on how they interact with the character you have created. Pearson is the person I'd like to be – the good bits of me, the caring, compassionate part of me. The person I'd like to think I would be if I were a copper; the copper that all coppers should strive to be.

Malcolm is probably the character in the book I can most relate to. He is the twelve- or thirteen-year-old version of myself that I recognise now, looking back from my mid-fifties.

Did you have to do a lot of research about police procedures?

Some. But luckily I have a good friend who used to work as a DCI in the Essex Major Investigation Team. I ask him how he might have investigated a particular scenario and then give it my best shot. Then I send him the finished result and hope he can correct the many inaccuracies. However, I am trying to tell a story, not write a police procedure manual, so I will try to use research where it is relevant and may sometimes use my 'author's privilege' to make it up.

Which authors or books have inspired you?

In terms of crime fiction, I owe a huge debt of gratitude to Raymond Chandler. I like crime fiction with strong or unusual characters such as Kate Atkinson's Jackson Brody series and the books of Gillian Flynn. But, as I said earlier, I don't limit myself to crime fiction; I think you can take something from every great author. Which is a polite way of saying you can borrow voice, writing styles, tricks etc. from them. One of the books that has stayed with me is *Empire of the Sun* by J.G. Ballard. I read this when I was around twelve, saw it as a film and then listened to it recently on audio. It survived all three formats which, in itself, must mark it out as a particularly strong and enduring story.

What's next for the Essex Police Major Investigation Team?

Gender reassignment, Government conspiracy, psychological experimentation and, for Pearson, a fatal accident on a railway track.

Now read on for the beginning of
Mark Hardie's new novel

TRULY EVIL

Prologue

i

The tide was coming in. His feet sinking as the silt became softer, less definite. Rivulets of advancing water reflecting the sickly dawn over the estuary. The air damp and chill, the haze yet to be burnt off by the warmth of the sun, so his stinging and streaming eyes could not make out the other side of the river, although he knew its contours and dimensions by heart. The County of Essex at his back. Somewhere in front of him, beyond the mist, lay Kent. In the occasional lull between gusts of a buffeting wind which had numbed and frozen his ears came the distant clanging of halyards on masts. The screech of seagulls.

The cold wind bit into his flesh, flapping his damp clothes around his body. His hands constricted into chafed and chapped claws. He looked down once again at the figure half-submerged in the mud. The eyes and mouth open. Grey silt had gathered and then cracked on the skin, so that now it seemed more like a statue than a human being. Sand flies already hovered, lining up to kiss the eyes. Mourning relatives filing past to give their last respects to someone they hated or hardly knew. A tiny translucent crab scuttled from the mouth, grains of sand dislodged by its claws. He took a deep breath, stepped closer and put the sole of his boot on the face. Applying a steady pressure. Pushing it under the mud. The slight sucking sound snatched away by a gust of wind. The sea rushing in to fill the space. A pool of brackish water forming. Before that too drained away and was gone.

ii

Extract from transcript of session held on 27 July

The subject was fairly unresponsive and questions often had to be repeated. The answers were faltering, hesitant; at times monosyllabic and numerous lengthy silences occurred. The subject was also frequently upset and very confused.

AF: Where are you?

RL: I don't know.

AF: What can you see?

RL: Dark ... Darkness.

AF: Okay. Try to stay calm. Try to relax. Look around you.

RL: Okay.

AF: Good. Can you see anything? Anything at all?

RL: Curtains? At a window. A small crack of light ... they have a ... weep? No ... weft? ... weave. They have a heavy weave.

AF: Nothing else? You can't see anything else?

RL: No.

AF: What can you feel?

RL: Metal. Under my hand. A metal frame. A hospital bed.

AF: What can you smell?

RL: Hospital ... sweat ... sleep ... pain ... body-stink ...many bodies.

AF: What can you hear?

RL: Cars? Outside ... a squeaky wheel ... metal on metal.

AF: How long have you been here?

RL: Here? I don't know ... weeks? Months? A long time ... for ever. Now ... here now ... before? I don't know before ... I know ... now ... I know here.

AF: Who are you?

RL: I don't know ... I was someone ... before ... I was someone ... before now ... before this room ...

AF: Good. Good. Well done.

PART ONE

DAY ONE

1

Barely half an hour after a fitful night had shuffled uncertainly into a gloomy dawn, Detective Sergeant Frank Pearson sat waiting in his car at traffic lights. The view beyond the windscreen blank, featureless, dull. It was going to be the sort of day, Pearson felt, when the sky went up and down – but never out of – the greyscale. A fine rain, barely more than a mist, started to fall from the leaden sky. Flicking the wipers on to their lowest setting he sat for a while, listening to the patter of rain on the car roof. The ticking of the indicator. The ponderous clunk and squeak of the windscreen wipers. Finally the lights changed and he swung the car right onto Marine Parade. Past the closed chippies and rock shops. The hushed pubs and bars. The mute arcades. And into the gusting wind off the estuary. The slow sweep of the wipers smearing the needles of rain across the windscreen on their upward arc before halting momentarily, then with a shuddering squeal of protest grudgingly clearing his field of vision on their downward trajectory.

He passed under the footbridge to the pier. To his right, the restaurants under the arches were shut tight. The chairs and tables put away, the metal shutters down. To his left, a jogger in a hooded waterproof jacket and shorts, head down against the rain and wind. The tide was out, the grey expanse of the mudflats exposed. But on the other side of the estuary, the metal tanks of the disused oil refinery were hidden from view.

As he reached Chalkwell, the seafront was already crowded. Haphazardly parked vehicles. Pedestrians in hi-vis jackets. Marked police cars. A solitary ambulance, the yellow banding achingly fluorescent in the dim light. Two uniformed police constables sectioning off the area with blue-and-white tape.

Pearson pulled to a halt, picking up his dark woollen overcoat from the passenger seat. Climbing out, shrugging it on, slamming the car door. Digging in the pocket for identification, holding the warrant card at shoulder height, nodding to the uniform on duty and ducking under the tape, he made his way towards the sea wall looking for the Senior Investigating Officer. He spotted the over-large navy anorak. The between-regular-sizes body and habitually ill-fitting clothes of Detective Chief Inspector Martin Roberts. His normally ruddy cheeks were now chapped red, his thinning ginger hair flapping in the swirling wind. Roberts was talking to a senior uniform Pearson recognised as DCS Andy Curtis. Between them stood the Crime Scene Manager, dressed in white forensic overalls. Six foot eight and stick thin. A couple having a furtive assignation under a lamp-post. As he approached, Roberts turned and nodded, 'Frank.'

'What is that thing?' Curtis asked, indicating a granite obelisk, about fourteen feet high and around forty feet away.

'The Crowstone?' asked Pearson. 'Historically, it marks the limit of the responsibility of the Port of London Authority on the Thames.'

'So,' Curtis asked, 'is she ours or theirs?'

Pearson looked out at the girl. Lying on her stomach, as if in obeisance at the foot of the monolith. Some weird kind of ancient fertility rite. The long black hair fanned out in front of her, obscuring the face from view. The black bra just visible under a ripped grey satin top. The black mini skirt. The boots. Some kind of wet-look PVC. A path had been marked out with tape from the sea wall to the area around the body and the Scene-of-Crime Officers in paper forensic suits were beginning to erect a tent. Somewhere above the clouds, the drone of a light aircraft.

'Her head may be in London,' said Pearson, 'but her heart is in Essex. She's one of ours.'